KEITH L. BROWN

Cross Country Hu$lin

By

Keith L. Brown

NORTH MEMPHIS PUBLISHING HOUSE

ST. LOUIS, MO

Cross Country Hu$lin

Copyright © Keith L. Brown, November 2023

All rights reserved. No part of this book may be reproduced in any form, except for brief quotations in printed reviews, without permission in writing from the author and/or publisher.

DEDICATION

This book is dedicated to all the lost souls in cells, prisons, and the feds. The street game never changes, just the players. And unlike most hood books, there's not one murder or shooting; only one or two acts of violence. Violence should never be the focus of telling the ins and outs of a fictional story,

I don't have to glorify killing, shooting, and robbing, although they're part of the dope game. It's not the center of attention of this tale about money getters.

I pray this book serves as a warning to whoever thinks that you gone get rich in the dope game. It's not worth it. If you're smart enough to sell drugs, try selling legit items cause the system is meant for you to lose. So please, love your life and never put money before your family and freedom!

Cross Country Hu$lin'
Don't try this at home!
I stamp that!

PRELUDE

Uptown Brown was a country boy born in the backwoods of Mississippi. He was raised in the mean streets of Memphis, Tennessee and went state-to-state applying his hustle to fame-and- fortune. His love for the almighty dollar put him in some life and death situations. Just as soon as he thought he had it all, he slowly, but surely, lost it. After years in the fast-lane, his hopes and dreams came crashing down. He soon learned that fast never lasts, and just like it started, every game must end. In the streets, only a few end up as winners!

TABLE OF CONTENTS

Chapter 1   Born Hustla

Chapter 2   Welcome to the Hood

Chapter 3   Getting to the Money

Chapter 4   My Family

Chapter 5   The Takeover

Chapter 6   Going Through the Motions of the Game

Chapter 7   World Domination

Chapter 8   The Top of the Mountain Comes Fast, But the Fall Comes Faster

Chapter 9   You Can Run But You Can't Hide

CHAPTER 1

Born Hustla

Willie Brown was born in Hernando, Mississippi. He was the fifth child of MaryLynn and Ivan Brown's fourteen kids. Life was extra hard on the Brown family. Like so many other Black families coming up in the South during the '70s and '80s, most were extremely poor. MaryLynn took care of the house while Ivan Brown picked cotton and worked on the White-owned farms to help feed and clothe the family. Lil' Willie learned early as a child that money was a very important tool to survive. He also noticed how happy everybody in his family would be when his father got paid.

One day, Lil' Willie asked his father "Paw, how come you are at work so much and how come we are so poor"? His father looked him in the face and said, "Son, us colored folks gotta hustle extra hard to feed our families"! That was his first time hearing the word "hustle" at seven years old. Then his father said, "When you get bigger, you'll have to work and hustle to help feed the family because to become a man, you need to be able to provide."

So Lil' Willie would watch and learn as much as he could. He admired his father's efforts and his grind to work hard every day, but they were still poor. In Mississippi, most kids went to the same school, especially the blacks.

One day at his school, he met a little boy whose nickname was Cotton. He was named that because he (and all his brothers) picked cotton and was always dressed in the flyest clothes of that time. He had long, permed hair and always was the life of any place he was at. Cotton had four brothers, and three sisters, but no daddy. His daddy was said to have been a White man because all his family was high yellow in complexion.

The two, Lil' Willie and Cotton, became good friends. Cotton was a true ladies' man while Lil' Willie was good with the girls. He learned a lot of his charm from Cotton. Cotton wasn't a fighter or a punk-ass kid; he was just a pretty boy. Lil' Willie on the other hand was born to brawl. At the age of fourteen, 6'3" and 235 pounds, he could whoop most grown men in his small town.

One day, Cotton asked Lil' Willie, "Man why y'all family so po"? Willie said, "Because nigga, my paw ain't got no two good jobs. My ma doesn't work either and it's hard raising fourteen kids." Cotton said, "Look my nigga," showing Lil' Willie about six hundred dollars. That's a true bankroll for a fifteen-year-old kid. Lil' Willie's eyes had gotten extra wide and he said, "Damn nigga, how did you get that much money"? Cotton said, "Nigga I be hustling." Willie said, "nigga I be working my ass off and never got that much money."

Cotton said, "Because I work smarter not harder. That trick ass boss your paw works for pays me every week just so that my older sister won't tell how he likes to buy black pussy. Meanwhile, I'm selling this," showing Lil' Willie a bag of weed that was a lighter green and very stinky. He said, "Nigga, this is why everybody likes to see me coming and that's why I'm always happy and smiling. I'm getting money nigga and I hate being broke"! Cotton told Lil' Willie, "You, my nigga and here is two hundred dollars. Let's go get some clothes, drinks, and some pussy. As long as you have a hustle, you have money and when you have money, you and everybody else around you gonna be happy." He handed Lil' Willie a fat junt and said, "Light this." Lil' Willie had smoked cigarettes before but never weed. He wasn't lame though, just never tried weed until now. As he lit and then hit the junt, he started to cough and choke. Cotton laughed and said, "Yeah that's dat good shit nigga! We gone get high, get fly, and get some bitches tonight!" This was his first lesson on how to get his hustle on. Lil' Willie had always dreamed of having more money than his paw and now he was about to start getting it.

Cotton and Lil' Willie walked to Cotton's house which was not far from the Cotton field where his Paw worked. As they walked past, they could see the men in the hot sun picking the white balls of cotton with the sun blasting down. Lil' Willie saw his Paw, but he didn't want to be noticed, so he looked off. As they got near the house, Lil' Willie noticed a lot of women, mostly light-skinned blacks, selling food and lemonade to the workers while the white men were buying food and drinks. Cotton lived in an extremely big house, bigger than most Black folk houses in his small town. Lil' Willie had known Cotton for almost three years, but this was his first time going to his house. When they got inside, there were many here too, all shades of color and sizes. One of the women said, "What's up bruh; let a bitch hit that junt." Cotton passed the weed to her and said, "What's up sis"! She said, "shit, trying to get a buck from a duck." Cotton said, "Hey sis, this my nigga Willie; he's my ace. I fuck with him tough because them other niggas at school be hatin on a real ass nigga. He's 100 though." He said, "My nigga, this my sis, Puddin." Puddin was tall and light-skinned like Cotton.

She was only sixteen years old but had the body of a grown woman with a fat ass and big breasts. She and Cotton were the youngest two of his mom's kids. They walked to the backyard where Cotton's older brother was. The oldest was named Mike. Mike liked to talk shit all the time bout how many bitches he fuck with but in reality, he just had a lot of baby mommas. Next to him was Nick a.k.a Slick Nick. Nick was a true con artist. He could talk a person outta anything. He had true game for a lame. After Nick, there was Big C. Big C was a super, big nigga who was 6'5" tall, 340 pounds, fat and muscular. He was a gentle giant, talked softly and smooth, but he would crush any nigga in a fight. Most niggas were afraid to fight him. Then there was Malcom a.k.a. Man-

Man. He was a real gangsta who had just got out of the Pen for murder. All of Hernando feared Man-Man. At the age of fifteen, he served eight years and extorted small-time hustlers in their town. He wasn't the biggest, but he was the most violent and short-tempered nigga in Hernando. The four brothers loved their Lil brother, Cotton, to death. They all were grown but Cotton and Puddin' were still kids, living like teenage adults because they weren't living like kids. They were in the back shooting dice and drinking.

Slick Nick said, "Cotton, I heard yo young ass got some more of that fye ass weed! Let me check it out Lil Bruh." Cotton handed the last of the junt to him and showed him the bag. He said, "The only way yo slick ass gone get yo hands on some this is you gotta pay for it, *bruh*." Nick smiled and said, "Cool, young nigga -- here's ten bucks. I respect yo hustle." Man-Man got up from the dice game and said, "what's up, Lil' Bruh, who's this nigga you got in our house?" Cotton said, "Big Bruh, this here is Lil Willie, my nigga from school." Man-Man shook Lil Willie's hand and said, "Any friend of my Lil' Bruh is a friend of mine." Then he asked, "you that Lil' Brown that broke that nigga nose who was trying to jump my Lil' Bruh, right"? Lil' Willie said, "Yeah, that's me"!

About a year after he and Cotton met, some niggas tried to jump Cotton in the schoolyard. Lil' Willie jumped in and helped his friend fight. Cotton could fight but wasn't as good as Lil' Willie with his hands. So, after that, Cotton knew Lil' Willie was a stand-up nigga who'll ride with him against anybody. Man-Man respected stand-up niggas plus he knew Lil' Willie's older brother Bubba's hand game was extra tight. Bubba would later fight professionally in Kansas City.

All the Browns were known fighters. MaryLynn raised her kids to fear nobody but the Lord, so that's just how they were. After Cotton and Lil' Willie got done smoking and kickin it outside, Puddin called Cotton and said, "Hey nigga,

Ma looking for yo ass upstairs." As the two walked up the stairs, they overheard this demanding voice yelling as they got closer to this big door at the top of the stairs. The voice said "Look here hoe, I don't give a flying fuck bout yo lazy ass baby papa talking shit bout yall gonna get through this. Fuck is he doing but nutting in yo pretty ass for free. I got you making money, paying bills, feeding yo kids and his monkey ass. Now you wanna take days off for him! Fuck him and fuck you, too! Go be broke and in love. We trying to get money over here and I don't need no sucka-for-love as a hooker in this stable. Now here's five hundred and don't come back when that nigga break yo ass and your back broke cause yo pussy ain't gone be worth a hamburger after that nigga finish with yo ass! Now get the fuck out, hoe!"

The door swung open as the female came rushing past them. As they entered the large room, Cotton said, "What's up, Momma"? She said, "The rent nigga." Cotton's momma was a light, brown-skinned heavy-set woman with extra big breasts. She had a cigarette and its holder hangin on the side of her lip as she talked and blew smoke out of one nostril. She was sitting at a big wooden desk counting a big stack of money. She said, "Baby boy" as she called Cotton by the name only, "Who's this Lil nigga with you"? He said, "This my friend Lil' Willie, Ma. He cool."

She said, "Okay"! "Look baby, you ain't been in no shit in that damn school have you"? Cotton said, "Naw, ma." I'm good." She said, "Ok, now where the fuck have you been lately? You been missing all of a sudden." He said, "naw ma I just been out with my nigga doing my own thing." She said, "Roll yo ma one of those good junts." He said, "Ok. Coming right up."

As he rolled the weed, Big Momma, as she was called, poured herself a drink from the mini bar that was in her office. She said, "Lil Willie, is that it?" Willie said, "Yes ma'am". She said, "You drank, Lil nigga?" He said, "Yes ma'am"! She poured all three of them a glass of Remi Martin V.S.O.P., got the junt from Cotton, lit it up and took an extra-long pull from it while inhaling only letting out a little smoke. She was a real pro at smoking weed. Her lips were dark too and she finished half the junt then passed it. As they all sat there smoking, she said hey Babyboy how much you got left of that batch?" He said, "bout a half pound ma. Why you need some to smoke?" She said, "yeah that too, but now that trick ass nigga from Seattle said he got more, and I'll buy it if it's selling good for you". He said, "yeah real fast". She said, "ok then I'll have it when he comes this weekend ok." Cotton said, "what's up with ole girl who just ran out of here." Big Momma said, "Aw, baby that young ass hoe wanna square up because of her broke ass, baby-daddy complaining about him babysitting and need her at home with him, but the hoe doesn't wanna work a real job and she don't want a real man who gonna support her and those kids she got. She a stupid confused young slut who likes to fuck and suck dick but don't know how to be responsible. Hoes like that always complaining about how hard life is but will go lay up with a broke ass nigga and never try to go get no money. They try to sell pussy, but they are afraid of what their boyfriend or friends going to say. I call them Wanna B's and ain't worth the trouble. Son momma telling you this. All women ain't whores but if you a sucka, a woman will play yo slow ass... real talk. That's why they call us females. This shit is for a fee and not for free!"

    Willie had heard of women with a lot of game, but this was his first time seeing and hearing this for himself. Big Momma turned out to be a Female Pimp or Madam. Now it was clear why Cotton didn't bring niggas to his house, he lived in a hoe house and his momma was the Boss.

    His mom was really open and cool with her children. Cotton's sisters were hustlas too. Puddin was a hooker and so was his oldest sister, Nyla. The middle sister just watched her momma's back and helped run things. Her name was

Moniqua, but everybody called her Money. The boys were all hustlas too, though they all worked from time to time in the fields. Their main thing was dice games, burglaries. Man-Man would sometimes rob and extort other hustlas. Big Momma gave her kids a lesson in how to survive with or without a job. In a small town like Hernando, there wasn't enough money to truly get rich, but they were doing okay for a small-town family. After they kicked it with Big Momma for a few hours, Cotton said let's roll over to the clothing store before it gets too late. Willie said cool.

As they were walking out, Nyla stepped out the door looking like a beauty queen with no panties on. She said, "Hey Lil bruh, leave me a bag of that fire ass weed." He looked at her and shook his head saying, "Hoe, go put on some damn shorts or something!" She said, "Fuck you, young ass nigga! This is my money maker. I ain't ashamed of this just like that damn weed you selling. Besides you and yo friends finna go buy some young hoes ass with all that weed money y'all got." Nyla looked at Willie and said, "Look young nigga, this a big fat pussy. Now don't be a sucka for none of this, ok. Y'all tell those young hoes y'all dick ain't for free and if they wanna give it up on the first date, they hoes too. Y'all ask them to come by the house and let a real hoe show 'em how to make real doe." She took the weed, shook her plump ass, and laughed at the look on their faces. Cotton said, "Never mind my crazy-ass sis." Willie said, "Naw, your family is cool as a fuck.

They went downtown to this clothing store. Lil Willie had gone downtown to buy clothes before but never without his momma. Plus, it had been over a year since he had new clothes because his family bought kids clothes one month at a time and it was fourteen of us.

It was a Friday night, and the store was packed. All the salespeople knew who Cotton was because he and his family shopped there all the time. The sales lady walked up and said, "What's good, Lil Cotton?" He said, "Shit, me and my nigga here looking to buy some fresh outfits and shoes for tonight." She said, "Y'all young niggas must be going to Lil Lisa's house party tonight." Cotton said, "Yeah, ain't you a little too old to be at a teenager's party?" She said, "Hell, yeah lil nigga! My lil sister Angie told me about it, so I got her an outfit to go. Besides, I don't do lil niggas, I fucks with grown-ass men. By the way, how's that fine-ass gangsta brother of yours, Man-Man, doing"? Cotton said, "He's out doing him." She said, "Tell that nigga he just gone fuck and leave and didn't even test the head game out yet?" Cotton laughed and said, "Damn, Bruh got it like that"? She smiled and said, "Enough bullshitting! Give me y'all sizes so I can hook yall up. Go to the bathroom and hook a sista up with some of that weed cause yall ass stank like dank." They all burst out laughing.

    She got both of them some fresh Adidas jogging suits. It was 1986 so that was the top-of-the-line outfit of that time. Then she came back with the tennis shoes to match. Lil' Willie had the Run-D.M.C., three-stripe jogging suits with the Shell Toes to match. Cotton had the plain logo jogging suit with just the Somoa shoes to match. He also had a Brim hat like D.M.C. would wear.

    After they left downtown, the two split ways to get ready. Cotton gave Lil' Willie a bag of weed to smoke with his sisters and brothers and told him to meet him in front of the gym so they could head to Lisa's house for the party. They bumped fists and headed their separate ways. He was so excited that he was walking fast, almost running to the house. Lil' Willie made it to his house in record time. His house was very old and small for the seventeen people who stayed there. Both his parents, fourteen kids and his nephew lived there. He had an older brother named Bubba, and older sisters named Pauline and Verlean. He also had three younger brothers, Earl, Glen, and Lauderdale. He also had younger sisters, Maxine, Henrietta, Fannie, Shirley, Lola, and Gladys.

His momma MaryLynn was called Mu-Dear by her kids and his paw name was Ike-Lee.

Mu-Dear was very religious, and always in the Bible. She would only listen to Gospel music and was really high on respect. Yet still, she ran the house with a iron fist. Nobody disrespected Mu-Dear! She was a tough, black woman from the dirty South, and she commanded her respect. Ike-Lee was a hard worker, but he was less strict. He drank, smoked cigarettes, and weed too. Mu-Dear didn't do nothing but go to Church even turning the living room of their house into a small Church with pews and an altar as well.

Lil' Willie walked through the door high as a mink coat smiling from ear to ear. Mu-Dear said, "what's so funny, Willie?" He said, "Momma, I'm just happy!" She said, "For what"? He lied and said, "I worked extra hard, and this man gave me a tip and some new clothes." Mu-Dear wasn't nobody's fool, but she just let her son be happy. All she knew was that he needed some new clothes. Lil Willie had one hundred and six dollars left so he gave his momma fifty dollars and said, "Momma, go buy yourself what you can with it." She smiled and hugged her son. Willie felt good giving his momma money and knew that he would do even more once his life started. He jumped out of the old-fashioned bathtub and got dressed. He looked in the mirror on his sister's dresser, and noticed a glow he had never seen on him before. He thought, "Maybe I'm still high because I've never dressed like I had money before now." He's looking at an image of the hustla he'll soon become. He said right then, "Man, this a good feeling! I'ma stay fly, till I die, no matter what!

As he was admiring his newfound look, one of his twin sisters walked in named Pauline. She said, "Damn, Lil Bruh! "You clean as the Board of Health. Where you going tonight"? He said, "to Lil Lisa's party. Me and Cotton going to get us some pussy tonight." His sister said, "Ok...lil bruh gone shine on them young bitches then." He said, "You better know it!" Pauline said, "Let me smoke some Lil Bruh." He tossed her the bag and said, "Roll a few for us and you can keep the rest." She said, "Now that's my lil nigga there"!

They went out the backyard because Mu-Dear didn't allow no smoking or drinking in the house. Ike-Lee had set up a chill spot in an abandoned chicken coup where he drank and smoked. Verlean, Earl, and Zina joined them out in the lil spot. They fired up three junts at a time, six in all. As they smoked and kicked-it, Ike-Lee walked up and said, "What the fuck you kids doing hangin in my shit?" From the smell, they could tell he was already drunk as a fish. He said, "at least let yo Paw hit that shit." So Zina passed him the junt. He said, "Damn son; you got this! This is some fire right here, nigga!" Earl asked, "Big Bruh, can I roll with y'all tonight"? He said, "Naw Lil Bruh. This ain't for kids. In a few more years, we'll be able to do just that." He looked at the clock on the wall and saw it was time to go meet Cotton for the party. So, he told his family, "I'll be in late and if I'm lucky, not at all." His dad said, "Yeah son go beat dem young pussies up, you a Brown. See all these kids I got; Ike-Lee Brown tears a pussy apart"! They all laughed as he headed on his way.

Lil Willie made it to the meeting spot in front of the gym before Cotton did. While he waited on his friend, he lit up the last junt he saved. Before he finished the junt, Cotton was walking up. The two bumped fists as their usual way of greeting one another. Cotton said, "You ready to go party my nigga?" Lil Willie said, "Let's do this my nigga!" Cotton said, "Hold on first," and reached into his pocket and came out with a bag of weed already sacked up for resale. There were twenty-, ten- and five-dollar bags, with another bag with about one hundred rolled up junts. He said, "These go for a buck," and Lil Willie said, "cool." He gave Lil Willie his first sack. He didn't know it at the time but at only fourteen years old he became a drug dealer. He then said, "This bag here is our personal smoke. We gone blow the roof off in that party. Cotton reached under his shirt and pulled out a small 22

Revolver and said, "Lil Willie, every hustla need to protect his or her investment". Lil Willie asked, "Where you get that?" He said, "my Big Bruh, Man-Man. You know niggas be robbing niggas for the sack but not us niggas; we can't take a lost." Lil Willie said, "dig dat. I'm 100% down with you on that". So, after everything was understood, they headed the short walk to Lil Lisa's house. As they approached the yard, they could hear the loud music blasting out of the door that kept opening and closing as people came in and out.

    The party was extra live. All the black teenagers in the town were there. Lil Lisa was known to throw the biggest teen parties in town. Her parents both drove 18-wheeler trucks and stayed on the road for weeks at a time. So, Lil Lisa and her brother Carlos would throw parties all the time. Soon as Cotton and Lil Willie entered the house, all heads started to turn and stare. Cotton had a junt big as his arm in his lip. All you heard from the crowd inside was what's up Cotton and what's good? The niggas in the bitches were like hey Cotton or hey baby! Cotton was more known in town than Lil Willie because he was a born hustla. A few people from school said, "What's up Willie, y'all shining in this spot huh"! Lil Willie loved his newfound attention as plenty party goers made their way to him and Cotton for a bag or junt of that stanky dank they were smoking. Like Cotton said of course the haters was there too. They were some petty hustlas from across town, but they came to party on our side because everybody knew Lil Lisa's party was the one to be at. The hater niggas had some bullshit ass brown weed. Nobody was feeling that headache weed so they were mad as hell when they saw all the people buying from Cotton and Lil Willie. Lil Willie noticed the haters mean mugging them, so he whispered in Cotton's ear asking what's up with them niggas over there putting they dog on us like that? Cotton said, "Man, them same low life suckas are mad because we getting all this money. I told you, niggas be hating, that's why we got this hammer. If they come wrong, then they gone get burned". Cotton smiled and said, "Fuck, them niggas! We came to get money and get some of this drunk and high pussy that's dancing through here. So, relax my nigga let's have a good night, its yo coming out a hustla party!" Lil Willie said, "Yeah, that's what's up; love yo haters because that only mean you're doing something worth another muthafuckas attention. We are shinning my nigga they love and hate us at the same time".

As they started to move through the crowd, Lil Lisa stopped them. Lil Lisa was a short, dark skinned fine-ass young girl with big hips and lips. She was well known in town and well-liked. She talks a mouth full and always cussing. She walked up and said what's up Cotton and Lil Willie, you niggas late to my big bash and I know yall brought a bitch some smoke for the House Lady. It's a rule in the game, if you are selling any drugs in somebody else house, you gotta kick them down some out of respect. Cotton said, "I gotta take care of you lil mama, you my nigga." So, he gave Lil Lisa a half ounce because they almost sold out fast. She was due a blessing. Lil Lisa said, "Good looking out. You niggas want something to drink and eat?"

They both said, "What you drinking"? Lil Lisa said, "Come back here with me." She led them to a room in the back of the house. When they walked through the door, it was What's good?" Carlos was a cool ass nigga. He fucked with a lot of young bitches because his sister had a lot of friends. Lil Lisa said, "Yeah, this shit back here for my VIP guest. Fuck that cheap punch everybody else drinking, we drinking that top notch shit in this room". Lil Willie said, "Oh, that's what's up!" She poured them a glass of Hennessy with a splash of coke on the rocks. She looked at Lil Willie and asked "Ain't your ass too young"? He said, "For what?" She said, "To be up in here getting fucked up". He said, "I'ma man, baby! Besides, how old are you"? She said, "Boy, I'm sixteen years old with two kids and I'ma full grown bitch"! Lil Willie said, "dig dat". She said, "Don't let the size fool you.. They call me Lil Lisa but ain't shit little bout me!" She asked him, "How tall are you?" He said, 6'3". She said, Yeah, now my bitches gone have fun with yo tall, fine, young ass. Cotton walked up and said, "Lil Lisa, you going hard on my nigga. Slow down, low down. Lil Lisa said, with her smart-ass mouth, "Fuck you Cotton, I know Lil Willie. I just never seen him at a party that's all. Look muthafucka this my shit and I can say what the fuck I want in my shit. Now shut the fuck up and roll this muthafuckin weed nigga!" Cotton just laughed. Lil Lisa had a foul mouth, but she was cool. Carlos said, "Man, you niggas got that A-1 weed, the whole party was talking about how high they was off that shit. Where y'all getting this shit from"? Cotton said, "The West Coast my nigga". Carlos said, "Cool, before you run out, sell me some, ok?" Cotton said, "I gotcha my nigga". Lil Willie asked, "Hey Carlos, what's up with the freaks in here? I'm trying to get my dick wet tonight". Carlos said, "Man they all in here, but my sister got friends who came just to get fucked. Holla at her. She'll hook yall up with some super freaks."

They were enjoying the scene when this thick, sexy young female walked up to Lil Willie and said, "Hi, can a sista hit some of that weed?" Lil Willie was star-struck. This young lady was the finest thing he ever saw. She had long hair down her back, a cute smile with perfect white teeth under a sexy set of lips. She was wearing a skintight bodysuit that was Adidas. He could tell the body under those tights was bangin. She said again, Can I hit that good with you or are you too high to hear me?" Just then, he snapped out of the trance she had him in and he said, "Sure - anything as fine as you, can hit whatever you want". She smiled as she hit the weed. Lil Willie had kicked it with girls before but never in a party setting. He didn't have a quick come up line. He remembered what Cotton told him. "Relax. We the *shit,* tonight! Just be yourself. So, he started by asking, "What's yo name, pretty? She said, "Angie" as she passed the weed back to him. He soon remembered the sales lady at the store say her lil sister name was Angie and that she was going to be at the party. He found a way to start up a conversation. He asked her, "Hey, don't you have a sister who works at a clothing store downtown?" She looked surprised and said, "Yeah, my sista Keisha works down there. Why?" He said, "Me and my nigga shop there all the time, so we know her like that, In fact, I got on this set right now from her." She asked, "You ain't fuckin my sista are you?" He said, "Naw. She messes with one of my older niggas". Angie said, "Ok then, cause my sister a cold slut. She fucks and sucks any fine-looking nigga who walks through the doors of that store. I know she was looking at yo tall, fine self. How old are you, Lil Willie, she asked?" He said, "I'm seventeen years old", lying because he knows she probably was older than he was. He then asked, "How old are you"? She said, "I'm fifteen years old". He felt stupid now for lying about his age because turns out she was only a year older than his real age. He then said, "I know yo boyfriend in here some place looking for yo sexy ass". She said, "Nigga please, I'm too young for a relationship. I'm here to have fun not find a husband."

  As they were chatting, Lil Lisa walked up and she was pissy drunk now. She said, "Angie, I see you met my nigga, Lil Willie." Angie said, "I sure did. We just getting to know each other." Lil Lisa put her arms around Lil Willie and said in his ear, "Bruh this my girl Angie. She cool as fuck and she be hooking a sista up on them fly outfits from downtown. She was telling me her last young nigga she fucked with just got locked up and she haven't had no dick in months. I'ma need you to dick this one down for me. If you do, I'll suck yo dick myself", as she smiled with a freaky grin on her face. Lil Willie said, "I got you, don't trip."

  So, Lil Willie turned his attention back to Angie. She was dancing so he slid up behind her and said, You having a good time?" She said, "Now I am", as they danced close. She then said, "It's getting hot in here with all these bodies. Let's go somewhere private". He followed her to a bedroom with a king-sized bed in it. From the looks, this was the master bedroom, Lil Lisa's parents' room. He asked, "Are you sure we good in here?" She said, "Yeah, me and Lil Lisa extra cool". Lil Willie had sex only a few times before, but he still knew what to do to please a female. Angie got straight to the point. She said, "Lil Willie I know we just met, but dancing with you made me extra hot and wet. I wanna fuck right now." He said, "Say no mo!" She took off the tights and like he thought, she wasn't wearing any panties. He started kissing her with his tongue down her throat and fingering her pussy. She was soaking wet. He soon got undressed as she started to take his pants off. Lil Willie was rock hard and as soon she saw his dick, she yelled, "Yes....you got hang time!". She said, " Now put that big pole in this wet hole and lay pipe daddy". Lil Willie started pounding her pussy hard as she moaned, Fuck me, daddy! That's right, fuck me hard!" As Willie beat her pussy up, he started to suck on her swollen nipples. She then said, "Lil Willie, baby, make me cum! It's been a long time, please, make me cum." Lil Willie was hitting her guts yelling, "Ok. I'ma make dat pussy cum." She then started screaming, "Oh, my God...I'm cumming, daddy--I'm cumming! As Angie's eyes rolled back in her head, Lil Willie put her legs over his shoulders and start drilling her. Her legs started to shake as she came. She said, "Now daddy; hit it from the back". So he flipped her over and started to hit it face down, ass up. She then said, "Smack my ass, daddy! Spank me. I'm your lil bad girl--spank this ass! So, he started slapping her ass. Angie was a real freak and Lil Willie was enjoying the whole thing.

All of a sudden, the door swung open, it was Cotton, Lil Lisa and another bad lil bitch. Lil Lisa said, "Don't stop, y'all good. This my house. We just came to join the party y'all having in here". Cotton said, "Yeah, that's how we do it my nigga, beat that pussy up dawg!" Lil Lisa drunk ass walked right in Angie's face and said, "Yeah, bitch -- I told yo ass you come to my party, you gone get some dick, didn't I?" She said, "Yeah" as Lil Willie kept hittin it from the back. Lil Lisa smacked her on the ass and said, "Say, that's some good dick then bitch. Say it"! Angie started to moan, "This some good dick, this some good dick."

    Then Cotton told the other young fine girl to get naked, so she did. Next thing you know, him and Lil Willie was side by side hitting two bad bitches from the back. Lil Lisa was coaching the whole thing, telling the females what to do. She said now you bitches put that dick in y'all mouths and start sucking, so they both did. As they started giving Cotton and Lil Willie head, Lil Lisa said, "Hold on, you dumb bitches! Don't know how to suck a dick? Let a pro hoe show you how it goes". She then jumped right on Lil Willie's dick first. Lil Lisa was a true head doctor. Her head was wet as a pussy plus she would go all the way down deep throating and gagging. Then she jumped down on Cotton. Cotton said, "Damn, Lil Lisa! Yo head game serious". She looked at him with his dick in her mouth and winked her eye. After that, she turned to the two bitches and said, "Now, that's how you hoes do it. Do it just like I showed you till you feel his dick jerk and taste cream in your mouth and be sure to swallow." The two did as they were told. Lil Lisa slipped off her skirt and started playing with her pussy as she watched the sex scene she helped start. She had the hiccups from being drunk. She said, "Now, I hooked you niggas up now one of you gotta fuck me too. I wanna cum too, muthafuckas. Don't matter which one of you niggas is first, nigga nuts gotta fuck me". They said cool. Lil Willie nutted first because he had been fucking and getting head the longest. Lil Lisa was a pro. She knew the second nut would take longer than the first, so she was about to have some fun. Lil Willie got up and started to lay Lil Lisa down. Lil Lisa said, "Hold on nigga this my party, I'm the one doing the fucking, you lay down". She then hopped on top of Lil Willie and start riding him.

    Lil Lisa had a big sloppy pussy for a bitch her size. But her foul mouth got extra foul. She started talking bad, saying, "Yeah, nigga. Yo punk ass gone remember this night I bet you." She was bouncing up and down and around on Lil Willie's dick making the bed rock still talking trash shit like, "Take this pussy boy! You can't handle this. I'll break yo dick off in my pussy nigga. Then she told Angie, "Come here bitch…suck my pearl tongue!" Angie did just that, her head went up and down as Lil Lisa started to moan. She said, "Yeah, now we fucking up in this bitch". She yelled, "suck that pussy bitch… I'm finna cum!" She started scratching Lil Willie's chest. He was getting mad, but she was riding his dick so good and hard, he just sat back and enjoyed the show. Lil Lisa hopped up and shot cum all in Angie's face and mouth, rubbing her pussy juices all over Angie's face saying, "You like that don't you slut?" Angie just shook her head and agreed. Lil Lisa said, "Now you finish Lil Willie off. I'm finna go wash up". So, Angie started back sucking Lil Willie's dick till he nutted again and she swallowed all of it. Yeah, Angie was a true freak swallowing two men's nuts and a woman's nut all on the same night. She was super cool with Lil Willie.

    After they were done, the two bitches joined Lil Lisa in the bathroom. Cotton and Lil Willie could hear them laughing and slapping fives as they knew they had pleased them. They all came out the bathroom at the same time. Lil Lisa was smoking a Newport. She said, "There are towels in the bathroom. Y'all can wash y'all stinky dicks and balls in the sink and don't fuck with my parent's bathtub. Take a hoe bath like we did, hit ya hot spots and roll." The women all laughed as they walked out the room. Angie said, "Willie holla at me before you leave". He said "ok" and they handled their business in the bathroom and headed back to the other part of the house where the party was starting to wine down.

    Cotton looked at Lil Willie and said, "My nigga…we had a blast plus we made bout a grand selling weed. This was an extra good night". Lil Willie said, "Yeah, this the best night of my life!" Angie walked up and said "Here's my number Lil Willie, call me. We can do what we did anytime you want to." He said, "Sure thing, ma plus you gone hook a brother up on some outfits, aren't you?" She said, "With dick like yours, you can have the whole store!" They laughed, hugged, and said, "See ya later!" Cotton said, "Hold on. I'm finna serve Carlos this last bag I promised him." Lil Willie said, "Cool--I'll be waiting at the door, my nigga."

Most all the people were gone except a few drunk people passed out on the couch. Lil Lisa was cussing this one nigga out saying, "Get your drunk ass outta my house, throwing up and shit." Cotton asked, "Where Carlos at?" She said in the other room, "Tell his ass to hurry up and help me get these drunk muthafuckas out our house when you see him." Cotton said, "Got you, Lisa!"

Cotton walked in the room to find the same girl he had just fucked on her knees giving Carlos head. Cotton said, "Here you go my nigga" and handed Carlos the bag of weed. He said, "Enjoy!" Carlos said, "Yeah, this weed fire." Cotton said, "Naw, that bitch head fire," they both laughed. He said, "When you're done, go help yo sister put them drunk niggas out, ok? He said, "Cool". Cotton walked back to where Lil Willie was waiting. They bumped fist and headed home. It was a good night, they got money, pussy, and the whole town talking about how they had the best weed in town.

Lil Willie made it home about six in the morning. Everybody else was still asleep except his momma. She was up listening to her morning Gospel show on the radio. She said, "Hi Willie, hope you had fun at your friend's house." He said, "I did." She said, "Look at this new radio I bought with the money you gave me yesterday." He said, "Good, Ma. I'm happy to see you smile. Hopefully, I'ma make you smile even more one day." She asked, "Are you hungry, son?" He said, "Naw, Momma. Just tired. I'm finna go lay down and get some rest." So, he went in the room he shared with his brother Earl, laid on the bed and went to sleep.

He woke up bout 3:30 pm still hungover from last night. His brother Glen came in the room and said, "Bruh you were out like a light. You good now?" Lil Willie said, "Yeah, I'm good." He then asked, "Bruh, you got some money"? Lil Willie said, "For what?" Glen said, "Because, I want some of those shoes you got on." Lil Willie said, "I got you Lil Bruh. He reached in his pants pocket, pulled out a fat bank roll and peeled off two hundred dollars. He said, "Go downtown to the store, get you and Earl some new shoes, and tell'em Angie sent you and she'll hook y'all up. Ask for Keisha ok". Glen said, "

"Ok, Big Bruh! Thanks for this." Willie said, "We Browns...we gotta look out for each other."

Willie got up, took a bath, and headed to Cotton's house. When he got there, tricks were in and out as usual. Willie walked up in the house, seen Puddin and said, "What's up?" Puddin said, Shit, I heard y'all shined last night!" Willie said, "We sure did!" Puddin said, "That's how yall do it my nigga. I'm finna go get Cotton for you, ok?" He said, Cool. I'll wait here". Nyla came by and asked, "What's good, Lil nigga?" Willie said, "I'm good. She said, "Did yall get some pussy last night?. Willie said, "For sho we did!" She then asked, "Did you tell them young sluts what I said?" He said, "Sure did. I told them. I got a bitch who gone get me clothes when I want." She said, "That's what's up, Lil nigga. You learn fast. Get money first and ass last. Be hard on a slut and treat a money getting hoe like a queen because as long as a bitch happy, she's yours!" Cotton walked up and asked, "What's good, my nigga? Willie said, "Nigga, I had a blast last night plus we got paid!"

He showed Cotton the money he had on him which was about four hundred and eighty dollars. Cotton said, "Cool. I got about one thousand and seven hundred dollars myself." He said, "Give me three hundred and I'll give this to momma so when the dude gets in from Seattle today, we'll be back in business." Willie said, "Bet and save some for us to smoke." Cotton said, "Now you know a nigga *had* to save some personal for the team." Willie said, "My man! Cotton said, "Roll up, nigga! Big momma walked in and asked, "What's good, young Willie? Is that right?" He said, "Yes ma'am." She asked, "Are you boys hungry? I got this hoe from New Orleans, and she make some good gumbo, y'all want some?" They said, "Yes ma'am!" So they went to the kitchen. The Black woman with a heavy accent asked, "Ya boys hungry, ya heard me"? They said, "We're starving." So she made them two bowls. Life was good, Cotton and Willie were booming weed in town and fucking all the bad young bitches.

    A year had come and passed then one day, Willie came home and saw his momma on the sofa in the living room crying. Willie asked, "Momma, what's wrong?" She said, "We lost it all son; we lost it all!" Willie said, "Lost what?" She said, "This house and this land." The house and land had been in the Brown family for generations, but Paw lost his job because machines was used on the Cotton fields now. The taxes are backed up and they owe the Farmers Bank for loans. Now, the Bank owns our house and land. "They plan to build a shopping center on it" momma said. Willie said, "Momma, I got twenty-five hundred dollars saved up. You can have it to pay the bills." She said, "Thanks son. We'll need way more than that. That'll help with the moving though." He said "Moving where?" She said, "To Memphis, Tennessee. My sister, Dina, and brother, Bo, live there now and they got free housing for families in need." Willie said, "But what about all our people and friends here?" She said, "Memphis only 45 minutes North of Hernando, so they'll be able to visit often." He said, "Ok, momma. I'm with you. Whatever we gotta do. I'll quit school and get a job to help out". She said, "No, you try to finish school ok?"

    Willie walked out the house crushed. All he knew in life was about to change. He had customers, a weed connection and a best friend. He lit up a junt and headed to Cotton's house. He got there in no time. Cotton walked up to him and said, "What's good, my nigga?" Willie said, "Shit ain't shit, good Bruh." Cotton asked, "What's wrong, Bruh? You alright?" Willie said, "My drunk ass paw lost his job. Now the bank owns our land and house so we gotta move to Memphis!" Cotton said, "Damn, my nigga. You gone be leaving ya boy? I'ma miss you, my nigga! You like a brother because all my brothers much older than me. Look, Bruh-- I got a cousin up in Memphis. He lives in Binghampton. They be hustling good up there. That's the *city*, my nigga. It's way more money in a city than a small town. So, don't be sad, my nigga. Just hustle up. I'ma come fuck with ya every chance I get". Willie said, "You're right, my nigga. I'ma handle business wherever I go!" Cotton said, "Yeah, nigga. A true hustla can get it wherever he at because money don't stop, believe that." They smoked a junt, kicked it, and said their goodbyes. Willie knew he would miss his nigga because they were tight. Still, he knew the lessons Cotton taught him would help him get money in Memphis.

    Before Willie left his house, Cotton also gave him a Q-P (quarter pound) of weed to get started. Three days later, Willie and his family were packed and ready to roll. They rented a van and a U-Haul with the money Willie gave them. They headed North on Interstate 55. It took them an hour to get to Memphis because traffic was bad. The city was super big compared to Hernando. MaryLynn said, "We're moving to Lemoyne Gardens". To the kids, the word Gardens sounded nice but as they would soon find out, the Gardens was known for crime and Memphis was a breeding ground for gangs, drugs, and murder!

CHAPTER 2

Welcome to the Hood!

L.M.G. MAFIA

As they got off the freeway on Crump Avenue, Willie looked out the windows and saw people everywhere moving and going. He wasn't used to seeing so many people out in the streets cause in Mississippi, it was slow and country. In Memphis, things were moving fast.

They made it to Mississippi Blvd. His Momma said, "Look kids--Mississippi street. This Mississippi wasn't like the one they knew. Niggas were all hanging out. The police had niggas laid on the ground searching them. Women hollering at them. The whole scene was live and loud. Then they finally made it to Walker Street, made a left, and they drove past Lemoyne Owen College.

They all said, "They have a College too!" None of the residents of the Gardens attended. Soon they made it to their destination--LeMoyne Drive. They turned left into the apartments. As soon as they entered, Willie could see that this wasn't like any place he had ever been. There were people hanging out everywhere on both sides of the small streets. Every time they hit a speed bump their bodies jumped. They soon reached the address they were looking for... 931 LeMoyne Dr. Apt A. Their Momma said, "Well kids…we're here. She already had a key cause Aunt Dina did all the paperwork and sent it to them. MaryLynn and all the girls went in first and started cleaning while Ivan Lee and the boys started to unload the U-Haul. Willie stood in front of the van and just looked around his new stomping grounds. Niggas was watching him the whole time. From the smell in the air, Willie could tell there was a lot of weed smokers in the

Gardens. Still, he knew he couldn't just open shop until he met someone who knew everybody.

So, he started unloading their things from the U-Haul. Out of nowhere, this real dusty guy came walking up, and said, "Y'all need some help with that?" Willie said, "Nah, we can handle it my guy." He said, "Cool, but if y'all need any help, my name is Big Bear and I'm the help man in these projects." Willie asked, "What's a project?" Big Bear laughed and said, "Yeah, y'all must be from Mississippi!" Then he said, "Look young nigga--this a project a hood, and a known ghetto. This where everything goes down." He said, "Come by later and I'll holla at ya." They started moving everything in the apartment. The next-door neighbor's door came open and two young niggas came out. They said, "What's up, y'all moving in huh? Willie said, "Yeah. We just came from Hernando, Mississippi. They said, "Aw shit, y'all some country muthafuckas! Hope yall didn't bring no pigs and cows with y'all cause ain't no pets in the jects" as they started to laugh. Willie didn't find it funny, but he didn't say shit. They asked him, "So, what's yo name nigga?" Willie said they said, "Dat's, what's up!" Then they introduced themselves. The brown skin one said, "I'm Darryl, but they call me Dee." The other black dark nigga said, "My name Money." So Willie asked, "Dat's yo real name, Money"? He said, "Fuck naw, but in the hood you never give out yo government name unless you really know a person and I just met you so it's Money to you, my nigga." Willie said, "I can dig dat. How long y'all been in these apartments?" They said, "Most our lives but we was born on 4-V in the Foot Homes but we die hard L.M.G., and you're in it now, nigga. We the MAFIA! We own South Memphis!"

Willie said, "OKAY...this South Memphis?" They said, "Yeah, nigga. This the Dirty South and there's a lot of Hoods in Memphis.They all don't get along but the Garden's the toughest of them all." Willie said, "How come?" They said, "Cause, niggas over here don't be fighting. They just shoot muthafuckas." Willie said, "Real talk?" They said, "Hell yeah, real talk. In fact, the nigga house y'all moving in got killed last week." He asked, "For what?" They said, "Cause he owe some niggas some dope money so they ran in and shot him in the face in front of his baby momma and kids, so the next day, they moved."

Willie was in total shock of the news the two brothers was telling him. Willie had heard that a lot of people get murdered in Memphis. He himself never knew anyone who actually was killed. Things like that rarely happened in Hernando but in Memphis, it was an everyday thing. They finished moving the things into the apartment, Willie told his new neighbors, I'll be back outside when everybody get settled. The brothers said, "Bet. We right next door."

His momma and sisters were busy decorating their new home. Willie asked, "Momma you sure you wanna stay here? "You sure it's safe"? She said, "Son, I know this ain't like back home and I know a city like this can be dangerous, but I prayed to God and we will be protected cause we have the Lord watching over us." Willie knew his momma would say that cause he knew her, but he also knew that staying safe meant looking out for one another. He knew what to do if anybody ever fucked with his family.

As they were chillin in the living room, a knock came at the door. MaryLynn opened the door. It was Aunt Dina. MaryLynn was happy to see her sister. They hugged tightly and screamed in joy at seeing one another.

Then the whole house hugged Aunt Dina. Aunt Dina was really cool. She and MaryLynn looked a lot alike but acted totally differently. Aunt Dina drank all of the time, plus she kicked it hard, loved the Blues Music and always kept a lot of candy, drinks and snacks for any kids who came over her house. Her husband was named Henry. He had a hole in his neck and talked with a device that helped with his words.

He was cool as well. Aunt Dina asked, "How was the ride"? Sis. MaryLynn said, "Not too bad, a lot of traffic." Aunt Dina said, "Yeah, it's a lot of cars in the city. MaryLynn said, "you telling me."

Aunt Dina was carrying a long bag. She told all the kids to go in the living room and let her and her sister talk some grown folks talk in the kitchen. Everybody left. Willie watched as the two sat down at the kitchen table. Aunt Dina sat the long bag beside her. She said, "Mae, I know you are highly religious and have faith in God, but this the ghetto you are living in now. I lived in these same apartments when I came to Memphis 15 years ago and I'm telling you shit goes on over here". MaryLynn said, "What you mean goes on?" Aunt Dina said, "Robbing, drugs, thieves, killings--you name the crime and it's here in the gardens." MaryLynn rubbed her face and said, "Well, why you tell us to move here?" She said, "Cause in five or six years, depending on the waiting list, they got a program called Section Eight that they put you on a list to put you in a house with little or no rent." Aunt Dina said, "I live in one now not far from here on a street called Lucy." MaryLynn said, "Ok. What's next?" Aunt Dina picked up the bag and put the bag on the table. She reached in and came out with a pump shotgun with a scope on it. MaryLynn said, "That's a big gun, Sis." Dina said, "I know you seen people hunting with these in Mississippi, but in Memphis, this is for protection. You'll be hunting niggas" as she laughed. Then she said, "All jokes aside. This is for your safety and to make sure nobody comes through those doors with no bullshit. If they do, shoot they ass right out the door cause the police in Memphis don't protect and serve, they just serve muthafuckas. You gotta look after yo own ass." She said, "Sorry for cussing Mae but I gotta tell you how it is." MaryLynn said, "I understand."

Dina said, "Still it's some good in the Gardens. There's a Boys and Girls Club, a playground and they also pass out free lunch in the park on the weekends. Plus, the best part is no rent and the light bill is only twenty or thirty dollars a month. So, you'll be able to save money." Mae said, "that sounds good. You know you've got to make the best of any situation," she said. "Well, I gotta get back to the house" Aunt Dina said. I'll be back tomorrow to take you places to get started." Mae said, "Ok." They hugged and said bye.

Willie watched as his Momma took the bag and headed to her room. Willie got his personal belongings and took out his weed he had stashed. He rolled up two junts and went and sat on the concrete wall in front of their apartment. He lit it, inhaled, and took a look around. The hood was always live with plenty of people moving around. The dusty man from earlier came walking up, and said, "What's up young nigga, let me hit that green." So Willie passed it to him. He hit it and said, "Damn baby…that's some fire my nigga." So, he passed it back, Willie said, "You cool, you can't handle good weed?" Big Bear said, "Naw, I can but weed ain't my thing, I fucks with that boy." Willie said, "Boy... what's that?" He said, "That boy, that dog food, nigga, that Heroin."

Willie never knew anyone who took hard drugs. Big Bear said, "Yeah, in this hood they on real drugs." Willie said, "Like what"? He said, "Heroin, cocaine, and pills." Willie said, "What pills?" He said, "T's and Blues, Tabs, Oxycontin, Dellotas, Volumes, etc. Now weed sells too, but the real D-Boys sell real drugs and that's the big money." Willie said, "I feel ya my nigga." Big Bear asked, "How old you is, young nigga?" Willie said, "Fifteen years old." Big Bear said, "You tall for a kid! Must be all that country food y'all eating in Mississippi," they both laughed. Big Bear said, "Look young nigga, this the hood and you've got to be able to adapt to this environment. These streets can either make you or break you. You young and you can go to school, play ball, or get a good job and be the best at whatever you choose. But if you get in the streets which so many do, the streets play for keeps and be the best at whatever you choose." Willie said, "I'ma hustla." Big Bear just smiled and said, "Awl ok, another Wanna B hustla. Well look…I was a hustla at your age and look at me now. I'm a junkie and I don't have shit." Willie said, "well I'm not gonna be like you." Big Bear said, "that's the best thing you said, but remember this; never get high on hard drugs, never! Never trust nobody with your money, your bitch, and your life, ok." Willie said, "Dig dat." Big Bear said, "I'm fixing to go do some hustling myself. Gotta feed this monkey on my back." Willie said, "What monkey? Ain't shit on your back." Big Bear just laughed as he walked off saying, "Boy---you've got a lot to learn."

Willie fired up his second junt and his sister Zina came to join him. She said, "So Lil Bruh, how you like it so far"? He said, "It's cool. How about you?" She said, "I'm loving it. I'll be able to get my own apartment through Memphis Housing Authority in a week or two, so I'll have my own first spot." He said, "Dig dat, sis. You know I'll be coming through fucking my lil bitches." She said, "Boy please! You already found you a new lil bitch in Memphis?" He said, "Not yet but you know hoes love my style, so it won't be long." She said, "Well you gone on, Big Playa. You know these women in the M-Town like niggas with a lot of money and a nice car." Willie said, "I'ma get mines, you'll see."

As they smoked, a clean Chevy pulled up. A muscular, brown-skinned nigga hopped out. Zina said, "Damn---that nigga got it going on. He looks as good as that ride he's in." Willie just laughed. She threw the nigga a seductive smile and winked hoping he noticed her. When he didn't, she built up enough courage to just try to start a conversation. So she said, "Hey Mr…That's a nice car! What kind is it"? He said, "It's a '76 Impala. You know anything about cars"? She said, "No but you can teach me. Oh, this my little brother." Willie nudged her and said, "Her Big, Little Bruh." She said, "Can I come look at it closer?" He said, "Yeah sexy, come on." So, she put her best stanky switch on, making sure he noticed her ass-throwing walk. Willie just laughed. He had plenty of sisters so he knew the game was on.

Willie said, "Hey sis, I'm fixing to go to the store alright." She said, "Alright bruh. I'll be out here talking to my new friend, Billy." He said, "Dig dat."

So, Willie started walking up Willie Street. He thought, "Damn…a street named after me in the hood." As he walked, he noticed all eyes on him. If you're new in a hood, people always look you up and down. They were being on their P's and Q's or as they say in the hood – awareness. Soon as he made it to the corner of Porter and Willie Street, there were four stores on Porter St. The first store he went to was the Chinaman store. There were people going in and out like they were in a hurry. The Chinese people who ran the store knew everybody by their names. They were selling everything from food, to beer, to clothes and all household items. Willie got some chips and a pack of Zig Zags. He walked out and noticed this other store next to the China store was extra live, so he walked next door.

The store was named Momma Strongs. It was a store/hang out. Soon as he walked up, niggas started approaching him and yelling, "Nigga, I got that blow! Another nigga said, "I go--that dog. Then another said, "I got that weed." Plenty of niggas was out trying to offer drugs for sale. He said, "No thanks" seemed like a thousand times. Then he went inside the store.

The man at the counter said, "You new here… haven't seen your face. What's your name son?" He said, "I'm Willie. I just moved from Mississippi." The man said, "Oh yeah, Mississippi. That's not far from here. My name is Albert Strong and this is my store. Me and my family run things in here. We sell most things you need, cut meat, beer, hygiene, household too. We also sell the best burgers in the hood." Willie said, "Yeah, how much"? He said, "Three bucks for burgers and fries." Willie said, "I'll have that, then." He said, "Coming right up!" then he told the woman at the grill, "Fix Willies' order." He said, "You wait over there. Don't hang out in front like those other dudes cause the police always messing with them." Willie said, "ok". He asked, "Did they have a phone?" and He said, "Yeah" and handed him a phone. So, he called his friend to let him know he made it.

Cotton's momma picked up the line. "Hello, who's calling?" "This Willie, Big Mama." "Oh, yeah?" She said, "Hey, Lil nigga! Heard y'all moved to the M-Town." "Yeah, Big Mama" Willie said. It's a big city and a lot to do". Big Mama said, "Yeah Lil nigga, I've had plenty good times in Memphis. You been on Beale Street yet?" Willie said, "No, what's that?" Big Mama said, "That's a strip where all the blues clubs are. A lot of people come to Memphis to visit that street. It's known all over the world as the "Home of the Blues." Willie said, "Ok, I'll check it out. Where's Cotton?" "I'ma go get him to the phone for you, ok" she said. "Thanks ma'am." "No problem, Willie! You take care of yourself, alright?" "Got ya!" said Willie. "Here's Cotton."

"What's up my nigga?" Cotton said. Willie said, "Shit's good, Bruh. Just at this store getting a burger." Cotton said, "So how's your new home, Bruh? "It's ok" Willie said. "The apartments live as hell with bitches and niggas out all day and night". Cotton asked, "Nigga, how's the hustle money out there?" Willie said, "It's plenty of hustling going on in the M-Town but these folks selling them hard drugs." Cotton asked, "like what?" Willie said, "Man, you name it---Coke, Heroin, pills...the whole nine. So, what's going on back in Hernando?" Cotton said, "Same ole shit...making cash off this good grass and Momma still selling hoes' ass." Willie laughed and said, "Y'all a muthafucka." Cotton said, "Oh yeah, I went to buy some clothes and seen your lil bust-it-baby, Angie. She said she misses you and to tell you to call her." Willie said, "Man fuck that slut. She'll be ok." Cotton said, "The way Lil Lisa was running those hoes, I should

[35]

pimp them bitches cause they going big time." Willie said, "Man I feel you on that. Go head get your cash outta hoe's ass, my nigga"! Cotton said, "You know that pimp shit runs in my blood. So, I'ma do me my nigga. Man, a nigga miss yo ass already but like I told you, I'll be up there soon. So, gone and get situated and I'll be up there in a few weeks." Willie said, "Bet. I'ma call you some other time. You stay sucka free and you taught me a lot Bruh. So, I'll be good here. Finna find my own hustle and get to the money here." Cotton said, "That's my nigga! Love you, Bruh and keep in touch." Willie said, "No doubt…Peace!" Cotton said, "Peace!" Willie hung up the phone and told the lady thanks. She said, "No problem, baby. Here's your food, young man. Enjoy! Come back and we appreciate your business!" Willie said, "Smells good. I'll be back depending on how good the food is." The lady smiled and said, "I'll see you later cause I throw down in the kitchen."

    Willie got his food and headed out the store. On Porter Street shit was poppin hard. Niggas was running back and forth to cars making drug sales. The shit looked like a movie to Willie. It was an open drug market with a hundred salesman. Willie headed back down Willie Street walking and eating on his food. Before he made it halfway back to his side of the drive, he was stopped by a group of young niggas who came from behind the stairs on the high wall. They all surrounded Willie. Willie knew how to fight and wasn't afraid but there were like seven or eight niggas. One of the niggas asked, "Who the fuck are you and why you walking through my hood? Willie said," Nigga, I'm Willie and I live over here now so why y'all surrounding me like this?" Another nigga said, "Cause, we don't know you tough ass, nigga and niggas we don't know could be an enemy." The other nigga said, "So where you stay at over here?" Willie said, "On the drive next to Dee and Money." Another nigga said, "Okay, he stay in that house where Cam's baby daddy got killed at. Is that right?" Willie said, "I believe so." The nigga said, "So where you move from?" Willie said, "Mississippi." They all laughed and said, This nigga a country boy." So, the head nigga said, "Look, my nigga. My name is Lil Horn and the other nigga said, I'm superman, and these our homeboys." They said, Nigga, this our hood and we can't let no new nigga walk through without checking to see if he a hater from a rival hood. It's for our and your protection." Willie said, "I feel y'all and I'm not from Memphis so I ain't here to get into it with nobody." They said, "Nigga, the L.M.G got plenty niggas who don't like us cause we hard on suckas who come through here. We be smashing on niggas in they own hood so, if you're going to live here you gotta know the reputation that goes with living in the Gardens." Willie said, "I can respect that, but I'm just here to get in school and stay out of trouble." They said, "school" and laughed. "What grade you in?" Willie said, "Ninth." They said, "Oh yeah. You'll be going to BTW (Booker T Washington High School) and trust me my nigga, coming from L.M.G you'll find trouble the first few days." Willie asked, "Why would I have trouble at school." They said, "Cause the school is across the street from Third Ward." Willie asked, "What's Third Ward?" They said, "The Clayborn Homes a.k.a. the Third Ward or C.H.P., our number one enemy. Shit stay poppin off with them. Hell that's why most niggas from the Gardens popped out cause it's always a fight or shooting. It's a real live war! But you gone find out for yourself. And remember if you get jumped, let us know cause we ride for our hood and if you're going to stay over here, you gotta stand like a real nigga cause ain't no suckas or soft ass niggas in the L.M.G. We da Mafia! We made niggas, win, or lose, we gone cause hell!" They all said, "Dig dat" as they flashed gang signs throwing up the L's. They all walked off.

    Willie headed back to his house. As he approached the porch, Dee and Money were hanging on the brick wall smoking weed. They asked, Willie, do you smoke? He said, "I do…like a broke stove." So, they passed him the junt. He took a pull and said not bad., but it got better as he came out his pocket with his weed. He said, "Go head role three or four junts, bruh." He handed the weed and papers to Money. Money smoked and said, "Damn, this looks like some fire like that Ink from James Street." Willie said, "Naw, that's from my nigga in the Sip. And I got that for sale if y'all wanna buy some. I'll hook y'all up good cause we're neighbors, ya dig." They said, "Now that's love." Dee said, "I got twenty dollars right now, my nigga. You gone hook me up?" Willie said, "Wait here." He went inside the house and up to his and his brother's room. He got his weed and headed back out the door. He gave Dee a fat twenty bag. Dee said, "Yeah, I'ma fuck with you bruh plus you right next door." He handed the bag to Money and told him to roll up some outta this bag too. We gone match bruh on two more junts. Let's get high as fuck! So, they all sat on the wall and fired up junts back-to-back blowing good green.

As they was smoking, a dark skinned, skinny big head nigga walked up and said, "Dee, let your boy hit that." He said, "you know what's up" and passed him the junt. He said, "Duck Head, this Willie our new neighbor and Willie this our homeboy, Duck Head. He stays up the drive. Duck Head shook Willie's hand and said, "What's up wit-cha my guy. How long you been in the hood?" Willie said, "just got here earlier today." Duck Head said, "Awl, shit. You smack brand new in the hood." Willie said, "Yeah." Duck Head said, "Well let me tell ya, the hood good and bad but we gotta make the best outta it ya dig."

It was just about nightfall when they heard the sounds of gunfire. Then a woman's voice yelled, help…..help! They just shot him. Then about three or four minutes later, a crowd started to form in a driveway across from where Willie and nem was sitting. So, Duck Head said, "Let's go see who's the new victim and I hope it ain't one of our niggas." Dee said, "you telling me. I'm tired of going to funerals." So, they all walked over to the crowd. As they walked up, they could see a large group of people standing over this lady holding a man who looked like he was lying in a pool of blood. She was saying, "Please baby don't die on me. Our kids need you. Please baby don't leave us" The man was gagging for air taking long deep breaths. Then an older lady came pushing through the crowd. She said, "Hold on son. Momma's here. Please son, momma's here." She then yelled, "Somebody call the ambulance!" A man said, "I did, they on the way now."

Money looked down and said, "Damn, man? Money said, "That nigga the stick-up man. He be robbing niggas. I guess he robbed the wrong muthafuckas this time cause they put big bullet holes in his ass."

They could hear the loud sirens as the police and ambulance pulled up around the same time. The crowd made a path and let them get the man. They brought a stretcher up and lifted him on as the two women held his hands and got into the back of the ambulance with him. Soon they pulled off. A policeman named Jack Owens started asking questions. So, everybody just turned and walked away cause everybody knows if you see anything, you'll be taking a trip downtown and nobody likes that. And most of all, snitches don't last in these projects.

So, Willie and his neighbors headed back to where they was chilling at. Duck Head said, "Yeah, see that's the bad shit I was talking about." As they made it back, they heard loud music approaching them. As the sound got closer, the cleanest Cadillac Willie had ever seen, pulled up. It was light brown with dark brown leather top with the humps in it. It also had tinted windows and a gold package with rims, trimming and grill. It had a solid gold flying bitch on the nose. Two niggas hopped out. They had on big gold chains, Rolex watches, and rings on their fingers with diamonds sparkling in the dark. Money said, "What's up Mitch?" to one of the niggas. He said, "What's up young nigga?. Yall hangin hard on the block ain't ya"? Money said, "Yeah trying to get money like you Mitch." He laughed revealing a mouth full of gold and diamond teeth. Then he and the dudes with him went into an apartment. Willie asked, "Who are they? They must be rich, riding a brand new Caddi that clean?" Dee said, "Man that's Mitch Boyd and his brother Mike. They some big time hustlas in the hood. They got plenty whips and they all clean. They got big houses too and a lot of niggas work for them over here and throughout the city. They booming!" Duck Head said, "Yeah there's a lot of big time hustlas that's from this hood. Still, you got niggas all over who making that big money, selling drugs, robbing, and pimpin." Willie thought to himself, "Damn, I want money like that. If they can do it, I can. I gotta help feed my family. I need some real money like them niggas." Duck Head broke him out of his daydream and said, "Nigga you still high cause you're in a daze. You never seen no rides like that in Mississippi, huh"? Willie said, "Nope. I ain't gone even lie, niggas in the Sip ain't eating good like that." Money said, "Yeah, I bet they ain't but in other spots it's plenty money to be made like in Jackson, Mississippi or Little Rock, Arkansas. Any city with a lot of people means a lot of drug users which equals a lot of fuckin money, my nigga." They all said, "Hell, yeah" and agreed.

Willie said, "Well, it's getting late. Gotta go get some sleep cause I'm registering at BTW tomorrow." Dee said, "yeah, I go there too, so I'll see you there and show you how we all walk the same way to and from school. Also, you'll be able to meet most the niggas our age that go to school even some who don't go to school walk with us cause we gotta be deep and stick together at school. Niggas be wilding sometimes." Willie said, "Bet, see you there." Money was younger so he went to Vance Middle School. Duck Head got kicked out and now go to school across town at Hillcrest High School.

Willie went into the house and got ready for bed. As he laid in his bed, he could hear sirens and gunshots in the night along with cars with music blasting all times of the night. It was like they never went to sleep in the hood. As soon as he thought he wasn't going to get any rest, he fell into a deep sleep.

Willie was awakened by his momma pushing him saying, "get up son, I got a lot to do this morning. I have plenty of schools to go to; plus I got to go get these food stamps started so we can eat up in here. Get up, there's toast and oatmeal on the stove."

Willie got up, went, and took a quick shower, grabbed a piece of toast, and jumped in the van with his family. They went to Cummings Elementary School first to get the younger kids in school first. Then they went to Vance Middle School and after that, they went to BTW. Soon Willie and his momma walked in, all eyes were on them.

BTW wasn't like the school in Hernando. It was a lot bigger and had way more students. They made it to the office and started the paperwork. The Basketball Coach walked in and asked Willie, "How tall are you? Willie replied, "Six-five (6'5") sir." Then the coach said, "Hi, my name is Coach Hayes, and I am the basketball coach here. Can you hoop, young man?" Willie said, "Yeah, a little but I'm not good at it." Coach Hayes said, "Are you interested cause I can teach you how if you like, but first you gotta get good grades before you can play." Willie said, "I'll see how things go." Coach said, "Ok, let me know alright." Willie did know how to play ball, but it never interested him like other kids. He liked to watch the NBA and his favorite team was the Celtics but that's as far as his desire went when it came to sports. Willie was a hustla. He enjoyed everything about hustling and was eager to learn how to master his trade. While his momma was doing the paperwork, Willie hung out in the hallway eyeing the pretty girls as they walked past. BTW had a lot of fine bitches and a lot of hood rats too. The girls would walk by throwing their asses hard making sure niggas were watching. Willie started doing a little flirting himself. He waved at the girls while grabbing his nutts and winking at any girl who would look his way. As he was styling and profiling, his momma smacked him upside his head and said, "Boy you're here to learn not find a baby momma" as she smirked and smiled. She knew her son was handsome. All the Brown men were, and she knew he couldn't help himself. Willie said, "Ok Mu-Dear. I got you." She said, "Here your classes are now gone to them. Make sure you get home at a decent time and don't be hanging in the streets around this school cause the principal said those Projects called Clayborn Homes are real bad and dangerous. You come straight home, you hear me"? Willie said, "Ok momma. Love you." She said, "Love you too, son. Now I gotta meet Dee so we can go get this welfare started today." They said their goodbyes.

    Willie headed to class and as soon as he walked through the classroom door, he noticed Dee. He said, "What's up, nigga? We in the same class? That's what's up! The teacher said, "I see you know people already, Mr. Brown. Don't let nobody get you started off on the wrong path" as she looked at Dee and frowned. Willie took a seat and tried to pay attention. All of a sudden he heard the thunder of a train roaring sounds in the air. Willie asked, "What the fuck is that"? A dark-skinned dude said, "Nigga, this school sits right next to a Railroad track." The nigga asked, "Where are you from? Willie said, "Mississippi, but I live in LeMoyne Gardens now." The nigga said, "Ok you're a LMG nigga huh." Willie said, "Yeah, I guess so." The nigga said, "My name is Chucky D and I'm from Fowler Homes." Willie asked, "Is that the Third (3rd) Ward"? He said, "Naw, that's across the street. My hood across those tracks off Crump and Mason Street. Also, Fouth (4th) and Latham". Willie said, "That's what's up." He said, "Yeah, you new to this city I see." Willie said, "Yeah, I'm still learning." Dee said, "My nigga, all the hoes around the south go to school here." Chucky D said, "Yeah, these hoes loose as a goose. All it takes is a drink, some good smoke, and then put dick all down they throat." They all laughed. Willie asked, "Y'all wanna smoke after school"? They said, "Bet."

So they focused on their schoolwork until the bell rang. After school they met up at some apartments that was across the street from the school. Willie met all his school homies that lived in or around the Gardens and they all walked to school together. There were a lot of crazy nicknames. All of them were tight, and they all grew up in the Gardens. You had LMG niggas going to schools throughout the city cause they kept getting kicked out. They stuck together wherever they were, and they were known to go to war with whoever, whenever, wherever, and forever. That was they motto. Fuck the rest, we the best or get laid to rest with that cocky don't give a fuck attitude. They made a lot of people respect them and hate them. They still had respect for other hoods. They were cool with hoods like 4-V, Hillview, and Trigg Street, but most of Memphis knew they was a deadly force to be reckoned with. Willie was impressed at all the respect they got in the school and the city. He had never been in a hood that was feared like the Gardens were but he rather be feared than to be from a pushover hood.

After the smoke out, they started to walk home. Some niggas had cars, and some even rode bikes, but they all had that get up and go about them. Also, they all carried weapons. Most had guns but they also had knives, brass knuckles, and special made belts with heavy steal buckles. Even the women had razors on them. When they walked together, they looked like a big Mob. If you weren't a part of their mobbing, you best to get out of their way or get rolled over. They would walk up Mississippi Street to Austin and make a left turn on Porter Street where everybody hung out. Soon as they reached Porter Street, Willie asked Dee, "What's selling that fast"? He said, Nigga them rocks and that boy. He asked, "What's rocks? Dee said, "That crack rock, and that hard cocaine. That's the new money rush and it's getting every crazy nigga rich." Willie said, "Hey my nigga, I got some mo' of that good weed for sale. You wanna help me down my sack?" I'll cut you in on the profit money. Dee said, "Hell yeah! I'm down, but it's a lot of weed selling niggas in the Gardens and they got all the customers on lock. If we gone get it off fast, we gone have to go hustle it downtown to the tourists. They be on Beale Street and the Mississippi River. A lot of White customers and out-of-towners too. Also, my Auntie lives on 4-V and we can sell a lot there. It's close to downtown." Willie said, "Bet that. I've heard of Beale Street, so I know it should be poppin." Dee said, "Alright we'll go this weekend cause on the weekend, downtown be packed." Willie said, "Ok, then it's a go cause I gotta get my hustle on. My momma can't afford to buy me the things I want and I like having shit so I gotta get mines."

They chilled on Porter Street for a while then headed back to the Drive. The Gardens was one hood but had four or five different main hangouts. You had the Drive niggas, the Porter Street niggas, Provine nigga, and Walker Street niggas, too. The Drive was where Willie lived. Porter Street had a lot of hustling going on. Willie got to his house and walked in. His momma was in the kitchen preparing dinner for her big family. She said, "Hi son! How was your first day at your new school"? He said, "It was ok and how was your day momma," he asked. She said, "It was good. Got a lot of business taken care of. I got all y'all in school, got the food stamps going, welfare check started and oh yeah, I put your Paw out, too"! Willie asked, "What do you mean you put Paw out"? His momma said, "For two reasons; first he's the reason we lost our house in Hernando. He was off work for almost three months before I found out he lost his job. He got up every morning and went out the door but never went to work. I don't know where he was going. He kept lying like he was paying the taxes on our land that my daddy left me. He also took out a loan just so I would think he was getting paid from a job. Really that was house money and he drank all his money away. He a low life and be pissy drunk. These apartments will charge me rent if a male lives here. We can't afford to pay rent cause he can't find work. Ain't no Cotton workers in Memphis and he ain't trying. So, he'll be staying on Trigg Street with his older sister. I've had enough of him. I love my husband. Don't get me wrong and he's a good father. I ain't gonna take that away from him but love ain't gone feed fourteen kids and keep a roof over our heads so, I had to do what I had to do and let him go."

Although Willie was hurt, he knew his momma was right. Ike-Lee was cool, but love don't buy food or pay bills. It was the harsh reality of growing up poor. A lot of fathers lose their families cause they can't afford to provide for them. Willie let that conversation go cause he knew that topic hurt his momma so he asked, "What's for dinner? She said, Y'all favorite, neckbones, greens, pinto beans, cornbread, and sweet potato pie". His momma loved to cook, she made everything from scratch like in the old days. Willie said, "That's what's up cause I'm starving!" She said, "Bet you are with all those left-handed cigarettes you smoke. His momma was highly religious, but she wasn't lame. She knew about weed and a lot more. She called junts left hands like they did back in the day. She didn't like the fact some of her kids smoked weed, but all she asked is that they didn't smoke it in her house, and they would always respect her no matter how high they got. His momma said, "Oh yeah son…you got a lot of cousins here in Memphis.

He knew his momma had a lot of brothers and three sisters. Most all lived in Memphis, but she had a sister in California and a brother in Milwaukee, Wisconsin. They all had plenty of kids, so the Browns were everywhere. He then asked, "Where at? She said, "Oh, they all over Memphis. They in Orange Mound, Westwood, North Memphis, Binghampton and Trigg St, Clayborn Homes, Fowler Homes, The Bay Area, and East Memphis." He said, "Ok. "When will I get to meet them?" She said, "In due time."

So, he ate and went back outside. He went to the Goodwill Boys Club the next day. It was live. He loved the games they had. There was foosball, ping-pong, pool tables, and table hockey. He met two cool brothers named Big Pale Moe and Lil Pale Moe. They stayed next to the Boy's Club on a side street called Beachwood. A lot of young niggas went there. It was directly across the street from the Gardens on Walker Street. Though the Boy's Club was fun, Willie's heart was in the streets.

When that weekend rolled around, Dee came over, and they went next door to his house to sack up the weed for resale. Dee's momma was cool. She didn't mind her kids smoking in the house cause she smoked weed, too. After all the weed was sacked up, they used Dee and Money's bikes to make the ride to Beale Street. Dee advised them to wear LeMoyne-Owen College sweatshirts, so they'll look like innocent college kids. They made it to the Foote Homes first, so they stopped by Dee's Auntie Ruby's apartment to let them know they had weed for sale. The Foote Homes was jumping like the Gardens. Plenty hustlas out making the block hot. They walked in Ruby's house. He said, "What's up Auntie?" She said, "Shit trying to make it." Dee introduced Willie to his Auntie. She said, "hi young man welcome to the Foote Homes." Then Dee told her he had some fire ass weed for sale and was trying to get it off and needed her to get the word out. She said, "I got you nephew. Give your tee-tee a junt so I can see what you working with." So, he gave her a fat ass junt. She said, "Thanks." Then he asked, Where Pink-a-Boo and Big Boo at? She said, "Them hoes on 4-V. Go check the pool hall and Nicely Pigs. You'll find em at either one of them, and I bet they'll buy some of this fire ass weed from y'all." Pink-a-Boo and Big Boo were sisters and Dee's cousins. They also were female hustlas. Pink-a-Boo sole dope while Big Boo sold pussy. They knew everybody on 4-V and everybody knew them.

They went into the pool hall. Dee spoke to a nigga named Val and another nigga named Big Ben. They each bought a quarter ounce of weed. Pink-a-Boo was in the back shooting dice. When she saw Dee, she said, "What's up cuz? What you got going?" Dee said, "Shit me and my nigga got this good weed trying to make a dollar." She said, "Cool give me a 50 bag. Anything to help the cause." Dee said, "Dig dat." She said, "Y'all need to sell these rocks; that's real money." "In due time cuz," he said. "Good looking out. I'm fixing to go to Nicely Pigs to holla at Big Boo." So, they walked out the pool hall and stood on the corner of Vance and Fourth or 4-V as it was infamously known as.

4-V was a known hoe stroll. Hookers were everywhere, all down Vance Street. The pimps were riding by blowing they horns checking they traps and handling they hoes. One pimp rode by everybody yelled, "What's up, Dun-Dee." He let his pinky ring out the window and sped off. Dee and Willie walked in the Nicely Pigs. It was a blues café slash hooker hang out. Plenty of hoes would run in there when the Police would sweat the block. The owner was a trick so he let them have their way so he could play! Nicely Pigs was live even in the daytime. The sounds of Bobby Blue Bland was playing on the jukebox. He sung, "Ain't no love in the heart of the city, ain't no love on this side of town!" He was right. Ain't no love in Memphis.

As they made it to the back, they saw Big Boo talking shit to some other hoes. Big Boo didn't have the looks or shape of your normal hooker. She was heavy-set and tall, but she had game and a hell of a conversation. She said, "Hey cuz, what's the deal?" Dee said, "Shit, coming to see my favorite cousin." She asked, "What you want, talking like that?" He said, "For you to buy some of this getty green." She said, "No problem" and reached in her bra and came out with a twenty-dollar bill. He gave her a bag. She said, "Smells good and who this young nigga with you?" "Willie," he said. "This is my partner in crime." She said, "Is that so? She moved in closer. Willie's breath was full of Newport smoke and whisky. She said, "Ok partner. "You better look after my Lil cousin." She blew a razor from under her tongue and said, "cause if anything happens to him while y'all out hustling, I'ma cut your balls and dick off and shove them down yo throat. Dee said, "He cool, cuz". Big Boo was a gangsta hoe-- bigger and badder than most hoes you'll ever meet. Willie knew she was just testing him, so he didn't sweat it. She said, "This some good and told all the other hoes to buy some cause they wasn't about to smoke all hers up. In all, they spent over a hundred dollars. Dee said, "Thanks cuz". We finna go to Beale Street and get some of those tourist dollars. She said, "Ok but be careful." So they headed down Fourth Street to Beale Street. It was live, a lot of music and plenty of street performers. Willie had never been to a place like Beale Street. It was a party spot where you could enjoy yourself and take in the culture of Blues music. People was selling food, souvenirs, and art. Dee said, "I told you this was the spot!" Willie said, "I see". He said, "Now, let's get to it." He said, First, be sure to ask them if they the police cause if they undercover, they have to identify themselves in order to make an arrest. Willie said, "Bet" as they walked up and down Beale stopping at Bars like Alfred's and Club 152. They made it to the River Front, and they sold all the weed. Willie said, "Damn...I never downed a sack that fast! He said, "Downtown is booming!" Dee said, "Told you my nigga. This is where people come to party." "Drugs and partying go together! Willie said, "I'll be here every day." "Just call me, Uptown Brown!" Dee said, "that's yo new nickname--- Uptown Brown. Willie liked the name, so they stamped it. From now on he was Willie to only his closest family and friends and Uptown Brown to the streets. Dee said, "so Uptown Brown it is or just Uptown."

And like that, his career as a hustla was born and Uptown was to make sure everybody knew who he was. Uptown and Dee started making trips to Hernando,

Mississippi re-ing up with Cotton and also shopping with a Memphis weed plug too. They was getting good money down on Beale Street and the Mall down by the river. Uptown's name was ringing hard. He bought his first car---an '84 Ford Granada. He and Dee was riding through the Gardens when a Ford Mustang pulled them over. The driver said, "Hey "Lil nigga…Greg and Ced wanna see you. Dee said, "Oh, shit." Uptown said, "What's up; who dat?" Dee said, "Them niggas run the L.M.G. MAFIA! They probably heard we cutting their weed sales in the hood." Dee said, "Shit…let's go holla at them." They pulled up on McDail Street and walked into the apartment. Niggas pulled M-16 machine guns on them and asked, "Y'all strapped?" They said, "Naw, we ain't." Niggas was snorting cocaine from a plate. Then Greg and Ced walked in. They was some stone cold killas and they had a lot of killas who worked for them. One of his goons named Deck was pointing a .44 magnum at Uptown head while Greg ordered him and Dee to have a seat.

    He said, "Look niggas…I run this hood and any nigga making money over here gotta get my permission. I don't care if you selling drugs, pimpin, robbing, stealing, or playing paper. Any and every hustla gotta get my approval cause if not you can't be in my hood." Greg said, "I heard bout y'all, Dee and Uptown. Y'all name been ringing but neither one of all came to get my approval". He said, "Look, I'ma let yall do y'all but I got to make sure if y'all reppin the L, that yall doing it right cause niggas be hatin and robbing. We the Fuckin MAFIA and we don't accept nothing. But if you killin and you rob the L, then you dead simple as that." He said, "Now Dee, I know you but this Uptown nigga new to the hood, so I'ma let you explain yourself. Uptown said, "I respect the L; I live in the L so I gotta rep it like a real nigga should." Then Greg asked, "Are you willing to die for the hood?" Uptown said, "This my hood now and if I gotta die, I'ma die getting money." So, Ced spoke up and asked, "so you're down to ride for the hood?" Uptown said, "On my momma!" Greg threw up the L and said, "So be it then…you're one of us! Now that means you're untouchable." They showed Uptown the L.M.G. handshake as he and Dee walked out. Dee wiped the sweat from his brow and said, "We made niggas now. Greg stamped us, so we on our way to getting the real bread now and ain't nobody gone stop us. We finna blow up hard." They both smiled!

CHAPTER 3

Getting To the Money

Everything was looking good for Uptown. He and Dee were moving a lot of weed on Beale Street, 4-V and the Gardens. The money got so good that his friend Cotton moved up to Memphis to help move the weed. Cotton set up shop with his cousin Splive in Binghamton. Before long, they had the Red Oaks Apartments jumping and they had a few young workers on Tillman and Jimson Street. Uptown, Cotton, and Dee started buying more weed. They went from getting two pounds to getting twenty pounds in a little over six months. By Uptown's seventeenth birthday, they each were playing with five thousand dollars apiece.

Then Cotton said, "Man we need more cars and some more spots to store and stash money and weed." So, they all pitched in and got a lil two-bedroom house on Walker Street. Uptown was enjoying his new life. For the first time he felt like a grown man. He would give his momma money to go buy food and clothes for his family. He would also go by his daddy's house and drop a few bucks on him also. Things were looking up for him. He also loved to see his crew happy. Cotton was getting money from Hernando and Memphis. He even started pimpin like his momma taught him. He had young hookers working on Vance and Brooks Road. He bought a Cadillac Eldorado and it was clean. Dee loved to buy clothes and jewelry. He would get a lot of his style from this master thief named Noon. Noon was a booster and one of the best in the South. He had clothes that weren't even out yet. He kept everybody in the L.M.G. fresh from head to toe. Uptown loved to see Noon coming cause he knew Noon would give good deals on the flyest clothes out. So, when they were out, they dressed like niggas with money. The young bitches started to take notice too. Everywhere they went, they pulled fly girls who wanted to be seen with them.

Dee was fucking every bitch that came his way. Cotton just bated them in so he can pimp on them. Uptown loved women and pussy, but he was always focused on making more money. One day as they were on the River Front, a nigga came up and asked, "Hey, y'all got some crack? I need to smoke." Uptown said, Naw Bruh; we sell weed. The nigga said, "Look Bruh...I'll buy a bag of y'all weed and give you a hundred dollars if you take me somewhere I can buy some crack. He said, I'm not the police, I'm from Arkansas and I don't have nobody to help me." Uptown said, "Ok, get in the car."

As they drove to the L.M.G., he went by his homeboy Gi-Gi crack house on Porter Street. The man gave him two hundred dollars. He said one for you and one for the rocks. So, Uptown went and got it. Then Uptown said, "I wanna see you smoke it". The man asked, "You sure I can smoke in your car?" Uptown said, "Yeah and this way you'll prove you're not a cop or snitch." The man said no problem. He took the crack and put a rock on a glass pipe he had. Uptown had never seen a person get high on crack before. The nigga said, Yup, yup...that's some good dope! Uptown said, "How you know?" The man said, "Cause I can hear them bells ringing."

Uptown just watched as the man smoked more and more. He said, "Look, drop me off at the Peabody Hotel and your beeper number so I can get more." That same night the man spent over two thousand dollars and Uptown made a thousand just for running him back and forth all night. Uptown got back to the spot at 5:45 am that morning. Dee was sleep in the bed with two bad bitches. He heard the front door open and close and got up, still hung over. He walked in the living room where Uptown was counting a stack of money.

Dee said, "Damn, nigga---you pulled an all-nighter didn't you?" Uptown said, "Hell, yeah! I did while your ass was laid up. I been getting this weed off, plus nigga I made another thousand selling crack." Dee said, "You lying?" Uptown said, "Look nigga, a thousand in one night." Now Dee said, "That's what real D-Boys make!"

Uptown said, "Bruh, we need to invest in cocaine. We can sell weed and cocaine, soft and hard. Everybody asking for it, so we need to have it. Let's get all the money!"

So the next day Uptown, Cotton and Dee all sat in the living room to discuss the new business venture. Uptown said, "Man my niggas...cocaine is the real money. Unlike weed, it sales all night long and it makes a lot of money. Niggas spend twenty to fifty dollars on weed, but niggas spend hundreds and thousands on cocaine." Cotton said, "Yeah there's a lot of cocaine users in Binghampton and Mississippi. We can charge more for it." Dee said, "Yeah all that sounds good, but that work as they call it, comes with a lot of extra drama too." Uptown and Cotton said, "Like what drama." Dee said, "Let me school y'all country slick boys on the work game." He said, "Cocaine ain't like weed. Those customers are happy and less violent while cocaine users are very mean at times." He said, "If a weed-head run out of weed, he just gonna wait till he gets some more money or he just won't smoke. Cocaine muthafuckas, on the other hand, gotta have it! They sprung---they steal and even kill for a high. They'll even steal their momma's T.V. and even make a man suck dick and sell his ass for a hit. Then you have them gangsta junkies, they usually be ex-dealers. They'll rob an old lady to get a hit. Then after you worry about the junkies, there's the other drug dealers. They always beefing over drug spots, always killing each other to take over territories. It's a dog-eat-dog world but the money is why people take that risk cause cocaine is a rich person's drug and it'll make whoever sells it, rich." Uptown said, "I wanna be rich, how about y'all?" They said, "Hell yeah, we do! But, where are we going to find a good connect?" Dee said, "There is a lot of niggas selling work in our hood but to make sure we don't run out, we gotta have a lot of plugs. Plus we gonna need a good team--workers and shooters--but first let's go holla at Greg. We need to get his backing and get some guns." They all said, "Bet. We'll meet here tomorrow and see how much money we got and how much cocaine we can afford to buy". They all bumped fists and hopped in their cars and went on bout their day. Uptown was riding down McLemore Street watching all the crackheads run the streets and thinking bout his new plans. He made it to his momma's house and parked his car. As he got out, Big Bear was just walking up.

He said, "Hey, Uptown...I'll wash your car for ten dollars! Uptown said, "Bet cause I need a quick beam up." Big Bear had a crate and bucket of water. He got his supplies out the crate and went to work. As he was washing the car, he noticed Uptown stuck in a daze. So he asked him, "What's on yo mind, young nigga?" Uptown said, "Shit, need more money to get my family outta the projects and in a house." So Big Bear asked, "What you got in mind?" Uptown lit a mack junt and said, "Let me explain. Weed is good. It helped me get the hang of hustling but the real money like you told me when I first met you, is hard drugs." Big Bear asked, "So you finna sell that, boy?" "Not just yet", Uptown replied. "Naw, I'm finna start selling cocaine, crack, and powder. Things going smooth with the weed and I'ma still sell it also, but I can make thousands a day selling work. Then I can afford to move my family outta these rat and roach infested projects. Also, I'ma get rich too." Big Bear said, "Now, hold on young nigga! Let me tell you a thing or two bout the dope game. I know I don't look like a hustla now cause drugs fucked my life up, but I used to run a lot of dope. I told you I use to be a hustla and I wasn't lying bout it either. I'm originally from the Third (3rd) Ward and I sold coke and heroin on Polk and McKinnley. We was making plenty of money, but dope money makes the police watch you more and niggas snitching in the dope game. A nigga ain't too quick to snitch on you about no weed. Cause if one of your workers get caught selling weed, he only facing a few months in jail or the Penal Farm. If a worker gets caught selling a lot of work for heroin, he headed to the Feds or Prison for years. Some niggas will fold like a lawn chair. But even if you're facing 20 years to life, never ever tell on your team or yo plug cause if you truly love your family, you won't put their safety at risk by snitching on niggas to cut your case down. You just don't do shit like that. I spent over 12 years in prison for dope cases. Then I started using drugs and now I have nothing but I'm still alive, so I feel blessed in a strange way". Uptown said, "I see you're a Vet in the streets, so I got to respect what you're telling me. So you still know a few plugs then, don't you?" Big Bear said, "Yeah, I still got family still getting it". Uptown said, "I'm trying to find a good plug with good prices. I don't wanna shop in the hood all the time cause I don't want a lot of niggas in my business cause my momma still lives over here. So, where can I go get plugged at?" Big Bear said, "I'll make a few calls for you in the Third (3rd) Ward, and you can go on College and McLemore. It's a million-dollar dope track, and you're bound to get a plug over there and it's right down the street from here." Uptown asked, "So how I'm gonna go over there and I don't know nobody on their block?" He said, "Take your home boy Pell-Pell with you. His family got family over there. Plus, there's a pool hall and AL's Tasty Burgers on the corner. Just pull up looking like you bout money and mix and mingle. You'll bump into a lot of hustlas who'll be able to help you. Cause trust me, plenty niggas got it over there." Uptown said, "Thanks" and handed Big Bear a 20-dollar bill and got in his freshly washed car and drove off.

    He made it back to the spot of Walker Street and noticed a lot of cars parked in front of the house. He rode passed and noticed all the cars had Mississippi tags on them. So, he busted a U-turn at the corner of Walker and Wellington Street and headed back. As he parked, he could hear music blasting from the house so, he walked through the door and was surprised to see all Cotton's family there. All his brothers and sisters were there. They were happy to see Uptown. They said, "Hey Bruh! We been waiting on your ass to show up…what's good?" Uptown hugged everybody and asked, "Where's Cotton?" They said, "He's in the back room. He's not feeling well." Uptown asked, "Man-Man, what's wrong with 'em?" Man-Man said, "We all sick Bruh, but I'll let him tell you cause I'm trying to get drunk right now." So, he walked in the bedroom and saw Cotton's sister standing over him as he sat on the edge of the bed crying real tears.

Uptown asked, "What's wrong, my nigga? Are you ok?" He tried to reply but couldn't get his words out, so his sister Nyla spoke for him. She said, "Big Momma passed away last night." Uptown said, "Damn, my nigga. I'm sorry for y'all", as he too felt his friend's pain.

Cotton was the youngest of his momma's kids and he was a true momma's boy, so it was extra hard on him. Big Momma died of Cancer, and she never told nobody cause she never wanted anyone to worry or feel sorry for her. Nyla said, "We'll be moving up here to Memphis so we can be close to our baby brother. So, we'll be looking for a house by tomorrow." Uptown said, "I'll help yall find one". She said, "Thanks, Willie" as she called him by his real name, but Nyla was like family, so it was cool. She said, "Big Momma loved you and she was happy Babyboy found a true friend." Uptown thought of what pain he would feel if he ever lost Mu-Dear. The very thought hurt his head to even imagine it, so he knew Cotton would never be the same again. His heart was crushed. Uptown asked, "So when's the funeral?" She said, "This Saturday in Hernando." Uptown said, "I'll be there Friday." Nyla said "Ok, Bruh. Y'all can stay here until then. Our house is y'all house. We family. Y'all just relax. There's plenty to drink, plenty of food and plenty of weed to smoke. So, make y'all selves at home." Nyla said, "Thanks. We all need a good rest. This has been extra hard on our family." Without saying a word, Uptown left out of the room and went back into the living room where everybody else was. He fired up some weed and passed it to Man-Man. He said, "So he told you bout Big Momma, right?" Uptown said, "Naw, Nyla told me cause he couldn't stop crying." Man-Man said, "Yeah...it hurts, Bruh. Shit ain't gone never be the same no more. My momma's gone." He let out a drunken tear. Uptown patted him on the back and said, "It's gone be alright, Bruh. Not the same, but it's gone be alright." Man-Man said, "Thanks, Bruh".

As they were chillin and smoking, Dee walked through the door. He said, "Bruh, y'all having a party and didn't tell ya boy?" Uptown said, "Naw, my nigga, these Cotton's family. They just came up from Mississippi". Dee said, "Where's my pimp friend anyways." Uptown said, "He not feeling too good right now. His momma passed away last night." Dee said, "Damn, I'm sorry to hear that my nigga". He then said, "Look my nigga...let me holla at you in private."

So they walked into the other bedroom and closed the door behind them. Dee said, "Yeah Bruh. I talked to Greg and he said he gots plenty of guns to sell us. He told us to meet him Saturday night to go over our plans." Uptown said, "Where we meeting him at?" Dee said, "At this club on Vance called Rayford's." Uptown said "Bet. I should be back in town after Cotton's momma's funeral." Dee said, "Oh yeah. You know selling cocaine gone cut into a lot of niggas drug turf and we gone need Greg's backing to keep the haters off our asses." Uptown wasn't worried about no haters. He knew how the game goes and mo money means mo haters. So Dee was right with Greg and his goons on his team. Nobody would dare try to cross or rob them. But Greg's backing came at a price. So the only way to find out that price was to go holla at him.

Uptown said, "Oh yeah, I gots plans on how we gone find a good plug". Dee said, "How?" He said, "We gone just start hitting known cocaine blocks and mix-mingle." Dee said, "We from the LMG so you know a lot of niggas don't like us." Uptown said, "Yeah, I know but the most important part is they all respect us." Dee thought, "Yeah, he was right. A lot of niggas don't fuck with the LMG but a lot of niggas still know not to fuck with the LMG or they'll get fucked up. He said, "Look here's two thousand. Do what you like to do best. Go shopping. We gotta look like money if we wanna get a plug with a nigga who bout money. And holla at that nigga Noon so you can save a few chips, alright." Dee said, "Dig that."

Uptown said, "I'm finna go swing by Trigg Street and holla at my Paw. Get with ya later." Dee said, "Okay" as they made their way back to their cars.

Before leaving, Uptown spoke to everybody and said, "Y'all welcome. I'll be back tomorrow. So yall enjoy, eat, drink and smoke as much as y'all like. If we run out, I'll get more so don't trip." They all hugged and Uptown was out the door.

Uptown drove down Walker Street and made a left on Wellington, passed McLemore. He made it to Trigg Street where his Paw lived one house from the corner in a big, white, aged house. The house was a rooming house. His Paw had a room for free rent cause his sister owned the house. He walked in and went to the third room on the left. He knocked on the door and his Paw yelled, "Who is it." He said, "It's Willie, Paw." So Ike-Lee opened the door as he hugged his son. Uptown said, "How you doing, old man. Ike-Lee said, "I'm good young ass nigga," as they both laughed. Ike-Lee asked, "You still got some more of that weed you gave me last time." Uptown replied, "Yeah, but I gave your ass an ounce. You smoking a lot of weed nigga". Ike-Lee said, "Hell naw, I ain't. I been selling that shit to these niggas over here. Plus I gots these young bitches sucking dick for a bag of that good." Uptown said, "Your old ass wild as hell." Ike-Lee said, "You want a drink, son? I gots that good whisky today---

Crown Royal, nigga" he said. Uptown said, "Naw, I gotta drive Paw." Ike-Lee said, "Shit young nigga, I can drive with a gallon of moonshine in my system from here to Chicago" as he laughed, showing off the Brown's trademark…big, gapped teeth.

Uptown said, "Bet you can, Paw. Bet you can." Ike-Lee said, "And you know this, man". He asked, "How MaryLynn doing?" "Fine", Uptown replied. He then said, "You know I love your Maw, don't you son? Uptown said, "I know, Paw."

Then Ike-Lee said, "Son, don't end up like me. Be somebody in this world. Get yourself in a position to never be without." He said, "I know you and your friends bet hustling. I can't knock it, Son. Just be safe and know money can help you live good but it can't buy you real friends and real love. So be extra careful of who you trust. The only muthafuckas I trust is my damn daughters. They my girls like Charlie's angels but I gots nine angels." Uptown said, "You sure do." Ike-Lee said, "Zina came by yesterday with this nigga named, Billy." Uptown said, "Oh, yeah…Billy's cool, Paw. Ike-Lee said, "Damn that! That's my first born and he better treat her right or my big foot going up his ass!" Uptown said, "She a grown woman, Paw." He said, "Fuck that. Them my girls, *my* damn angels. I just told your monkey ass that boy." Uptown said, "Okay Paw, I hear ya." He said, "But you good? You don't need no money or nothing do you"? Ike-Lee said, "Naw. I'm good for now. Made some money selling that damn weed. What I need is some more of that weed". Uptown said, "I'll bring some by tomorrow." Ike-Lee said, "I do a little hustling myself." Uptown said, "Okay, old man. Don't have no niggas run in here and rob your old ass." Ike-Lee said, "Nigga, I'm good on Trigg Street. All the young people call me Pops plus my sister knows everybody and they families, so we good over here."

Uptown thought about it. Trigg was booming too, so he planned to set up shop on Trigg Street once he got a good plug. They talked a little more and Uptown said, "Paw I'm fixing to go now. I'll bring that weed by soon." Ike-Lee hugged his son and they said, "See ya later."

Uptown got into his car and began his ride down Trigg Street. He made it to Mississippi Street and made the left at the light. He drove to the corner of Mississippi and Walker Avenue and stopped at a restaurant called the Four-Way Grill. So he parked his car as he went inside for a bite to eat. The Four-Way Grill is a classy soul food spot where people from all over Memphis go to eat and enjoy the culture of Southern soul food. Uptown ordered his favorite, which was chitlin's, collard greens, lima beans, and hot water cornbread with a sweet tea and lemonade mix. As he sat waiting for his food, he began to daydream about his next move. Dee was right; cocaine was a different game than the weed game. He knew if they were going to be successful, they would have to expand their hustle territory. Beale Street and Downtown Memphis were good for weed selling but cocaine is an all day and night thing, and he knew you couldn't be downtown all night. It was too risky. Plus, he knew he had to establish new markets in the city and outside the city. As he was daydreaming about his plans, his food arrived.

The waitress was a fine paper sack brown skinned woman. She had beautiful long black hair and a perfect smile with a dimple in one of her cheeks. Uptown paid for his food and gave her a 50-dollar tip. She said, "Thanks, Sir…you're too kind." Uptown said, "No, I'm not kind. I just like what I see." She said, "I bet you say that to all the women you see." He replied, "No I don't and I don't just like what I see, I love what I see." She grinned and said, "Are you high, Mister?" He said, "Yeah, high on the sight of your sexy self. By the way, what's your name, baby?" She said, "My name is Mo-Mo." He said, "Short for Mona, right." She said, "You're right but I gotta get back to work. So, if you would like dessert…just let me know!" He said, "I sure will cause I want me some of that sweet thang. Look, here's my beeper number. Call me when you get off work." She said, "Okay. I'll hit you up later." Uptown finished his meal and headed on his way.

The next day he went back to the house he and his crew shared. Cotton was feeling a little better than before, so Uptown sat down at the table beside his friend. He said, "My nigga, I feel your pain". Cotton replied, "Yeah, Bruh. It hurts but we gotta move forward." Uptown said, "Look, me and Dee can go take care of the business. Cotton's a true hustler at heart." He said, "Naw, Bruh...I'm still going with y'all to handle that business cause we gotta get our game down tight." Uptown said, "Okay Bruh. That's what's up!" Cotton said, "Yeah, Big momma was a business first type of lady and from this point on, I'ma be gettin my money and stay hard on a hoe just like my momma taught me. So when is this business going down?" Uptown said, "First, we going to go to Club Rayford's and holla at Greg to get some more guns, and a few of the goons to come work for us cause you know that nigga got a real army that'll handle any hating ass niggas who think they might wanna take something. Next, we gone go to College and McLemore and find us a good cocaine connection. Then we gone set up new territory so we can get money all over the city." Cotton said, "Yeah, we can set up shop in Mississippi and Arkansas, too." Uptown said, "Bet that, my nigga. Yeah we gone get money wherever we go, state to state, city to city, coast to coast. The earth is our turf. We gone go cross-country hustling making our presence felt. First, we get the money, then get the power and everything else will fall in line." "Sounds like a plan to me," Cotton said. They bumped fists and went over the details more before leaving.

Cotton took his siblings house hunting. Uptown drove over to 4-V where Dee was. He pulled into the apartments. There were police everywhere so Uptown parked in front of Dee's aunt's apartment. Dee was standing with a big crowd of onlookers. Uptown asked, "What's going on over here?" Dee said, "Oh yeah, nigga. That nigga named, Lil Poo just came through here and robbed a few niggas and they called the police. So, he came back ski-masked up and shot at the police with an Uzi." Uptown said, "Damn, we need a nigga like that on our team. He extra wild." Dee said, "Yeah, niggas piss in they pants when he comes around."

    They went inside Dee's aunt's house and sat down and started discussing the plans. Dee said, "Yeah my nigga, I'm 100% down with you on that. Plus I got niggas who will work for us when our money is right." Dee said, "Oh yeah, I talked to this nigga named Table and he said he can sell us whatever we need." Uptown said, "Yeah, you're on point, I see my nigga. Plus we gone connect on College and McLemore and our weed will still be selling also. Dee said, "Yeah, we gone have every high ass muthafucka want. And we gone get our money right." Uptown said, "Yeah, get rich and get our families out of this project shit. Dee said "Yeah, I'll smoke to that my nigga. So when we going to holla at Greg." Uptown said, "Friday night. We gone go to Cotton's momma funeral Saturday morning and after that go holla at a plug so we can buy some dope." Dee said, "Cool. I can go get off the last of my 5 pounds of weed before then." Uptown said, "Yeah cause we gone need all the cash we can get on this re-up." They finished the weed and waited till the police were gone, then got in their cars and parted ways.

    It was getting late so Uptown headed to the house but before he made it, he remembered that Cotton's family was all at his house. So he headed to his momma's house in the LMG. When he made it to the house, his beeper was blowing up. Usually, a customer would leave an amount of how much weed they wanted behind the number but this one didn't have an extra number one it. He grabbed the house phone and called the number back. Who is this he asked. A smart voice said, "This Mona, and why the fuck you took so long to answer my damn calls?" Uptown said, "Is this Mona?" She said, Yeah, it's me nigga!" He said, "What happed to that sweet talking ladylike woman I met?" She said, "Ah, nigga… that was just my work talk but this is me. Take it or leave it." Uptown said, "I can dig dat, lil momma. I hear ya." She said, "Lucky for you I like you cause how long it took you to call back I should've just said, fuck you! Uptown replied, "Well you didn't and what's up? How's your night going? She said, I been thinking bout you all day and I like your laid-back attitude. Plus, you are tall and handsome just like I like em. Uptown said, "So where you from Lil lady? She smiled and said, "I'm from Orange Mound but I also grew up in South Memphis and Whitehaven." "Where you from, Mister, she asked." He said, "I'm from Mississippi but now I lives in the Lemoyne Gardens. She said, oh that's down the street from my job." Then she frowned. "You're not one of the LMG thugs, wanna be pimps are you, cause my pussy ain't for sale." He said, "Naw not a pimp nor am I a wanna be thug. I'm a Hustla, lil momma. I gets my money." Mona said, "Oh, yeah I heard that a thousand times. So how many baby mommas and hood rats you got cause everybody knows hustlas have a lot of women fans wanting a baller who can support them and they'll do whatever to keep him around, spending that cash." He said, "So you're hip, huh. Well let me tell you this lil momma."

 Women ain't my weakness and I only talk to one woman if I like her ways and personality. Don't get it confused. I like good pussy and head as much as any man does but ass come and go. And if I care, I'll put effort into getting to know you but I'm a true hustla. My money comes first. I got mouths to feed. My momma is poor so I gotta help support her."

CHAPTER 4

MY FAMILY

She said, "I can dig it. My brothers helped us out too. They are in the streets also." He said, "Okay, dig that. So you respect my hustle, right?" She said, "Of course I understand that. Gotta get your money. That's why I work. I'm not like these lazy females out here depending on a man to take care of me. I am independent. I get my own and do what I want." Uptown said, "Dig that baby." She said, so when can we spend some time together or are you too busy to give a woman some of your time, Mr. Hustla? He said, "Soon baby, soon". She said, "Okay. Come by the restaurant tomorrow on my lunch break." He said, "Okay, lil momma." They talked till 5 a.m. and then hung up. Uptown thought to himself, "Damn, she's down to earth, real cool to talk to, plus she had a fat ass and little waist. She was fine. He thought of her plump round ass and made him think about that ass naked. He hit the weed and smirked as he fell into a deep sleep.

Uptown awakened to the smell of bacon and eggs in the kitchen. It was early. He grabbed his beeper and realized he overslept. His momma was cooking him breakfast cause he missed it earlier. It was almost 1:15 in the afternoon. He usually would be up counting money by now. His momma said, "Come on son and sit down and have some breakfast." He loved his momma's cooking but when she cooks for only one child, there's going to be a long talk that comes with it. Uptown washed his hands and sat down to eat. He went for the fork and his momma smacked it out of his hand. "You know we pray over our food in my house, she said. Ain't nothing changed since you moved to Memphis." She gave him her I am dead serious look, and he bowed his head and waited while his momma prayed. She began by saying, "God, bless this food and please watch over my son and his friends as they run those wicked streets. Jesus, forgive them for their hustling ways. For you said if thou ask for forgiveness under God's name, thy soul shall be saved." They both said, "Amen" and ate their meal.

Uptown kissed his momma on the cheeks as he headed out the door. He drove to the spot that he and his crew shared. Dee was there but Cotton had headed out to find his family a house and to prepare for his mom's funeral. Dee said, "Bruh I went and collected all the money from the niggas who owe us plus here's my part of the stash. It was about $6,500 dollars. Uptown said, "Damn, nigga you been getting yo money, huh? I thought you been buying too much pussy to stack yo chips." They both laughed. Uptown said, "Bet cool. I got about $8,300 and Cotton got 20 thousand. Dee said, Damn, Cotton making plenty of money, huh? Uptown said, "Yeah, he taught me how to hustle plus unlike yo trick ass, he get paid off hoe's pussy on top of that. I'm sure Big Momma left him some money when she passed. They said, Cool…now it's on! We finna take our rightful place in this game and get this real money so we can move our families out those projects so we can really live. Dee said, "That's a plan my nigga!" Uptown said, "Okay, everything is set. Now I gotta go get fitted for this suit for Big Momma funeral." So, he took the money and gave it to the one person in the world he could trust---his sister. She and Uptown were extra close. Plus, he knew his momma wouldn't take no dirty money. His sister was a hiding pro. She knew how to keep her mouth closed too, so that trust he had in her was extra solid. The next day he went over to get his suit. Before going to Mississippi, he stopped by Betty's house to catch up with her. He asked, "Is your mom home, cause I wanna try on my suit. She said, "Naw, she is at work but go ahead." She said "You can be my model for today". So, he went into the bathroom and put on his suit. It was a smoky gray suit, English cut with black shirt and tie, with black wingtips to match. Betty said, "Damn baby, yo ass is sharp!. But hold on, I have something for you." She gave him a pair of Ray-Ban sunglasses, all black to match the suit. He took a look and said, "I see you got taste, baby. He got back into his street clothes, a t-shirt and Levi's. She said, "You gone come back and take me out when you can, right?" He said, sure thing baby. I got ya. She kissed him on the cheeks." He looked at her and just smiled cause she was so cool, not fast like all the other women. She was just so laid back and easy to talk to. He liked that a lot. So he said to himself, she's a keeper. I got to show her a good time.

    Uptown jumped into his car and headed south on I-55. Traffic was real slow leaving Memphis, so he fired up a fat Mack joint. He was smoking and enjoying his high listening to Bobby Womack "Across 110th Street" when out of nowhere he sees the flashes of a cop's blue and red lights behind. He said to himself, "Damn! He grabbed his chronic killer and sprayed it, then fired up a Newport and pulled over. The cop got out, walked over to his car. Uptown rolled down the driver's side window and asked, "Is there a problem officer?" The cop said, "You were going 75 miles per hour in a 65. Can I see your license, Sir?" Uptown passed him his license and said, "I'm sorry, officer. I am just in a rush to make it to a funeral." The cop asked, "Oh, yeah…are you one of Big Momma's kids? He lied and said, "Yeah. The cop said, "You are good, young man. Carry on."

    Big Momma was one of the Magnolia State's best. She was a sweet lady so he didn't write Uptown a ticket. Uptown thought to himself, that was close cause the pigs in the Sip don't play especially with niggas. But he remembered how there were all types of tricks buying busy at Big Momma's house, even cops. That's why Big Momma never got busted cause pussy is a drug every man and even some women are sprung on. He just laughed and turned up the Bobby Womack song and headed to Hernando.

    As he pulled into his old hometown, he drove through the neighborhood where he was born and thought,

'Damn...Mississippi is country compared to Memphis. He pulled up to Big Momma's old house. Cotton and his family were already there. Cotton walked over before he got out the car and said, "Damn, bruh, what took you so long?" Uptown then said, "Nigga, the traffic was slow when I first left plus I got stopped by the pigs. He knew Big Momma so he let me go without a ticket." Cotton said, "See, that's Big Momma watching over us from heaven."

Uptown got out of his car and headed into the house to change into his suit. Puddin, Nyla and Money was all busy in the bathroom. So he changed in Cotton's old room. He got dressed and headed to his car to join the funeral procession when Man-Man said, "Hold on nigga, you family, you ride in the limo with us. Big Momma would have wanted you to." Uptown smiled as he headed to the limo.

The church was a small one in the country. Big Momma wasn't a church-going woman but her heart was big. She would help a lot of people out in the small poor town of Hernando. So the entire town was at the funeral. Big Momma was a lady pimp and hustler, so, all the hookers and hustlers came to pay their respect. They funeral was very sad but happy because she knew how to bring her town together. Even in death, she put on a show like no other the town had seen. Yeah, Big Momma will truly be missed.

After the funeral, everybody headed to Big Momma's house cause one thing the town knew was Big Momma's house was the party house and this was going to be the last and the biggest one yet. Big Momma kept a fully stocked bar, plus all the local bootleggers brought all the country moonshine and corn whiskey you could drink. Plus Cotton laid out a whole pound of some superlight green skunkweed from California. The local DJ played nothing but the Blues which was Big Momma's favorite. Everybody was enjoying themselves. Cotton and Uptown were sitting in Big Momma's office room discussing the business that they were about to get in when they got back to Memphis when they heard a knock at the door. They both stopped and said, "Come in." It was Lil Lisa and Angie. Uptown said, "Hey home girls, what's good?" Lil Lisa said, "It's shit...sad to hear about Big Momma. How you holding up, Cotton?" He said, "Good, home gal. Thanks for asking" he said.

She said, "You know we from da Mud and y'all are my niggas." He said, "That's what's up," as he took a sip of his Yak. Angie said, "What's up, Willie? You just forgot about us country folks since your up there in big mad Memphis. I guess us country gals are too slow for you, huh?" She was drunk as a fish. Cotton and Lisa laughed. Uptown said, "Naw, Lil Momma. It ain't like that. I just been busy getting my money." She said, "Yeah, I bet," as she stumbled across the room to get close to Uptown's face. She got close enough to his ear and said, "So you don't miss this good pussy and fire ass head," she said sticking her whiskey-smelling tongue in his ear. Uptown jumped back and said, "Girl, you are drunk." She said, "Fuck you, Willie. You ain't shit nigga." He said, "It's Uptown, Bitch. Willie is family and we sure ain't kissing cousins! They all laughed. She said, "well, kiss my ass then." Lil Lisa said, "Sounds like somebody got sprung," and started laughing. Angie said, "Fuck you, bitch" as she sat on the couch head swinging back and forth.

Lil Lisa then asked, "Hey Cotton...what are y'all doing in the M-town?" Getting money. You know me!" he replied. She said, "Cool...maybe I'll come through with y'all! Cotton said, "You know, it's pimping with me, right?" She said, "Yeah, I know what's up with you plus you know how I get down. I'll charge a trick and break on a hoe. I gots to get mine too cause this town is too slow for a boss hoe. I'ma get at ya as soon as I can, alright?" He responded, "Dig that, Lil Lisa." Cotton knew Lil Lisa went both ways plus she had game so he respected her hustle. He then said, "You make sure yo home gal gets home safe cause she is fucked up." Lil

Lisa said, "I got her", as she left the room. Uptown said, "Damn our home gals still wild." "Yeah, ain't that the truth," said Cotton. "I might put Lil Lisa down in my new stable cause she someone I can trust plus I have known her all my life.' Uptown said, "That's what's up Mr. Pimpin." It's in my blood my nigga", Cotton replied, as they made a toast to that.

"Now back to the business at hand, enough about them hoes," Uptown said. "Yeah but hoe money for sho money," Cotton said. Now, Dee already set up a meeting with Table, Cotton said. "Who the fuck is Table?" he asked. "Table from Foote Homes but he's nationwide with the cocaine. Dude is a major player in this Memphis dope game." Cotton then asked, "Why you can't get coke in the LMG, Uptown?" He said, "I could but I want our business to be our business. The less they know, they more we can move, you dig? Plus, it's time to expand all over the city and beyond. It's time for us to get the real money and one or two spots ain't gone move the amount of drugs I'm trying to move. Also, we got Greg backing us with all the muscle and killas we need in case niggas wanna rob us. This is Memphis so we gotta play the game how it go, "get money and fuck a hater. They can die. Ya dig." Cotton said, "That's why you my nigga. You smart as hell". Uptown said, "Yeah, we finna blow up. Plus we gone get other connections on College and McLemore, and wherever else so we don't ever run out of product." They smoked and finished their Yak. As they bumped fists, Cotton said, Okay my nigga, let's do this then", as they walked out the room heads held high. As their plans started to take form, it was time for them to advance and graduate in the game. Game on now. Ain't no turning back. The future is now and they plan to master the trade.

CHAPTER 5

THE TAKEOVER

The next day, Uptown, Cotton and Dee all met up at their spot. They carefully counted the re-up money making sure every dollar was accounted for. Altogether they had 42 thousand dollars. They planned to buy 2 kilos of coke, but Cotton reminded them that they needed to save some money for their weed re-up also. So, they decided to buy 1 ½ kilo's. Dee then said, "I set up the meeting with Table." Uptown said he had a meeting on College and McLemore in a few days. Cotton asked Dee where the meeting was and he said, "On 4-V at Nicely Pig's Café." Cotton said, "You mean we bout to take all this cash in a known dangerous project?" Uptown spoke up. "Listen Bruh, we good. Greg gave us three shooters. Deck, Low-Down, and Big Munchie, plus here as he handed Dee and Cotton a .45 magnum and 9 mm. He also had a .357 Bulldog pistol. "Damn, this game is real," Cotton said. Uptown said, Yeah, we gotta stay ready so we don't have to get ready, ya feel me." They all were nervous, palms sweating, young and ambitious. But they all wanted to the same thing, and that was to get rich. So they bumped fists and hooped into Cotton's new Cadillac.

As they drove down Vance Avenue, the shooters riding in a station wagon with tinted windows drive up. They approached 4-V. The corner was live as usual. Hookers and dope boys on all four corners hustling, getting they money. They parked right in front of Nicely Pigs Café. The shooters parked behind them and they all walked into the café together. Dee noticed his cousin at the bar, so he said, "What's good, Big Boo." She said, "What's up cuz…what brings yo to my hood? He said, "Just kickin it with my LMG crew, enjoying the weather." She said, "Yeah nigga, right… this ain't no park! This a dope/hoe block so either you want to get high or get in a hoe's thigh" They all laughed. Big Boo was a real slick talker and she was from the streets so she had plenty of game for a Big Gal.

She then asked, "You got some of that smoke on you?" Dee said, "Yeah, here you go cuz as he handed her a fat half ounce of some fire weed. She said, "Now that's my favorite kinfolks right there. What are you and the crew drinking", she asked. Dee said, "Don't even ask. You know it's Yak in our glasses! So she ordered them rounds as they ate barbecue and listened to the jukebox.

After about an hour and fifteen minutes, they started to wonder why Table hadn't showed up yet. So, Dee called his number and after the fifth time, he answered the phone. He asked, "What's good?" Dee said, "Me and my niggas been here for over an hour, my guy." Table said, "My bad. You know my I'm a busy nigga so time is very limited. But I'm outside right now so y'all can come out." Dee told Uptown and Cotton to come on, he out there now and they walked outside the café. All they saw outside was a long black limo. They all looked at each other like damn this nigga here gotta be rich riding like this. As the door swung open, a big baldheaded nigga hopped out. Dee knew how Table looked so the look on his face told them that this ain't Table. So he asked, "Where's Table?" The big nigga said, "Boss told me to come get you lil niggas so if you wanna go, let's go. If not, let me know now." They knew they had come this far so there was no turning back. So, we said, "Let's do this." Cotton said, "what about our security." Uptown told the shooters to wait across the street at the pool hall. So, they jumped into the limo and headed down Fourth Street to Uptown Memphis. On the way there, they all were silent. This, after all, was the biggest deal of their young lives. All kinds of thoughts raced through their heads. They all knew what was at stake so the butterflies were all through their stomachs but they wanted to look confident in front of their new plug. This wasn't like copping weed. They were about to meet one of the most known kingpins in the city, so this was huge. As the limo pulled in front of the Peabody Hotel, they knew it was serious now. They all knew about this famous hotel off of Beale Street but neither of them had ever been to the 5-Star world renown hotel.

They got out the limo and the valet took the long car to the garage. They followed the big nigga through the big brass doors. There were White people and rich-looking Blacks everywhere. There was a big fountain in the middle of the lobby. Also, there were real ducks being escorted by a White dude in a butler's suit. Cotton said, "damn even the ducks are rich in this bitch." They made it to the elevator and got in. The big nigga pressed the big red button that read Presidential penthouse suite, top floor. It took less than a minute as the doors swung open. They exited the elevator and headed down a long hallway. At the end of the hallway, they came to a big door with two ducks in brass on the handle of the double doors. They all took deep breaths at the reality of what was about to happen. The doors opened wide as they walked into the biggest, cleanest, plushed out room they had ever seen. There was a 360-degree view of the entire city. There was an all-white grand piano sitting in the center of the room. All the furniture was leather with nice soft, thick wall to wall carpeting throughout the room. Along with that, was a fully stocked bar with a full kitchen, dining room with a big table that seated 12 people. The room had gold trimmings everywhere. They were all amazed. The big nigga said, "yall have a seat. I'll go and get the boss. So, they sat down as the big nigga walked through another door in this super large room. Soon, the door swung open and a slim Black nigga with more gold on than Mr. T. But this wasn't the A-Team.

This was Mr. Table, a legend on the streets of Memphis. Dee said, what's good Table. He said, shit young nigga how's yo mom's doing? He said, "she good. Dee then introduced Uptown and Cotton to the legend. Table said, what's up with yall cats. So yall from the LMG, huh. They both said, yeah, that's our hood. Table said, yeah I gots a few business partners over that way. He then asked, did they know the Jones family and Greg. They said, hell yeah, we fucks with Greg. He our big dog. Table said, yeah, dude a bonafide hustla, but his brother Ced is a stone cold killa. They both said, "we know." Table then said, "so nigga, what you and your homies want to do. Dee spoke up. First, Sir, we are trying to buy a key of that good white and I know you're the man who can help us take our business to the next level. Uptown spoke up and said, "yeah man, we trying to make some real money and get our families out the ghetto." Then Cotton spoke. Yeah, we got mouths to feed, plus I just lost my momma so I'm trying to make sure my siblings are taken care of just like Mom Dukes took care of me, ya dig. Table said, 'ya did, huh. I likes this lil niggas word play. He said, I can respect yall grind. I started out just like you lil niggas. All I had was a dream and I stayed down till I came up. Now I'm one of the biggest in the city. I'm a millionaire over and over. But, I must say this is a none-winning game. You only survive. You gotta make the money and don't let it make you. Ya feel me. They said, thanks for the words of wisdom, my nigga. We just trying to eat, learn and teach.

Now, let's get down to business. As he snapped his finger, the big nigga sat two shoe boxes on the coffee table in front of them. Then Table asked, so where's the money? That's when Cotton came out of his pants with three Crown Royal bags. He put the bags in front of Table and said, "it's all there." The price of the kilo was 20 thousand, so there was 30 grand in all. As Tablet counted the money, he smiled and said, "no small bills. I like that. Yall do business like yall been doing it. He finished counted and said, "30 grand on the nose". They said cool. Table then said, "but we have one small issue. They looked at each other and said, what's the problem. He said, "there's two keys here and I don't do halves, so yall gone owe me 10 large. Can yall handle it? They said, so when is the deadline to pay. He said, "a week or two if that's okay with yall. They said, sure thing. He then said, this is a test for yall. I know Dee, so I'm taking a chance on yall on his word. Make sure your word is your bond cause businessmen, that's all you have. They said, dig that. We won't let you down and we appreciate everything. Thanks for your time. He then said, "my drive will take you wherever you need to go. They said, "we left our cars and homeboys on 4-V. Table laughed. It's in y'all's best interest to go somewhere and stash yall drugs first and make sure you cut that shit cause it's 100% pure straight-8 from Miami. Cotton asked, "what about the niggas on 4-V? Table said, "I know the niggas at the pool hall. I'll give em a call and tell your guys to gone back to the LMG and they'll watch yall cars until yall go pick it up. They said, thanks, you on point. He said, "I'll call you, don't call me. As they walked out with the two boxes in a shopping mall bag.

  They drove to their spot, got in the house, and took the dope out of the boxes. They sat there staring at the two big bricks of coke. It was so white with light blue sparkles in it. It was wrapped in 4 layers of plastic. As they unwrapped the bricks, each layer of plastic they took off the smell got stronger and stronger. They began to get dizzy from the fumes in the air. Yeah, this shit was strong so they knew it was A-1 coke. They had to put on masks because of the smell. They looked at each other and said, "damn, what and where can we get some cut at"? Dee said, you know the VIP head shop on Mississippi and Walker Street. Cotton said, oh yeah, across the street from the 4-Way Grill. Uptown said, yeah I've been through there. That reminds me. I gotta get up with this beautiful gal when I get free. But we got to split this dope up and hide it in a lot of different places cause like momma taught me, you never put all your eggs in one basket. So, they packaged everything up in 8 quarter birds and they took each one to a different location. They all said they would meet up first thing in the morning.

Dee drove Cotton to pick up his car off 4-V and Uptown drove to his momma's house. He pulled up on Lemoyne Drive and got out his car. Suddenly out of nowhere, a crackhead named Mike-Mike stopped him. He asked did Uptown have a dime rock for sale. Uptown replied, nah bruh catch me another day. Then Uptown thought to himself, he and the crew didn't know how to rock yup the coke they had just bought. So he asked Mike-Mike, "say bruh do you know how to cook up crack? Damn skippy I do. Hell, they call me the south Memphis chef. Crack be so good you'll be licking yo fingers. Uptown laughed, and said, "well you teach me how to cook and I'll give you a rock so big you'll be able to smoke all day long. Mike-Mike said, you got a deal young hustla. Can we do it now? Uptown said, nah but here's 20 bucks to let you know I', for real. Mike-Mike said, you gone need some baking soda, a stove and some ice water, and a tube depending on how much you plan to cook up. That'll let you know what size tube to use. You can get everything at the VIP on Mississippi and Walker. Uptown said, cool, I gotta go there anyway tomorrow. Mike-Mike said, what time you gone need me. Uptown said, first thing in the morning about 7 a.m. I'll be here at 6:45 a.m., he said. Uptown said, bet.

Uptown left and as he entered his momma's apartment, his momma was out shopping at the Big Star Store. So, he went to his bedroom and picked up the phone and called Betty. She said, "Hello…hey sexy! How you been, he asked? "Good," she said. "How was the funeral? You know, it was sad. But happy she don't have to suffer no more," he said. "Sorry to hear that," she said. "So, when can I see you, handsome?" "Tomorrow," he said. "By the way, I gotta come through their first thing in thing in the morning. Do you have to work?" She said, "Yeah, but I have to be there at 9 a.m." "Cool," he said. "Meet me in front of the job at 7:30 a.m. We will go get breakfast and chop it up, okay?" "Cool," she said. "It's a date. So don't be late." He said, "I'll

[75]

be there baby, can't wait to see your sexy ass. Talk to you then, sleep tight." "You too," she replied.

As he hung up the phone, he heard the door opening. It was his momma and Aunt Dina. She said, "Boy, go out there and help us get these bags out the car." He said, "Yes ma'am." Uptown brought all the bags in and sat them down on the kitchen table. He said, "Damn, Momma, you bought the whole store, didn't you?" She said, "Big family and we eat a lot." They both smiled. "Besides, I gets a lot of stamps, so we okay. Uptown told her to close her eyes and hold out her hand. She did exactly that and he dropped 10 one-hundred-dollar bills in her hand. He then said, now open your eyes. She looked at him and said "boy where you getting all this money? And, before you lie, just promise me yo'll stay praying for forgiveness. He said, I do Ma, I do. Okay, then, thanks Son. Aunt Dina said, damn nephew, where mines at. He said, here you go Auntie" as he handed her 20-hundred-dollar bills. She said, thanks baby. Tee-Tee loves ya. Uptown said, 'yall" my everything. I do it for yall and where's something to drink. I know you got some yak, Tee-Tee. His mom said, don't be giving my kids liquor. Aunt Dina said, "Hell MaryLynn, them kids been drinking. You late," as they poured up two glasses. His mom then left the room. She didn't mind her kids drinking or smoking weed, she just didn't want to see it. As they drank, Aunt Dina said, "Willie, you be care out here getting this money okay. This city is a MF nephew. I know these streets. I am old but I seen it all, believe me. Plus, I'm on Lucy Street if you need me. Okay, Uptown said. Thanks Tee-Tee. We Browns, she said. Remember that comes first and family is the only people who can be trusted, know that. Dig that Tee-Tee. So he went and laid down for the night early so he could get up early since he had a lot on his plate the next day.

Morning time had come. He was 5:30 when he woke up, the sun was just coming up. He got up and took a hot bath, brushed his pearly white teeth, and took his freshest outfit out the closet. He then put on his favorite cologne, Drakkar. And started thinking, I've got to be looking good and smelling good for this early morning date with Mona. He knew the first impression is the best impression. So, he wanted to impress her and be on his best behavior cause he really liked her. He had had women before but this was different. He really enjoyed her down-to-earth attitude. Plus, she had a beautiful body with a ghetto fabulous fat round ass that all Black men would love. He pulled up in front of her job on time. She was there looking like a Black Queen. He got out the car and went over to open the door for her trying to be on his gentleman shit. She smiled and said, 'thanks." He said, "I don't mind cause you're worth it."

    They drove down Mississippi Street and made a right on Crump Avenue. He turned up the music as the sounds of Sade came blasting from the speakers. Mona leaned back in her seat as she took in the view. She then said, "I love this song," as she turned up the volume on the radio. She turned to him and said, "So you are a smooth operator huh?" They both laughed at the mention of the song that was playing. He said, "yeah I can be smooth and I can be hard, just like my Remi. Betty said, okay. I likes that cause I love my man to be hard all the time. He said, "what you mean hard"? She said, I like my man like I like my dick, hard and staying up. Cause no bitch want a soft lay down ass nigga. If a man not a man's man then the woman won't respect him cause he too weak. And how a weak nigga gone protect his woman or be the head of a household. That's lame and I don't fuck with lame niggas. Uptown said, "okay. You're mature. I can dig that. She said, "I gots a lot of Auntie's and all of 'em teach and not preach. So I know a lil sum-sum." He said, "That's what up."

Uptown fired up a joint and Mona said, "You smoke a lot of weed, huh?" He said, "Yeah, it helps me eat and sleep. She said, "I tried it but it's not for me. I likes to drink so I only drinks when I party. He said, okay. I'll remember that. They then drove down Crump until it turned into Lamar. They pulled up at the Waffle House, got out and went inside. They sat at a table in the back near the jukebox. Uptown gave Betty 5 dollars and said go pla y some nice music 'while I go make a few phone calls. She said, okay Baby. I'll be here waiting on yo tall handsome self. So, Uptown stepped into the phone book, stuck in a dime, and called Dee and Cotton. They both were at the spot.

    He said, "what's good my niggas." They both said, waiting on you so we can go handle this business. He said, "look I'm out having breakfast but when I'm done, I'll be right there. Cotton said, "what's up with the cut and bags," Uptown said, don't worry bout that. I'll head that way soon as I finish eating. So I'll get everything we need. Oh yeah, plus I got a nigga to show us how to cook crack so we'll be on top of everything. They both replied, okay my nigga, we here. Holla at you then. He hung up the phone and returned to his seat. Betty was playing NWA Boys in the Hood. He said, "so you bump Rap too. She said, I,' from Da Mound so I been a gal in the hood, ya dig. They ordered their food and talked and laughed and really enjoyed each other's company. She then looked at the clock on the wall and said, 'damn I gotta go get ready for work. So he said, don't trip. I'll hit the E-way and get you there in no time. So they paid the bill and left.

    He drove down Lamar, jumped onto the I-240 freeway, and headed south. He then exited on Crump. He pulled up on Mississippi and Walker Street just as the 4-Way Grill was opening. All the other girls saw Mona getting out the car and leaned over to give Uptown a nice long goodbye kiss. She said, "Thanks for the breakfast and your time. Cause she knew a street hustla's time was very limited. She felt good as her coworkers all watched and yelled, "we see ya Betty. And girl he is fine too." That made her day. She said, talk to you later okay. He said, sure thing Lil Momma, bye. He waited until she was in the building as he drove across the street to the VIP Headshop. He parked his car and walked inside. As he entered the door a bell rang. Then a big black nigga came from the back to the front counter. He said, "what's up nigga. What you need? Uptown looked around at all the drug paraphernalia. There were weed pipes and bongs, scales, every size baggie in the book, crack pipes and needles. Every drug shit you needed was there on display.

He was in awe of all the shit. Then he broke out of his trance as he heard the big nigga yell, "come on nigga, what you need. I ain't got all fuckin day." So Uptown said, I need some cut. He said what cut coke or H. Uptown said coke. Then he said hard or soft? Uptown said, both. Plus I need scales, baggies, and a tube to cook it. He said, okay you need the whole hook up? Uptown said yeah hook me up and here's 50 bucks for your time. The man looked at the 50-dollar bill and said, "now I likes the way you do business. See, Cotton taught him to always tip the people who help you cause they working people who needs a lil extra cause they there to help you and he knew he'd be back. So, why not look out for any and everybody who can help him get more money. He brought him some Vita blend and B12, two scales, two tubes, 4 sizes of baggies and 3 big boxes of baking soda. He then said, you know how to cook it don't you. Uptown said, nah but I got a junkie who gone show me how to do everything. He put all the things on the counter and said, now look the Vita blend is to stretch the powder for the blow sniffers, and the B-12 is to stretch the crack, and the baggies are 5-, 10-, 20-, and 50-dollar sizes. The scares are one for small amounts and on for large amounts. Also, the Purex tubes are the same; one for once's and up and one for 8 balls, quarters, halves and to re-rock the shake. Also, here's a box of razor blades to cut the rocks. So, yo junkie gone show you everything else you need to know, right? Uptown, said yeah. He said, that'll be 225 dollars Sir. Uptown gave him 250 and said keep the change. He said, 'dam you're too kind. That'll take you a long way in this game. Yeah make sure you only cut it with a 4th. You want your dope to be big but still good. That way, your customers will always be satisfied and stay coming back to spend they money. Uptown said, thanks, see ya next time. He said, nah thanks for your business, and I'll give you a deal next time. Uptown said, bet that.

He drove down Walker Street and made a left on Lemoyne Drive. He pulled up in front of Mike-Mike as he leaned on the brick wall on the side of the apartments. He was smoking a cigarette as he smiled. When he saw Uptown's car, he thumped the cigarette and ran to the car. He jumped in the passenger side and said, "damn, I been waiting on you my nigga. Uptown said, "my bad, I had a date, plus I had to go get all the things we gone need. Mike-Mike said, "cool, I'm ready to work boss mane as they drove out the LMG headed to the spot where his crew was waiting. They got to the spot and went inside. Cotton and Dee were shooting dice in the living room. Uptown said, "my bad for being a lil late my niggas. Dee said, yeah cause this slick nigga was bout to win all my lil money as Cotton laughed holding a fist full of cash while he smoked a fat joint. Dee said, you get the shit we need? Uptown said, yeah here's everything and this here is, and before he could say anything, Dee said yeah I know this Mike-Mike nigga. Where's my money muthafucka he said. Mike-Mike said, I gots ya Dee baby I been fucked up. Dee said, "I know just like last time. I should beat yo ass now but my nigga said you the cook we need, so you gone get a pass nigga. But don't ever do me like that again cause I don't play bout my pay. Mike-Mike said, I gots ya cause he knew Dee was known for beating the shit out of niggas who owed him. Uptown said, enough of that. Let's get down to business. They went in the kitchen and took out a half a key of coke on the table. Uptown said okay, chef Mike-Mike; work yo magic. He went to the kitchen sink and filled it with cold water. He then took out a bag of ice and poured it into the water. Then, he got out the big Purex tube and the baking soda. He put a pot of hot water on the stove and let it come to a boil. He put 4 ½ ounces in the tube with some baking soda. The dope instantly started forming into a big round white rock. Mike-Mike said, yeah this that good dope. I can smell it. It ain't no OPL base. It was all coming together fast. Then Mike-Mike took the tube out the boiling water and put it in the ice water in the sink. Then he heled it up, shook the tube and the big round rock made a cling cling sound. Mike-Mike smiled and started singing "Solid as a Rock." They at started laughing. Mike-Mike took the rock out of the now ice-cold water and put it on a paper towel that was on a plate so it could dry off. Then Uptown took out the scale and placed the big rock on it. They all looked at each other and said, dam, the dope weighed 5 ounces and a quarter. It had jumped to 21 extra grams. Uptown looked at Mike-Mike and said, yeah nigga you could. Mike-Mike said, yeah nigga I told you. I'm one of the best. I been cooking crack back when they used to call it freebase. Then he smirked and said but this shit ain't for free, it's for a fee, so what you got for me. Uptown said, here and gave him 7 grams. Mike-Mike said, damn, thanks, my nigga. This more than I usually get. Uptown, said, naw. Thank you for showing me yo recipe. Now I can say you taught me that. With Mike-Mike paid and happy, it was time to chop and package the crack. He and Cotton got out sandwich bags and started bagging up 5's, 10's, 20's and 50-dollar pieces. They sacked up all the dope and hid it behind the dray walls of the house. Then they both said, this shit here finna take us to another level. They already had the weed and powder doing numbers, now with the crack starting to sell, they were sure to get rich quick. They finished up and both headed in for the night. As Uptown drove down the highway, his mind started wandering about how he planned to get his family out of poverty. He knew his momma wouldn't understand why he was doing what he was doing but he hated the fact that his family came from nothing and as a child, he promised himself that he would do whatever it took to make a better life for his family, even if it meant taking his freedom and life to do it.

He was already making money but he wanted more. So, that night he went to sleep with dreams of getting rich and he knew it was about to take off.

That morning, he got up early and called Cotton and Dee and told them to meet him at the spot. They got there early and all sat the round table to talk about their plans. Uptown spoke first saying, look my niggas, now that we got the crack on deck, we gotta expand our operation. Then Cotton said, well we got our team working in a few hoods now, but we need to network with new clientele in other markets. Dee said, yeah now you talking. He said. I gots family in Nashville and Chattanooga. Cotton said, plus we can move in cities and towns in Mississippi and Arkansas. Uptown said, yeah that's cool but I want to be all over this country, some real franchise shit like McDonald's nigga. I am trying to have a billion served just like on the sign. Cotton said, okay, Pablo, how we gone get enough dope to do that. Dee said, we gone need a real plug from Texas, Miami, and LA. Uptown said, well we gone go get it my nigga. Cotton, said, okay, one step at a time my nigga. I'm down in the meantime. Let's get this money up so that we can go cross county hustlin. They all agreed as they went out to distribute the crack. They went to all their workers. Dee had a lot of young niggas in the LMG rolling for him. Cotton had his brothers, sisters and about 5 of his hoes selling for him. Uptown had his crew working Uptown Memphis and a few towns in Mississippi. They all supplied their workers with good crack, powder and weed. The first few couple weeks went by and the money kept growing and growing. It took them by surprise how fast the dope was moving. They had to beef up their crews as the more money came in, the more dope they needed. They Seattle weed plug was so happy that he started sending 5 times the amount. Their coke plug was highly impressed as well as in a few weeks they started to double their order to meet demand. Things were finally looking up. They money was good. Uptown, Cotton, and Dee all bought new cars and new homes. Uptown bought 3 new house one to put up the stash of drugs, another to hide the cash and one big house in Southaven for his family. Life was good. Then out of nowhere, things went from sugar to shit real quick!

CHAPTER 6

GOING THROUGH THE MOTIONS OF THE GAME

Things were going as planned, then one day Cotton was riding down Third Street when an unmarked car started following him. He drove a little more heading pass the movie drive-in. He felt this unnerving sense come over him. He played it cool hoping it was a routine traffic stop. So, he didn't speed or act out of the norm. After all, he had no drugs or weapons in the car. So he felt secure when they finally turned on the police lights behind him. Cotton pulled over to the gas station on Shelby Drive and Third street. He had his license, so he didn't panic. They out of his rear-view mirror, vans and SWAT cars started pulling up. Then he realized that this wasn't a regular stop but a sting operation. The guns came out as soon as the pigs jumped out of the vans. Cotton knew that police would shoot a Black man quicker than a speeding bullet so he thew both hands up high so they could see that he was unarmed. They were all yelling and acting aggressive.

Cotton saw this a million times before. He was a young Black man riding in a new Cadillac in the revel south, so this was nothing new to him. They swung open the door of his car and grabbed him by his collar. They then slammed him face down to the hard pavement. They cursed him so loud that he couldn't get his word out. They yelled out, you low life drug dealing pimp, we go yo ass now. You won't be going home today or this decade nigger. They threw the handcuffs on him and put him in the back seat of a squad car. Cotton knew his hustling was the reason but decided to ask why he was being arrested anyway? He said, hey officer what did I do to deserve this harsh treatment? The two officers looked at each other then laughed and said, "harsh treatment?

You niggers beat women, sell they bodies, sell drugs to kids, beat each other over drugs, and now you're the one who feels mistreated? Well, fuck you, you loser as they hit the gas on the E-way speeding to the county jail. That was the longest car ride Cotton ever had.

They ran every stop sign and streetlight. Cotton slumped. He didn't want to get in a situation like that again. He chilled when he got to his house. All he wanted to do was get a hot bath and some much-needed sleep.

Uptown got up early the next morning and called Cotton's phone. The phone picked up. Hello, who is this Cotton said in a muffled voice. Uptown, he replied. "This yo celly nigga? Phone check, homie as they both laughed. When Cotton realized it was his other brother on the other end, he shot back, "Yeah, that shit was a nightmare and a half. Uptown said, "I don't want to find out." Cotton said yeah bruh. I gotta make sure this shit like this never happens again. Cotton said, I'ma call you soon. I get up with you O.K.? Uptown, said, Okay, hit me when you do. I'ma come pick you up. I got some important shit to run pass you. Cotton said, "dig dat, get up later."

Uptown hung up the phone, called Dee, and told him to come meet him at the spot. Uptown pulled up early cause he liked to survey the block before pulling up at the spot. He did this to make sure that no police were in the area and the riff-raffs or jackers. He had to secure the scene at all times cause in this game, sometimes being a lil paranoid helps you see everything coming yo way good or bad, ya dig.

After they made sure the coast was clear, he drove up, hopped out and slowly used his key to open the door. After the door opened, he lifted up the burglar bar and removed the kick proof stand away from the floor. The trap house was highly secure and well protected. His look out was in the living room. Eyes bucked wild with a shot gun pump beside the chair and a 45 mag in his lap. Uptown said, what's up Young Dee?" He replied, "what's up big homie. Just holding it down like yall showed me. Uptown then asked, "them knuckleheads still sleep huh? He said, yeah you know how they get full of that weed, drinking and them hoes. Uptown said, "yeah the usual."

He had 4 workers plus security, so there were 5 young niggas holding down the spot, making all the hand-to-hand serves all night. Like the casino, the trap was always open for business, fuck 7-11, it's 24-7, 365 in the trap. Uptown didn't wake the young hustlas cause even though they party every night, they are also up getting that money.

He went to the stash spot behind the sheetrock and open up the safe so that he could count up the night's take. Uptown headed to the office so he could sit back and conduct his business. He began to count up all the cash. He then heard the familiar sounds of Dee's bass banging the loud rap music he loves. He could hear Dee from two blocks away. The closer he got, the sounds were so loud that they shook the pictures on the walls as he pulled up. Dee came through the door talking loud as he liked to wake up the young niggas. He yelled, Cotton, Cotton where you at my nigga"? Uptown said, he still sleep nigga and why you always so loud, car loud, mouth loud with this loud ass outfit on? Dee said, I like it loud. I'ma in yo face type nigga. You gone hear me before you see me cause I'm bigger than most lame niggas. So that's me; love me or kill me. They both laughed,

Uptown said, "here nigga, fie up that weed and calm yo loud ass. down. They sat at the table and smoked as they both started to count up the money. Uptown said, "dam, these young niggas moving the shit out of this coke and weed. Dee said, "of course they are, mainly cause of that crack-rock. That shit do numbers." Uptown said, "sure in the fuck do. We making triple the profits we used to make. Dee said, bet that plus we starting to open up new traps in new areas every other week" This shit getting good, Bruh. We bout to move up to the big league. Uptown said, yeah bruh. Now that our money right, we need a bigger connect. Dee said, "yeah it's time to go holla at dude-nem on College and McLemore. They are the biggest in South Memphis.

    They had a million-dollar operation going on in a lot of states throughout the United States. If you needed a lot of weight, they could handle any order you ask for. They were the plugs. This was a crew from the 60's and 70's; old heads who knew the game inside out. They got rich off the big entertainers like Al Green, The Bar-Kays, Earth Wind and Fire, and also Blues legends who used to record at Stax Records. So there was plenty money flowing through that area. And now Uptown was in a position to meet these kingpins and get more than just a plug but to suck up a lot of game from O.G.'s who knew how to make a lot of cash, but more importantly, how to make it last. This was a chance of a lifetime in his young career in the dope game to meet major players at this level. It was a new high he hadn't felt before. It was like opening the doors of a kingdom with endless resources to get to a place where your only worry was how to spend all the big money. And that was a worry he didn't mind having.

    Dee got back in touch with the old heads and set up the meeting. It took place at a pool hall next to a burger spot called Al's Tasty Burgers. The room was slightly dark as he and Uptown entered. The smell of heavy cigar smoke filled the room. A few old heads were acting like they were shooting pool but street niggas know that those old guys didn't shoot pool, and the only thing they shoot was niggas, white boys, cops or whoever came in trying to violate or take anything.

The men had that cold killer look on their faces, not a smile, but shit straight stone-faced ready to do whatever needed if you come in thinking these old heads slipping. You gone end up on the news, "man found shot dead at pool hall," typical street shit. They knew how the game went. More money means more protection. Even the banks did that.

Dee introduced Uptown. They already knew Dee cause he was from Lemoyne Gardens, which was only two blocks away. A lot of dudes from the projects used to come on College and McLemore to do business, party or just hang out. It was a live corner with clubs, liquor stores, pool hall, arcades, barbershops, and the world famous Stax Records, it wasn't as famous as the legendary Beale Street. But a lot of black cause could was hood where you cause it was in the any vice you was into. Dee asked could he smoke a junt to ease the tension in the room. The old guy who went by the name Fox said, "go head young blood, make yourself at home. This my place and a lil weed don't hurt nobody. Now what can we do for yall young hustlas"? Uptown spoke first, "well OG, we trying to expand our operations and we need some solid suppliers who gone keep us stocked up with good product. The other old head spoke. "We can do our part but you must know that or you wouldn't be here now. Now what I ask is what can you do for us. And can we trust yall cause trust is a must with us. He continued, "we don't need no money we good on that so don't come ty in here talking bout you gone help us get rich cause we already that. Now as they say for all business dealings, what's in it for us?

Uptown sat back and carefully thought for a minute cause he knew his response had to be good in order to seal the deal. But before he could respond Dee spoke up. Well, for starters, we don't want no fronts. We will pay for our packs in cash and full every single time. If we can't buy it, we don't want it. Cause if the money always right, won't be no fights, ya dig? The old heads said okay, I respect that cause most don't come in ready to do business like that, so that's cool. Uptown smiled at Dee cause he impressed everyone in the room. Also, Dee said, we got a Seattle plug on some good Canadian weed and that they would allow the old heads to buy from them at a good price. Uptown spoke, "yeah, we got it coming to our doorsteps so ain't no transportation fees. We will deliver it straight to you. One of the old heads said okay, I've heard of yall. Y'all those Mississippi boys who been selling all that good weed. We old but we keep our cars to the streets and we know who's selling what. Now, let's get to the important shit, numbers. How many can yall buy and when and where do y'all want it.

    Uptown said, "well it depends on the price. If the price is right, we can get started tomorrow. The old head Fox said, "well now.... much yall getting now and how much you paying"? Uptown said, well right now we buying a half key here and there with no real solid connection. That's why we here cause we trying to level up, serve more weight, and help our team eat more you know. Uptown said, we paying 14 thousand a half key so that's about 27 of 28 a key but it's got to be that good dope to make sure our customers stay coming back. The other old head said, "our core is the best we stand by that, in fact most people get there dope either from us or from our people. So we know it ain't stepped on cause our people come from where they grow that shit at, ya dig. So the niggas who serving you, hell, our lil homies might be serving them. Then Fox spoke again, "okay we can do 25 and if you do two, it's 24, and cheaper and cheaper the more you buy. How about that? Uptown and Dee said, "hell yeah we can do that. In fact, we gone need two tomorrow if that's okay. The old heads said, yeah that's fine. Here's the number. Call it tomorrow. They'll let yall know when and where. Okay, and oh yeah please no small bills; only 20's, 50's, and100's. Ain't got time to be counting all that lil cash ya dig. Uptown said, "Bet that. We will call yall in the a.m.

Then Fox said, "Yeah and bring me an ounce of that Seattle weed so that I can tell my young pothead hoes to test the product. Maybe we can work out a trade or we'll buy from yall to keep that money flowing, ya dig. Yall shop with us and we shop with y'all." Uptown said, "I'ma make it two ounces on the house cause we appreciate y'all fucking with us." Then the two old heads looked Uptown and Dee directly in the eyes with a hard stare and said, "Look young hustlas, this is big business. We play no games. Our business is our business. And we don't talk about our business to no one who's not involved in our business, ya dig, Uptown said, I promise. I respect that and honor your words OG. Thanks for taking this meeting with us. On my word, we gone stay loyal and learn gone... thanks.

Uptown and Dee quickly left and walked back to their car with their heads held high. They held their composure "until they got back on the E-way then they yelled, "hell yeah – hell fuck yeah. We did it. We finna get on bruh, no more nickel and diming it. We finna get real money now.

Uptown looked at Dee and said Thanks bruh. You really gave me the game bruh. You heled me to realize it ain't about how good you hustle but it's how you speak up for what you want. That's real talk. How the fuck did you learn how to use words to get into more favorable situations, cause they wasn't feeling us at first. Two young niggas walking in talking bout they wanna get on but they heard that a million times. But you sold the deal and made them respect our grind. You the voice of this crew from now on bruh. Dee said, yeah my guy I learned that most successful people be the talkers and not the workers. It's like this in order to become a true boss gotta talk like one first. Plus good conversations run this nation. All politicians, lawyers, public speakers, and preachers, talk for what they want & they don't do it hard they do it smart-

Uptown said, "Nigga you wise as fuck. You a city nigga though. I'm just a country boy from the Sip, still learning this shit but thanks to you bruh. I'm learning fast ya dig. Yeah, Dee said, I was born in these projects and when yo situation like that, people in a poor struggle situation, yo natural survival skills kick in automatically. Cause by all means you gotta eat and feed yo family. That's all we live for. Plus I'ma teach you like my big homies taught me. Pass on the game so yo people can eat, ya dig. Who taught you how to talk like that, Uptown asked? Shit, old-school pimp Roboe. He was a legend in our hood, a pimp/hustla with the power of a gift of gab; using words like art to paint his picture of success. He could sale anybody a tale and sale water to a whale. Dude had skills. He passed, but his game lives on through the minds of hustlas not only here in Memphis but across this country. He should've won an award; but plenty money and women was his trophies, plenty gold, and diamonds on his wrist, on his neck-and fingers, even had a 24-karat smile. He talked money and looked like it too.

That's what's up, Uptown said. I appreciate him giving you the game so you can share it with me, my nigga. Dee said, no problem bruh, but I thank you, bruh. You're the brains, the calm, level-headed, leader we need. You smooth and hard like a rock of ice. I respect how you handle yo business no feeling involved. You just get yo money. Plus niggas know you got them hands so they know you don't play. You moved here a few years ago and showed me. I could make a good living here in Memphis only if I move around more. I was stuck in the hood. Now I be all over the city plus Mississippi, St. louis, and Arkansas. See you go that discipline me and Cotton want the money and fame and yo love it cause you love the game. You want to help people and they family. You keep this shit going. You the star of our team and we couldn't win without you, my Bruh. And oh yeah, let's go wake Cotton's ass up so we ca tell him the good news.

They can pulled up to Cotton's house, knocked on the door and this tall, dark-skinned woman answered the door. Who's there, she asked. Dee said, you gotta be a new hoe if you don't recognize his brothers. She said yeah I'm new and I don't know you. Let me go get Nicky-red. Dee said, "go head bitch. Go get the queen you simple hoe. Uptown laughed. Dee loved to talk shit to the girls mainly cause they wouldn't talk to him like they liked him. Cotton would tell him he too gangsta for a pimp, playa, or Mack. He runs all his women off cause he too hard for em. Nicky-red came to the door and opened it. She said, look Dee you shit talking tender dick ass nigga stop harassing our hoes with your short, big head ass. They call you Dee cause, you fucking every bitch or hoe. Dee betta stop with all them dam kids you got. Keep on Dee and your D gone fall off you nasty ass nigga.

Uptown laughed cause Nicky-red could talk shit with the best of em and Dee know Nicky-red didn't play. He was a light weight in the shit talking ring and Nicky-red was a heavy weight champ trained by the best, Cotton and his momma, Big Momma, rest her soul. Dee yo said, fuck you, where's my nigga Cotton at? She said, he back there in the room. They went to the back of the house into the den area. Cotton was chillin in a thick smokey terry cloth robe with leather slippers smoking a junt. Dee said "dam my nigga, you went to jail now you back here looking like the black Hugh Heffner. Cotton said Dee you wouldn't understand. I'm a PIMP and this how I suppose to be, ya dig. Stay fly and always look your best even when you at your worst. Always look like you worth sum cause that represent that your bout sum, and that you're a somebody.

Uptown said, "Preach pimp, preach. Man, I'm happy to you free, my nigga" as he gave Cotton a warm handshake. Uptown grabbed him and gave Cotton a brotherly hug. Yo nigga you free bruh and boy do we have some good news for you! Cotton said, is this bout business, Dee said, yeah it is good business. Cotton said hold that for a minute. Then he called Nicky-red in the room and said, hey baby, get the hoes together and yall go out and go shopping. Yeah, and get your hair and nails done too. I gotta get these lawyers paid. So he gave her 2 thousand dollars and the keys to the car. She said okay Daddy. I need yall gone so I can rap with my brothers in private. She said, gotcha and then walked into the living room and yelled, "okay hoes who want to go on a shopping spree? Get yo shit bitches we riding out now. Five hoes all jumped into Cotton's big Lincoln Continental and peeled out the driveway.

Cotton sat back in his recliner chair and fired up a cigarette and said "so what's the biz Bruh's. Uptown said, we just left off College and McLemore and got the plug we been trying to get. We good now bruh. We finna make some real money now my nigga. This that shit that's going to take us to a higher level. We straight now. Dee said yeah nigga you can buy a hundred suits now my most pimpest partner. Cotton said, bet that. Yall did the deal, that's mayor, Bruh: Uptown said why you looking all gloomy nigga. We should be way more happy than that Dee said right you ain't been in jail long enough to be institutionalized now. You sad faced all the time mean muggin mac. That's what I'ma call you. Cotton said naw my niggas I'm happy for us real shit but with good news always comes bad news. Uptown said, Bruh don't tell me somebody died bruh. Cotton said naw bruh nobody died. But I talked to the lawyer this morning and he told me my case could go federal cause it involves other states. Uptown said, other states. The lawyer said you was good lawyer cause Hernando ain't nowhere from Memphis. Cotton said yeah that was true for the bond hearing but these crooked prosecutors and DA's were highly upset that I got a low bond. So they sent the case to the U.S. courts trying to make sure I get a lot of time, shit crazy. They didn't catch me with shit but yet they wanna lock me away cause of what a hating ass snitch said. The system fucked up. Dam Bruh what do we do now? The plug is waiting on us tomorrow to get two bricks, Uptown said.

Dee said, look it ain't the end of the world. We just gotta move different now. Plus it's a drug case. You can just go on the run. Fuck them. Run bruh. If you run for so long you can outrun the charges. Uptown said, nigga you crazy. He can't run. They'll be on all our trail and we got a business to run and people to take care of. Dee said yes we do and how we gone do all that if we in prison. We got caught up. Cotton said, yeah, he's right bruh. We gotta get out we of here in order to maintain cause if the feds looking at me, y'all most definitely are under radar. Shit we be together every day, and as soon as I don't show up for court, they will be kicking yall doors in.

Uptown just sat there in a daze. He wasn't ready for this. He knew about the up's and down's of the game, and this was a down time and he could see the worry in Cotton's eyes. Things were about to change real fast but he being the levelheaded leader, he had to make it look like he had it all under control. Things were about to change. They got a good connection and had the clientele to move. He just sat back and took in all the things going on. He had to make sure there next move was there best move and one thing was for sure he was going to make sure Cotton was safe.

Uptown said, "well you most definitely ain't turning yourself in and if they looking for you they gonna be looking for us. So we gotta split up and capitalize on our new environment. Dee said, "yeah we can still make our money here and still distribute our product in other states, get money everywhere we go; real cross-country hustling, ya dig. Cotton said, "yeah my nigga, and have a chain of trap houses, like McDonalds over a billion served. Okay, Uptown said. That's it then. We stay on the go getting our mutha fuckin doe. Yeah, we gotta take our show on the road. Cotton said, "yeah I got a lot of people in Dallas, Texas. Plus my hoes can work down there. Another plug there too, its plenty Migos that got that sack in the big-D. That stands for big dope my nigga. Dee said, yeah, I got a bitch in Milwaukee. She's from Chicago but she lives in Milwaukee and she down with the Daddy.

Uptown said, okay I gots folks in LA and Las Vegas, so I'm a be in Cali and all over the west coast. We gone connect the dots and get our money. Most importantly, stay off the feds radar, live on the road, buy houses then retire to big boy houses when we all get rich. It's going to be what dreams are made of.

But in this dream, it would go from the American dream to a real live nightmare cause, in this game ain't no winners just survivors and losers.

CHAPTER 7

WORLD DOMINATION

Uptown said, "First let's get these two keys and flip a couple of times before we hit the road cause we gotta make sure our people well taken care of before we leave. Also, we gotta have plenty money for when we hit these new cities. We must get established and maintain a low profile while we peep out the scene cause street niggas know every city don't take kindly to newcomers getting more money in their own city than them. Yet, it happens and it's more money for the out-of-towners cause they can move all over the city cause they not from there. They don't have a hood of their own nowhere for hustlas to label you. You can get in and out, get yo cash and dip. It was easy, yet most niggas don't have the social skills to interact with other hustlas and street niggas. But when you come up in the dirty south, you learn you gotta speak for what you want. A closed mouth don't get feed, ya dig." Uptown, Cotton and Dee all grabbed a glass of Remy Martin and made a toast: To the hustle and may we aways stay close no matter where we at. We still gone stay up as one family. We global now niggas. The earth is our turf. We are gone get money in every city and town we hit. That's how we moving now like true bosses. They finished sipping their yak and they all left in separate cars. They had to get ready for the upcoming day so they could cop the bricks and put them out on the streets.

  Also, their Seattle plug was on the way in a few days with that good weed. They were getting low and their stash of weed was moving fast. Life was good and about to get better. As Uptown drove, his mind was wandering about his upcoming future and how he was going to tell his family about his leaving the city. He knew the news would be hard on his family cause he was the breadwinner. His sisters were all on their own except two of them. His brothers had jobs, but he was the main person who they all could come to when they needed help. They all loved each other and this would be hard to tell them, but he knew that he had to go. He decided to go see his dad, Ike-Lee. Although their relationship wasn't like it should be, he knew the love was real. After all this, he loved his pop, and knew he could trust him without a doubt.

He pulled up on Trigg and Wellington Streets. Ike-Lee was coming from the corner store with a tall can of beer. Uptown pulled up alongside him behind tinted windows. He honked his horn 3 or 4 times then rolled the window down so that Ike-Lee could see his face. I -Lee said, "Dam Son, I almost shot yo ass. Don't be creeping up on me with all these strange ass cars. How many fuckin cars you got anyways." "Three," Uptown replied, "and besides why you walking to the store. You too old to be walking around by yourself. And I know you got a young chicken head to do that ripping and running for you." He said, "yeah, I do but they want to get paid for everything and I ain't got no money to be just giving bitches for every lil thing. These legs can move real good." Uptown said, "yeah I know yo ass will move for that ice cold beer." Ike-Lee said, "betta got dam know it. Soso what to do I owe this visit. I haven't seen you in almost a month." Uptown said, "Well pops I gots some important news for you. I'm about to move out of town. I gotta get out of the city. The shit getting too hot for me here plus you know Cotton got popped, and that's my right hand. So you know they'll be after me next." Ike-Lee said, "Dam son. I hate that for you. But I know you hustle to take care yo family and I respect that. Still at what cost. Yo freedom is all you really have and Black people got it extra hard. Anyhow, where you going son"? "California Pops," Uptown said. "Okay son, that sounds good. You know you got a lot of family in LA, don't you, on my side and yo ma side too." "I know," Uptown said. "I'ma be a Hollywood star, Pop." "Okay I hear ya son, well this news going to be hard on yo momma." "I know," Uptown said, "but it's for the best. I'll be back and forth Pops. Plus when I get settled you can come visit me." "Bet that son. I'll be on my way and no matter where you go best remember you're a Brown and I'll always love you." "I love you too, Pops."

They hugged and Uptown got back in his car heading to Orange Mound. He had to go and visit his mom and tell her the news. He had her set up in a nice one-bedroom house on Mashaneil Street off Park Avenue. She had turned it into a mini church where she had a podium and pews. His mom, MaryLynn, was a highly devoted Christian. She would get her amp and microphone and would preach to the crowds. That's where he got his fearless ways. She was afraid of nothing or nobody. She spoke her mind and never held her tongue. Uptown pulled in front of her house and knocked on the door. She would always peep out the window before letting anyone in. She learned that from living in the projects. She would say I trust God not people. She opened the door and hugged her son. Uptown said, "hey momma, how you doing today." He then sat down low on the pew. Uptown looked around the small house and said, "Momma, you deserve a bigger house." MaryLynn said, "son, I came from a shack in Mississippi to the projects in Memphis, and now to this house. It might not be much to you, but this my little place to worship the Lord. I know it and love it." "Okay, Momma. I hear ya," he said.. "Well why you here son," she asked. Uptown said, "I can't just be wanting to see my Mu-Dear kids. She said, "now boy I know all my children, and you're not here to just visit and ain't nothing wrong with me, so just tell me what's on yo mind son." Uptown took a deep breath and then began. "Well Ma, I can't tell you no lies. Cotton got into some serious trouble and I believe I'll be next cause". "Son, why you doing this, she asked. I never complained about you hustling cause I always knew everything you do is for your family, not yourself. I understand that it's hard for Black people in the south to get ahead. So, I don't judge you, Son, but I don't understand why y'all young folks are willing to risk freedom and life for a man-made piece of paper that really holds no true value. Son, money is a means to help get things you want and need but it ain't worth your morals and your freedom. Freedom ain't free for Black people. Our people paid for it with their lives and we still got a long way to go to get equal freedom in this country." "I know momma and trust me I be listening to every word you say cause I need your wisdom to help me make the right decisions,"

Uptown said. "Well son," she said, "what you gone do, and how is Cotton? I heard he went to jail but he out now. Tell my other son to come see me. I know it's been rough on them kids since his momma passed. I know she you might have hustled but she loved her kids and I respect that as a mother." "He good, Momma. I'll tell him to get through here before we leave." "Leave, where y'all going," she asked? "Well momma that's what I came to tell you. We leaving town so them crooked pigs won't get us caught up in their crooked system." "I understand son," she said, "but let me know where you gone be. I'll come to wherever you at. Okay. and I'm gone work." Uptown said, "I know I love you too and I'ma have it set up to where big sis, Henrietta will bring you money every week on time as long as I'm able, okay." "Thanks son," MaryLynn said. "Come here and let me bless you with some of this holy oil." She got out the oil and made a cross on his forehead and prayed for him. Uptown loved his momma with all his might. It was the main reason why he was hustling to take care of her and his family. After leaving his momma's house, he drove to the LMG projects to get up with Dee. Dee was out collecting the money from all the traps and the street hustlas. They had to get the money ready to buy the two keys in the morning. Dee had three trap houses in the projects: one on the drive, one on Porter Street, and one on Provine Street. But he used his momma's house on the drive to count up money cause he only trusted his momma when it came to his cash. In the streets, only momma will have your best interest at heart. Uptown walked in and said to Dee's momma, "Hey Miss Lady where's my guy"? "He's upstairs smoking that shit," she replied.. Uptown headed upstairs. He could see the thick cloud of smoke coming through the cracks in the door. Dee opened the door and it was like a scene out of a Cheech and Chong movie. Smoke poured out the room.

    Uptown said, "Dam D, you smoke like Cheech and Chong." Dee said, "betta know it. Gotta stay high to deal with all this madness in the game." "Pass that shit my nigga," Uptown said. Uptown hit the junt as they both started to count up all the cash. Uptown said, "Dam all the 1's, 5's, and 10's. We gotta go change them for big bills." Dee said, "I know just the place who'll do all of it for us as long as we spend a lil sum sum." Uptown said, "where is that cause we show can't take it to no legit stores or bank." Dee said, "naw nigga, we going to the strip club. They always need more small bills. We can do it there plus have a ball while we taking care of the business." Uptown looked at Dee and said, "nigga, you sure you gone find yo way to the club. You a real party animal my nigga." Dee said, "Strippers, spend money too." Uptown said, "Yeah. I know they do when they getting money from trick ass niggas like you." They both shared a laugh as they finished smoking and counting the cash up. Uptown called Cotton and told him about the strip club situation and to be ready to party tonight. It was going to be their going away party too. They all agreed on a time to hold all their closest family, friends, and workers together for a big leaving Memphis with a bang party! This was the beginning of a new era. Time to go on the road to see what's out there for sum real hustlas. Uptown went to the Mall of Memphis to pick up a fresh outfit for tonight. He had to be at his best cause this was going to be the last time they saw him for a while.

After he left the mall, he headed west on Lamar Street and made a right on Airways Street, then a right on Carnes Street. Then he rolled through Orange Mound for a minute pulling up on known drug spots like Brentwood Park, Pendleton, and Inez Street a.k.a. the 4-Way. Then he pulled up to Church's Chicken to grab a bite. After a quick meal, he headed to Mona's house, which was around the corner. He knew everybody would understand him having to leave, but Mona had developed strong feelings for him, and he cared deeply for her also. This was about to be hard cause unlike Cotton and Dee, Uptown wasn't a pimp or playa anyway. He believed in her like a queen and she was a woman who knew how to handle a street nigga in his position. Still this was a touchy situation. He never meant to hurt her, but if he stayed in Memphis it would hurt her in the long run, so he had to do what he had to do.

He walked up to the door, rang the doorbell. Mona opened the door with a big smile on her face. Uptown always made her so happy with his presence. Uptown said, "hey baby, how you doing? I was just riding through yo hood and I couldn't come through the mound without checking on my baby." Mona said, "just riding through? Yeah, right. Anyhow, I'm glad to see you handsome. How's your day"? "Going fine I hope you're good," Uptown replied. "Well, I haven't seen you in a few days. I thought you forgot about me," Mona said. "Hell naw, baby. I'll never forget about you. You my sweetheart." "Ok. Come have a seat then," she replied.. Uptown sat beside Mona and wrapped his arm around her and pulled her closer to him. Then he looked her in her eyes and said, "You know I care about you don't you"? Mona looked at him and said, "hold on. Don't come over here with no bad news." Uptown asked, "why you say that"? She replied, "cause every time somebody starts a sentence with I care about you first, usually there's bad news." "Well it's not per say bad, or good news, it's just life," he said. Mona said, "come on give it to me. "Who is the bitch, how long y'all been talking. Don't play. Keep it real. I ain't no girl. I know your type. We grown. I can handle grown woman issues." Uptown said, "naw baby it ain't no bitch. We real with each other." They weren't a couple and Uptown never asked who she was seeing nor did she. They were an attractive couple and they understood until they settle down they was just living life and enjoying each other's company. Uptown said, "look baby, Cotton got locked up on charges and his lawyer said it is serious and could go federal. That they would be looking for him and all his associates, and you know that's me right? I'll be one of his co-conspirators. In short, they'll be on my dick ass too, and I'm not trying to go to prison for no time. Can't do it." Mona said, "Dam Baby, I didn't know you was wrapped up in all this madness, I know you hustle, so I guess that's part of the game. Damn. What you gone do now"? Uptown said, "Well me and Cotton gone skip town. He'll be on the run cause he's already under indictment. I would just be laying low keeping off their radar so I don't be caught up on no pics, wire taps or indictments." "So where y'all going," Mona asked? "I don't really know yet but soon as I get settled in I'ma call you and send for you. Are you afraid to travel, he asked"?? "I love to travel, Mona replied. So what about all yo business here in Memphis, how you gone support yourself out of town"? "Well, Dee gone handle the business here in Memphis, plus Mississippi and Arkansas. He'll be in and out the city, but he's from Memphis so he'll have to duck off spots. We still gotta feed our families, so he'll be the person in charge while we are away. Also, I'ma born hustla. I'll be hustling wherever I go, it's money in every city and town, and the earth is my turf, and I'ma get it if it's there, ya dig." "Boss Daddy, I hear ya, well baby let's celebrate your new nationwide job." As she rubbed his dick through his pants, Uptown said, "naw baby not now. I got a lot to do before the big party tonight." "What party," she asked. "The big going away party. Me, Dee, and Cotton getting all the family, friends, and closest workers together tonight for a big bash at the Pure Passion Strip Club on Brooks Street. We taking over the whole club. It's only going to be our people, drinks, weed, and coke on us all night long. It's free to get in but please bring the ladies tip money. Gotta tip the twerking moms." "Ok. I'll be there. Can I bring my homegirls." Uptown said, "sure, Hell, bring the whole mound if you like. The mo the merrier. Plus the mo doe for da hoes, cops I mean, stripping moms of America," as they both laughed. Uptown said, "here," and handed Mona a fat bank roll and said "go to the mall and get you sum sexy to wear and here's a little for your hair. And be so kind as to get a room at the Peabody for me and you for after. Buy me a robe and you some sexy party thongs. Make sure you get those long inch heels cause you'll be my personal private dance later on." Mona said ok baby we can do that." Uptown gave her a shoebox stuffed with one-dollar bills. He said, "that's for the strippers." Mona said, "Uptown if I'ma be your personal stripper where's my tips"? Uptown reached in the bag where the shoebox came out of and came up with two big chunks of cash wrapped in rubber bands. It was his re-up money for the next day in Memphis. This is called flouging, showing off shit that ain't really yours or not telling the truth. Uptown said, "This yo tip plus you gone get to lay naked on top of all this cash while you get only the tip of this nigga." Please, she said, "You gone drop all yo inches in this pussy nigga. Stop playing. I'm from the hood too don't make a bitch take sum." Uptown said, "you can take what you want baby, I won't resist." "You bet not" Mona said, "so what time the party". Uptown replied, "it starts at 8:00. I wanna be in and out by 12:00 cause we rented it for 4 hours. That's enough time to party, have a meeting with our crew and dip so they can still stay open till 6.am. It's all figured out."

    Uptown hugged his sweetheart and headed towards his house in East Memphis. He had rented a nice house off Mendenhall. It was low key plush only. He came to the house once or twice a week. He didn't want to bring no unwanted attention of his hustling to his neighbors, mostly old people or single working-class people. This was a quiet suburb that most people in the city wanted to be in. His two younger brothers Earl and Glen lived with him. They both had jobs so they all pitched in on the bills. But Uptown paid the big bills like the rent and utilities. Earl paid the furniture bill and paid the yard cutting people and Glen paid the cable bill and phone bill cause he loved sports and talking to girls on the phone. They all bought food. Plus all his sisters and momma would come by and cook. Uptown's family had been in Memphis for 6 years now as he looked around his 4 bedroom/3 bathroom, and 3 car garage home. He just smiled to himself thinking, Dam, came a long way from that broke down old shack in Mississippi to a small 4 bedroom rat and roach infested project apartment to a big home in East Memphis. "Dam I'm blessed, thanks to God and the hustle. Now about to take is game worldwide, get rich for real. This just the beginning of more riches to come."

Uptown walked in the door and Earl was in the living room dancing to some old school Blues music. It was some Jimny Taylor. In the south, Blues and ole school R&B or soul music was always in style, no matter how old the song is. Earl turned around and said, "what's up big bruh, how's it going? Yeah momma, and all the sisters called and told us bout you leaving town, you leaving us big bruh"? Uptown said, "not leaving y'all just going to handle more business and stay safe and free while I do just that, ya dig." "Let me hit that hen-dog bruh. Earl passed him the bottle he was sipping on." "So, where you going big bruh, Earl asked"? "I'm going to the west coast bruh. to LA or Vegas. Hell all over, Arizona too. I'm going to be on the west side the best side for now. I might move around state to state. Gotta spread my wings and fly high. I'm trying to secure a good future for me and y'all, the whole family. We can't ever go back to being poor. I would die or do a thousand years before I sit back and watch my people suffer and want, never again. That struggle made me hunger for more -now I have more and more is all I'm living for." "We gone be good bruh, that's my word". Well I love ya and soon as you get settled, I'll be on my way. Just got my license back so I'll be traveling too, I love ya bruh. Oh yeah, can't wait till the party tonight. You know I'm the life of the party." "I know bruh," Uptown said.

"Where's lil bruh Glen at" Uptown asked. "He's in his room big bruh." Uptown walked down the hallway to Glen's room and opened the door. Glen was ironing his clothes, on the phone, and watching Sports Center all at the same time. He liked his clothes crispy sharp. He would spray his clothes with heavy Stay Flo Starch and you could stand his pants up on their own they was so stiff. Uptown said, "what's up bruh? Glen said, "I'm good big bruh. Heard you moving out of town. Who gone look after me now, bruh"? Uptown said, "me lil bruh. I'm leaving not the money. I'll still be taking care of the bills, taking care of you and the family. Y'all gone be alright. In fact I'm leaving so I can do more for y'all. I'm trying to put us in better situation. You'll be straight bruh. I've already set up a fund for you and all my sisters, brothers, and momma, and oh yeah, Ike-Lee too. Y'all still can call me for whatever whenever, all I'll do is have Dee bring the money to you, and there's Western Union, money gram and I got a few bank accounts set up in momma and my sister's name. So, you'll have plenty access to get money. As long as they print it, I'ma get it, and if I got it, you got it. So don't worry lil bruh. You still gone have money, stay fresh and ride clean. How's the car riding by the way"? "It's running smooth bruh. Just got a tune up on it". Uptown had bought Glen a clean two-door Monte Carlo, jet black, for his 16th birthday. "Okay" Uptown said. "Yeah always take care yo ride bruh." "I gots to," Glen replied. Uptown loved all his siblings, but Glen and Gladys were the babies of the Brown family. So he helped raise them. Glen said, "big bruh when you get out of town can I come see you"? "You better come see me lil bruh ..can't wait to go to new cities with you, plus I'ma open up some legit, businesses so y'all can have something to do that belongs to us, we'll be our own bosses, make our own work hours, but more importantly it'll be a family-owned business that no matter what you won't be fired." Glen said, "I can dig dat bruh."

  Glen worked part-time with his bruh-in-law, Clem, at a sign company called Simmons Signs. He liked his job but he knew his big bruh would make him a boss and that was what he wanted. He didn't like people telling him what to do even at work. Uptown reached in his pocket and handed Glen a few hundred dollars. Then he said, "that's for now a lil gas money for you. When I get situated, ma will let me know what you need and I got you." Glen said, "bet. Can I go to the party tonight? Uptown said, "Hell naw Bruh. I love you but Mu-Dear would rebuke me to the cows come home if I took you too a strip club. Maybe when you come visit me on the West Coast. I'll show you a good time I promise, okay."

Uptown went to his room and called Cotton and Dee. He had em on three-way: Uptown asked, "What's good my niggas? Everything ready for tonight night? Cotton said, "betta know it. Me and my family and my hoes ready to go and party." Dee said, "you know I'm ready. I'ma regular at Pure Passion." Uptown said, "I bet you is nigga. Dee said, "Oh yeah, I got. d. j. Lil Larry spinning and I got Ray the Jay on the mic." Cotton asked, "did you tell the whole city we trying to be packed; a party to remember." Dee said, "yeah nigga, every hood in the city gone be there. We gone be live just wait and see. They'll be talking bout our party for years to come my niggas. Uptown said, "okay it's set can't wait. Finna take me a power nap before the big night." Cotton said, "okay bout the business. What time we going to get these bricks." Uptown said, "bout 11 or 12. Cotton asked, "why so early?" You know we'll still be hung over from the party." Dee said, "yeah but these old heads like to do business as early as possible. They move doing business hours during morning, noon, and night rush hours to get blended in with the traffic. They professionals and we need to learn to be more organized like them. That's how they got rich by paying attention to the details. That's the key." Cotton said, "okay I'll be ready to go to work gotta get it cause shit finna be different but I'm ready" Uptown said, "okay, I'll holla at y'all when I get to the party. Dee don't be late. Cotton, I know how you like to make a grand entrance like you Goldie da Mack." Cotton said, "nigga that's tv. I'm bigger than that nigga. They call me pimp Cotton cause I sure know how to pick 'em, ya dig." They said their goodbye's and hung up the phone. Uptown got comfortable and relaxed in his California king-sized bed. He is tall so he liked big beds. When he was a young boy, his momma couldn't afford a long enough bed for him, so he slept on the floor. He promised himself once he got some money he would spare no expense when it came to a good night's sleep. He dosed off for a few hours and got up around 6:45p.m. He jumped in the bathtub, got out and got dressed. He had he learned from Cotton you gotta keep your appearance on point cause if you bout yo business, you gone dress the part. And if you talking bout money, you gotta look like money. After a quick check in the full body mirror, Uptown headed to the car and drove to a car storage lot off Shelby drive and Tchulahoma Road. He had bought a classic 1957 Chevy Bellini. It was candy apple red, chrome everywhere with icy white leather interior with wood dash- and steering wheel. In other words, it was extra clean. Uptown bought the car over 9 months ago from a rich car collector in Germantown, but this was going to be his first time showing it off. The time was right and tonight's party was perfect to show up and show out. It was his and his crew's time to shine. Uptown and Cotton were about to show off all their hard work in the years since moving to Memphis. It would be bittersweet cause after tomorrow they both would be gone not for good but for a while however long it took to keep the pigs off their backs. Uptown headed to south Memphis to let the crack heads wipe the dust off and clean the chrome rims. He pulled up to the car wash on McLemore -n-Lauderdale. The junkies all knew him so they knew he paid extra good. Uptown understood that these men were still somebody just with an addiction so he would pay them and even buy them food and beer. After a good wash up, he went by the frap to go talk to his workers to let them know even though they were having a party, product still had to be sold. So he had 3 workers working the club; one in the men's bathroom, one on the floor, and one in the parking lot, all selling party favors like weed, powder and pills. Cotton had a few of his hoes hustling the women's bathroom, but you gotta be careful cause in a strip club there are plenty of women in there hustlin. They knew not to step on nobody toes cause those women were there every day. Everything was set. It was now 8:30 p.m. Uptown drove pass the club to see how crunk it was. He told all his family and friends to come early so that the parking lot was packed cause that's how party goers judge if your party was jumping or not. The lot was jammed packed. Cars were lined up off the expressway just to get on brooks street. Uptown saw that and instantly thought about money. All these people coming out for us. He then started to daydream about owning his own club or being a party promoter cause he knew people meant money and you only as big as your clientele.

    After circling the block a few times, he pulled up to the parking lot and headed to the v.i.p. line where the owner greeted him. The owner had a big smile on his face and said, "dam my nigga. Y'all got this place packed. I mean, the whole city been talking bout this party. My bar is making money, my food selling and the girls cleaning up bags of cash. I thank y'all for this. It's like the talk of Memphis right now. You ever thought bought being a club owner or a promoter"? Uptown said, "yeah in fact after tonight I'm seriously considering it." The owner said, "you should cause can't anybody do what y'all did tonight and trust me I know I've been in this business over 30 years now. You've got to be a well-liked person to draw large crowds just on yo name alone, that's a gift and a talk that could pay." Uptown thought about what he said and then asked for his phone number. The owner said, "yo crew is right over there and I gots that private room for you in the back for your meeting.," Uptown slapped fives with him and headed to his section with his people. All his loved ones were there, his brothers, sisters, uncles, cousins, and all his friends from Mississippi. All Cotton's family and friends along with all his hoes who were dressed alike. Cotton had on a white mink coat with a fur white pimp hat, alligator shoes, with a smoke grey silk suit with enough jewelry to make Mr. T. get jealous, year he was big mamas son to the fullest. Dee was there with all his family, even his momma and daddy were there too. They all hung out together. They were a very tight-knit family. Also, Greg, Ced and the whole mafia were there along with plenty of others from the from all across the city of Memphis and Arkansas including Walker Homes, Binghamton, and Westwood. It was a true hustlas ball and Uptown, Cotton and Dee were the main attraction. The bottles of Moet with the sparkles were flowing everywhere. The DJ had the dance floors crunk and Ray the Jay was talking his shit telling tricks to tip the girls. Then Ray the Jay said, "ugly hoes the parking lot is for y'all. Then he said, "yeah my nephew is in the building. What's up Dee from the LMG. What's up pimpin ass Cotton, and what it do, my nigga Uptown? Y'all got this muthafucka off the chain. What's up Greg and Ced, I see y'all. We up in this piece. Uptown took a seat between his sisters. The youngest, Gladys and Earl were too young to attend, so they were at the house. His brother, bubba was in the army in Sacramento, California. Mona was on his other side with her brothers and sisters. She was dressed in a sexy tight dress with six-inch heels. She looked at Uptown and said, "you like these" as she pointed to the heels. Uptown said, "yeah baby, they look fly on you. Mona said, "yeah they got yo attention cause I have been preparing for this all day long, and oh yeah, here's the keys to the room at the Peabody. We on the top floor baby presidential suite." Uptown kissed her and said, "thanks baby you on point." Mona said, "when I say I got you, I got you. They hugged real tight while the party was in full swing. All the D-boys and D-girls were throwing money everywhere. The strippers were doing they thang, twerking, and working,

Cotton and his hoes hit the dance floor. Cotton loved to be the center of attention that's what he used to recruit new hoes. He showed them a glimpse of the life they would have being with a pimp; all the money, cars, cloths, the ice, the gold, it was very tempting to a young broke girl who was still fucking for weed, drinks and a ride somewhere. Cotton understood early on in life from his momma that most women were raised on the teaching that a lot of women use their sex appeal to get money from men and a lot of em think that's how you get ahead. But in true reality, you only get used. But a pimp doesn't judge her but shows her hot to capitalize off of anything she does. It's a normal agreement; hoe's need pimps and pimps need hoes. It's how it's always been. Wise words from big mama, R.I.P. Cotton was high enjoying himself. Dee had started up a dice game That nigga always hustling. He was cutting 6 and 8 getting plenty money. The young homies were moving weed and powder packs throughout the club and in the parking lot. Uptown was chilling when he noticed Lil Lisa and her crew coming towards him in her along with Angie.

Although Uptown had fucked a few out of Lil Lisa's crew including her, Angie had a lot of liking for Uptown. But he was there with Mona and he knew lit Lisa was cool and wouldn't cause any issues with Mona. But Angie was a lil mouthy and slow-slick ghetto country crazy bitch, yet cool. They all were cool. These were his home girls from Hernando. Lil Lisa walked up and spoke to everybody, Uptown's family and Cotton's family who all have known Lil Lisa and her whole crew. Uptown grabbed her hand and hugged her. He quickly introduced her to Mona to make sure he didn't disrespect her in any way, shape, form, or fashion. He cared a lot about Mona so he made it his business to always make her feel secure whenever they were together. Uptown said, "hey baby, this Lil Lisa. She's a close family friend. We grew up together. My family knows hers, and my momma is friends with her momma. You know we from the Sip, ya dig. Lil Lisa smiled and hugged Mona and said, "nice to finally meet you. He talks bout you all the time. We all heard good things bout you, and he's like my big lit brother so you take good care of my family, okay? Also, whenever you in the Sip come fucks with us. We country but we know how to party, ya hear me." Mona said, "thanks I make him happy every night and in the morning too."

Uptown looked at Mona and said, "now that's how a boss bitch handle her issues without getting low down. She keep it classy yet aggressive." Right then he knew he would someday marry her. Lil Lisa with her foul mouth self said, "enough of that small talk shit. Where's ya weed at Uptown? A bitch need to smoke. All these sweaty, naked ass hoes shaking and pussy popping. Where's the male strippers at." Uptown said this a strip club for men only; ass and titties and hoes." Lil Lisa said, "well hook us up with some of yo Memphis home boys. Let them niggas know the Sip is up in this bitch, ya hear me." Uptown said, "I gots you Lil Lisa. Let's drink and smoke. He handed Lil Lisa a big bag of that Seattle indoor weed. After Cotton got off the dance floor, he returned to his section with Uptown. He whispered in his ear, "Bruh, this the life. We shining in this muthafucka. Niggas raisin their cups to us. Niggas, bitch ass strippers telling us we threw a dam good party. They love us bruh. I hate we gotta leave all this shit bruh, I hate that shit bruh." Uptown said, "nigga this only the beginning. We bout to do this all over the country now. We finna be international hustlas. We finna get rich for real then we gone buy big houses and retire young and still have fun." Cotton said, "I can dig it, bruh but Memphis and Mississippi is our home. It's what made us who we are and to leave that and our loved ones behind is hard on a nigga, Bruh." Uptown said, "I know bruh but you can't go to prison. Yo family could come visit you behind a fence and barbed wire jails or come visit you on a beach or big house in the suburbs; which one you want bruh." Cotton took a mouth full of that Remy Martin. I choose the big house on the beach with the sand and freaks. Fuck prison. I don't ever want to see that big house ya dig." Cotton said, "that's why I love you big bruh. You always know what to do. I'm blessed to have you family. Coming to Memphis changed my life you a real nigga." Uptown said, "you gave me the hustle game nigga. I owe you my life. You gave me my first pack. You was my first connect. Nigga I wasn't shit before I met you. All this cause of you and the game you gave me." Cotton said, "nigga you elevated the game. You a true boss nigga. Y speaking of connect, we good on the business tomorrow right"? Uptown said, "yeah everything ready and it's a go. Oh yeah go get Dee so we can have this meeting with our crew. Gotta let them know what's going on in all situations-and issues." Cotton said, "ok, let me go get em." Cotton told his hoes to wait here and be cool but don't slip on a trick and turn yo back on other Macks, ya dig." They all yelled, "okay daddy." Mona looked at Uptown and said, "dam he good. Got them hoes well trained." Uptown said, "Oh yeah, it's in his blood. Real talk, his big momma was a pimp. He was born to do that." Mona said, "I couldn't be no hoe. My pussy ain't for sale plus no man can have control over me like that. I'ma boss my muthafuckin self." Uptown said, "yeah you're a lady. It's a difference between hoes and ladies." Mona said, "as long as you know baby." Uptown said, "I know. Tonight you gone be my lil stripper." Mona said, "yeah tonight I'll be yo stripper hoe, bitch, freak, slut whatever." Uptown said, "baby, I gots to go get with my crew." She said, "okay baby I'll be right here waiting on you. Cotton, Dee and Uptown headed to the private room. Their whole crew was waiting inside. After a few more members got inside, two big young niggas locked the doors stood in front of them arms folded while two more stood outside hands clutched on their guns on their waist."

Cotton spoke first: As yall know, they busted a pimp a few days ago and now the crooked ass Prosecutors trying to take the case to the feds. And as you know that means long sentences, but a pimp like me can't go. I'm too smart for that lame ass shit. I'm not a lay down ass nigga. They gotta catch me. So in other words, I'll be leaving for a while. The room fell quiet. Crew members was shocked. They had heard rumors but now it's coming from the horse's mouth. Cotton was in really in trouble. This was a nigga they all looked up to. Niggas were upset. They had love for Cotton. He was the leader who always would show them how to talk to females, how to dress, let em drive his cars, and even gave some of them his old Cadillacs. He was somebody they loved to see coming. They all were stunned. Cotton said, "now look, I know this a shock but now we finna take our hustle nationwide. We bout to get some serious paper now. Y'all been loyal and that's what's going to keep us together loyalty. It's more important than love ya dig. Who wanna get rich in here raise yo hands." Everybody in there raised their hand. Cotton said, "we gone be alright. I'ma be alright now Uptown will tell y'all the details. Uptown stood and spoke. But unlike Cotton, Uptown was all business, no fun, and games. They all loved Cotton and Dee. They respected all three of them but knew who was the tough one, and who was going to be on their asses if they weren't in line.

Uptown said: As y'all know, Cotton gotta leave town. In other words, he'll be on the run. It is what it is. Talk to no one bout his or our business. If a nigga or bitch ask bout his whereabouts, you don't know o.k. Never talk bout the crew business, never. Always throw em off and lie to em. We finna be in and out of town so never tell where you going or when you coming back, only yo crew-n yo closest family members like momma, daddy, brother, or sister if they don't gossip a lot. Yall know who in y'all family talk too fuckin much. Gotta throw everybody off. Tell em you going here but in reality you over there, ya dig? Gotta keep em in the dark and stay one step ahead. Can't snooze cause when you snooze you lose and we winners. We ain't got time for no setbacks; gotta stay focused and move right so we won't get jammed. Things are going to be a lil different cause we're constantly on the go, but the goal is the same get money get money and get mo money. Thats all life's about. Now, me -n-Cotton will be out of town opening up new markets, getting new plugs. Dee will be in charge here in Memphis and Mississippi. When we out of town we gone need drivers to move product around so anybody with valid driver's license would be good for that. It's good money in that too. Also if anybody want to change location and come on the road it's all good. We finna be global now; get money in every city and town we land in. We finna get rich and whoever don't wanna do this or scared to leave town, speak up now. Cause if this ain't for you, you could leave now. We ain't trying to force nobody to do something they don't want to do. Now Dee has some words for y'all.

    Dee stood up and began to speak: As y'all know, I'll be in charge here in Memphis as the head charge boss of our operation, but I'll be in out of town also but close by driving distance. I gots business in Nashville, Atlanta, and New Orleans. We'll have houses and traps in those cities as well as on the west coast, east coast and up north. We bout to franchise the game. Just like McDonalds or Burger King, we trying to get money everywhere. We gotta make this a professional business. No more thinking hood rich shit. We trying to get enough money so all us can be well off. Yall young now but in due time y'all will grow older and have y'all own crew. We trying to create bosses, y'all will be future bosses, and we got to follow the blueprint of the people whose doing it the right way. We still learning ourselves but ask questions that's how you learn. I'll come by each spot and explain more. Remember loyalty and trust, that's the only thing that truly matters. Now this meeting is over. Y'all can go back to partying. I gots a crap game to get back to. Y'all enjoy tonight cause it's back to business tomorrow. As everybody left, Uptown, Dee and Cotton stayed a few seconds longer. Uptown waited till the last man closed the door behind them then Uptown spoke. "Yeah my niggas, after tomorrow we ain't finna see each other for bout a month. That'll give us enough time to get the ball rolling, you know get somewhere to live, get ID's and driver's license in the city we're in." Cotton said, "I'ma be in Dallas. I gots a hoe already working down there. She setting everything up for me now. I'm only going to take two more hoes with me and I'll be networking in no time." Dee said, "yeah I'ma stay in Memphis till everybody situated and I'ma go to Atlanta and see can I open up some shops down there. I got a house already there. My cousin let me take over her lease when she moved back to Memphis." Uptown said, "yeah soon after we re-up today, Dee you go put the work up, and wait till we out of the city to package up and take em to the traps. I love you niggas; y'all the team. We the Big 3. We going to the top. All there is to do now is stay focused. Well, we gone get up tomorrow morning. I got everything up for the re-up. Y'all gone enjoy y'all self. I gotta go." Cotton said, "yeah I seen yo lil honey dip, Mona, sitting close like to hip nigga. You into her, I can dig it bruh. As long as your happy that's all that matters. Cotton said, "oh yeah, Dee, how much you cut off the crap game so far?" Dee said, "about 27 thousand and it's still on. I gotta make sure both of y'all leaving with a nice bank roll to go anywhere and already be up." Uptown said, "I'm out. Y'all get at, see y'all in the a.m." Uptown returned to his section. Mona was there dancing with her friends, poppin bottles. She clearly was drunk. Uptown approached her from behind and started to slow grind on her thick ass to the music. She noticed him on her and began to smile as she turned around to pace her man. She hugged him tight and said, "I been waiting on you to come dance with me" as she pulled him closer then kissed him passionately on the neck then spoke soft and sexy in his ear, "I ain't wearing no panties. I want you to fuck me like the world was ending tonight." Then she looked him in the eyes with those bedroom eyes coming out for us blushing. Uptown whispered, "I gots you baby. In fact, we can leave right now. I want it now." Mona whispered back, "you gone get it now. I might suck that dick all the way to the room, Mr. Uptown." "You sure you ready to go Uptown? I got a lot for you to do down there. This cream ready to be licked." They left the club after saying goodbyes.

Uptown and Mona got in his clean 57 Chevy Bellini and headed down Brook Street, then went north on the I-55 till they reached Poplar Street. They then took the exit and drove through the Uptown area till they reached the world-famous Peabody Hotel. The Peabody is an old 5-star hotel where all the important people who come to Memphis usually stay. The theme of the hotel is southern hospitality and luxury. It is also famous for having well trained ducks that do a walk from the elevators to a small little fountain. They then swim around.

Mona-n-Uptown had one of the best rooms they had to offer. The room was beautiful, real high class type shit. Uptown knew this was going to be his last night in the city so he wanted to make it special; something to remember. He had preordered two racks of ribs from Rendezvous Barbecue

Restaurant. Memphis is the barbecue capital of the world. There are more grills fired up in Memphis than anywhere else in the world.

After a bite to eat, Monan and Uptown made love all night and going to sleep around 5.a.m. Ater 4 hours of good sex rest, they woke up, took a shower together and left the Peabody.

On the ride back to Mona's house Uptown could tell by the expression on Mona's face she didn't like the fact that he was leaving town but more importantly leaving her. She knew he had to do what he had to do cause nobody wants to go to prison, but she was falling in love with him and if that meant being there for him no matter what, she was willing to do that. Still it was exciting to know that real soon she'll be on the road with him and knowing that all the big cities they used to watch on tv, she'll be seeing with her own two eyes.

They pulled up to her house. Uptown got out and opened the car door for her. Mona liked the fact that although Uptown was a street nigga, he knew how to be a gentleman. They kissed goodbye and Uptown assured Mona that he would come to see her later on in the day right before he left town.

After dropping off Mona, Uptown headed to the spot to get ready for the re-up today. Cotton and Dee were already there. Uptown walked in the door. Cotton was finishing up counting all the hundred- and fifty-dollar bills. Dee said, "Well my niggas, y'all ready? This is the start of something extra good with our connect in Seattle on the weed, Table out the Foot Homes, and now the kingpins off College and McLemore as our supply in the city is well secured. But they knew bigger and better were still to come. They had the

Memphis game down-packed, so now they were ready for world domination. The shit street legends are made of.

After all the cash was counted, they all got in separate cars; one with the re-up money, another with the guns-n-shooters, and another for the look out. This was big business and although they felt the kingpins were on the up and up, the game can be really wicked. You learn to trust no one when it comes to large amounts of cash. That's why you gotta learn how to move like the bank's Brink trucks. You never reveal how you moving so you can see any crosses before they come. The pickup spot was typical of some paranoid old heads. It was at a car rental spot off Airways Boulevard.

The two old heads were parked in front in a low-key old-school Ford pickup truck with working shit on the back cab. They were dressed like dusty working men nothing like the fly kingpins off College and McLemore. They knew how to handle business, never calling attention to themselves, again, they were professionals.

Uptown got out of his car and walked over to the truck. They gave the usual pleasantries and began business. Uptown said, "Hey, I got the cash so what we doing"? The old heads said, "Well go into that car rental place and take the money to the bathroom. There's a guy in there. You will give him the cash, and then go to the counter. The young lady will hand you the keys to that red rental car. It's already in a secret stash spot. All you have to do is go under the floor mat, lift up the lever, push a button, and like magic, the product will appear.

Uptown followed instructions and pulled off the rental car lot making sure not to speed and following all traffic laws.

After making it to the spot, all the butterflies in his stomach settled down. He was nervous cause he had never seen a crew so well organized. After they all pulled up to the spot, they pulled the rental car to the backyard where they couldn't be seen. They had properly protected themselves from being seen by building high wooden fences around the place. After getting the bricks out of the stash spot, they looked and noticed there was an extra half brick in the packing. They immediately called the old heads to make sure they didn't give them the wrong package.

Uptown said, "Hey OG, you know there's an extra half key in that package." The old head said, "Yeah we know. It's a gift from us to y'all. We did that to show yall we bout our business and that it's plenty more where that came from. If y'all shop with us, our business gone always be good. You learn to always keep the customers smiling and that way they always come back to do more business." Uptown said, "Well, you got our business and I really appreciate it." The old head said, "Oh yeah, remember that lil weed yall gave us, we need more." Uptown said, "yeah, we got you. Just let me know when and where." The old head said, "Well take it to the young girl at the counter when you return the rental car. She's my lil weed tester and if she says it's good, we'll be shopping with y'all." Uptown said, "I gots you OG. It'll be on the way. In fact, I'ma make it a whole pound to show you we thank y'all for all y'all doing for us. We business partners for life and I'm ready to learn more from y'all OG's." The old head said, "that's cool young blood. Yeah, she'll have plenty to smoke now so she'll be very happy. Yeah, I hear ya, young blood. That's the plan. Keep em happy. That's how you be successful. thank you." "I believe that OG," Uptown said.

Uptown hung up the phone and told Dee and Cotton about the free half of brick. Cotton said, "now that's how you do business. I haven't met them OG's yet but I like how they handle they shit." Uptown said, "yeah, thanks to Dee. He knows all the big dogs in Memphis." Dee said, "yeah my pop and mom's from South Memphis. They been on they hustle since I was born"! Cotton said, "just like I was born in a hoe house raised to be a pimp." Uptown said, "well I'ma country boy born in poverty and raised in the church, but one thing we all have in common is we all want more. So this is why we some certified hustlas, real hood niggas and now we bout to go global"!

Uptown, Cotton, and Dee each went to their own houses to pack up for the trip on the road. Cotton was headed to Dallas, Texas. He had never been there, but he knew people through his hoe who had been back and forth from Memphis to Texas. She got Cotton a condo in Plano, Texas. Uptown had aunts in Las Vegas, Los Angeles, and Oakland. He called each one of them asking about prices for houses and that he would be in their city in a couple months but in reality he wanted to surprise them cause he would be there in a couple of days.

    After going by his momma's house, visiting his family and Mona's house, he met up with Cotton and Dee. They all split up the cash they had been saving up plus the money from the crap game. They all put back some cash for their families. Dee almost teared up knowing he wasn't going to be able to see his niggas every day. He grew to love his Mississippi brothers. They weren't original LMG niggas but they showed him the true meaning of loyalty and he really enjoyed having them in his everyday life. Likewise, they loved Dee for showing them how to hustle in a city like Memphis. He would always tell them that if you can make it in Memphis you can make it anywhere. They were going to miss each other but the thought of jail made it clear that they had to keep pushing forward so they wouldn't have any setbacks.

    They all had about 35 thousand each. Now that's not a lot of money but for some 22-, 23- and 25-year-olds, it was a nice little startup bankroll. Plus they still had the two and a half bricks put up and the weed plug from Seattle was still sending pounds of that good light green stuff. So, the money was still going to be made. But when you're on the road, you have to create more opportunities so the money won't slow up.

They chilled together for a few hours and then Uptown and Cotton got in their cars and headed west on the I-40. Cotton took Nicky-Red and two more of his hoes with him. He let them drive cause although he had his driver's license, he knew he had that case over his head. So, he didn't want to get pulled over and the police run his name to find out he had an open case. There wasn't a warrant yet cause he didn't skip court yet but he wasn't taking any chances.

Uptown liked to drive solo. It was his peace of mind time. He always got on the road with snacks like chips, cookies, candy, water, sodas and most importantly a big box of chicken wings from Crumpies. He never liked to get off the highway for food, only gas and the restroom could stop him from driving. Uptown also only listened to the old school Blues while he was driving. He liked R&B and other music but the Blues always reminded him of his southern roots and he enjoyed it. The soul sounds helped to keep him relaxed and focused. He also kept the bible on the dashboard; a lesson his Mu-Dear taught him. This wasn't just for luck, but to let God know no matter where the road of life takes him, the word of God will never let him get lost and will keep him safe along the way. Uptown grew up in the church so his faith was always strong. But the struggles of growing up in poverty gave him reason to want more, so he hustled. It was a must that he help his family situation. He could've taken the legit route but that meant years of school and hard work. He just chose to take a shortcut to success, something that always looked good in the beginning.

As he drove west on the I-40, he caught up with Cotton's car and they both stopped to get gas in Little Rock, Arkansas. After getting their gas, Cotton and Uptown went to the back of the gas station and took a weed break. They always had a rule; only smoke weed at a rest stop or gas station but never in the car, mainly because you're from out of town, and if you do get pulled over, they won't smell weed or alcohol. Uptown never would drink and drive not even a beer. Now Cotton on the other hand never really had that problem cause when he gets drunk his hoes usually drive. So he could lay back, ride and sip yak and talk that pimp shit all day long. They smoked and chit-chatted for a few minutes knowing it would be a few months before they would reunite either in Texas or in California once they both got settled.

Uptown said, "Win my nigga. I'll be seeing you in a minute, my brother." Cotton said, "Okay big brother. Make sure you get a big house." "Okay, you know I rolls deep; hoes and bros plus family." "I'll come to Texas nigga and gone get me some snakeskin boots and a big cowboy hat nigga. I'm coming to see you Bruh, you can bet your life on it, Uptown said." "Love ya, bruh, we gone see each other soon," Cotton said trying not to tear up. They finished saying their goodbyes and then got into their cars and got back on the e-way.

As Uptown looked into his rearview mirror, he could see Cotton's car get on the 1-30 west exit heading to Dallas. He let about 3 or 4 tears run down his face. This was his best friend, his brother, leaving him for the first time since they met. He hated the situation that led to their departure from the city, their families, and their loved ones.

The thought of all the people they had to leave behind to get money entered his mind. It was bittersweet. He enjoyed the money the hustle provided for him and his family, but this is the same hustle that's taking him away from those who love you the most and the reason why you do what you do.

After a few minutes of daydreaming, Uptown turned on some Bobby Womack, the song was "California Dreaming." It was his way of saying man up nigga; what's done is done. Let's make the best out of this situation. I'm free, I got money, and I'm on my way to the land of sunshine, good weed, good wine.

Uptown drove for 16 straight hours till his eyes got tired. He pulled into a motel off the freeway. After 6 hours of sleep, he got back on the road. He fell in love with all the beautiful mountains on the west coast. In Memphis and Mississippi, the land is flat but with lots of big hills and valleys. Here were beautiful mountains; a sight to see for a wide-eyed southern boy.

After reaching Naples, California, He went south on the I-15 to west on the I-10 driving towards Los Angeles. It was a wonderful sight to see. After reaching the top of the mountain, you can see LA in the distance. The city was so big, so wide. As you drive down the valley, you get closer to the city and things look much bigger than the small cities like Memphis and Little Rock. The sun was shining like a beam of light. The weather was great.

Uptown rolled down his window to smell some fresh clear air, but there were so many cars on the road that the only thing he could smell was the smog. He continued to drive as the traffic seemed to get worse. He wondered how much longer before he arrived into the city itself. The buildings were so tall and there were palm trees. Now that's something you would never see in the big M. The very sight was so amazing.

As he got into the heavy Uptown traffic, he could see the tall round shaped ivory white Wilsher building. He seemed to have seen these buildings a million times. He got on the 110 exit and headed south. That's when he noticed that there were two LA's; the one you see on tv like Hollywood, Malibu, the beach and Beverly Hills, and the other east L.A., South L.A., South Central, Compton, Watts, Inglewood, just to name a few. In other words, in every city there is the money side and the poor side. The poor side is where you'll find the most Black people and Latino's. In L.A, Mexicans are the majority and even the name Los Angeles tells you who this city is named for. Unlike Memphis, streets are numbered and have names. The number streets usually run east and west while the name streets are north and south. But the big city is different. You have to know where you are cause there's L.A. County and San Bernardino County, so the streets are long and go through plenty smaller towns, cities, and neighborhoods.

Uptown made an exit on East Broadway, then drove to 54th street and went down to the corner of Avalon and 54th. He stopped by the corner store to buy a case of beer for his auntie. After getting the beer and a few snacks, he went a few houses down till he reached his aunt's house.

He got out and went to the door and rang the doorbell. His aunt asked who it was. Uptown said, "it's Willie, T-T as he called her." The door flung open and she ran and hugged her nephew saying, "dam you got tall boy. What you been eating"? Uptown said, "that good ole country food". "Okay dam nephew I didn't expect you so soon I thought you was going to be here in a few months, why so soon," she asked? Uptown said, "cause I needed to get away from Memphis. The south is home but I want to see more you know." She said, "well, I been trying to get my sistas and brothers out of that old slave mentality south. It's home and where we're from, but the system in place down south wasn't meant for Black people to succeed. Here, everybody understands this is a melting pot of different people. The culture here is of many different people from different backgrounds. A lot of different countries are represented here. So that brings a lot of open-minded people that call L.A. home. That's what makes it so different from down south. This the new USA and those old black vs white down south ways don't exist here. Anyway let me call your cousins so they can come see you. Are you hungry? Let yo T-T make you some good ole soul food." Uptown said, "yeah, I'm hungry but I wanna taste some Cali food, some good taco's." She said, "O.k. You wanna taste some of our west coast food? I know a spot around the corner on King Street called Bill's Taco's. It's our hood spot. Let's go around there and you know your T-T got some of that good west coast weed to smoke." Uptown said, "good, cause I'm almost out of the weed I had."

   They got into this old school station wagon. She reached into her purse and pulled out a small dime bag of weed and handed it to Uptown. Uptown said, "Now T-T, I'ma need way more than this. I smoke a lot." She said, "Well you know I'm old and a lil pin junt is cool for me but, I gotcha nephew, and by the way how long you gone be here"? Uptown said, "I don't know I might make L.A. my new home; so I'll be needing you to help find me some place to live okay"?

They got to the restaurant and ordered what looked like everything on the menu, and then returned back to his Auntie's house. Uptown's cousins and some of their friends were waiting to see him. As the car approached the house, his cousins, Mario, and Cam were sitting on the porch. They ran over and hugged him. They were so happy to see him. Mario said, "Hey Willie, how you been. It's so good to see you." Uptown said, "good to see yall too cuz, and I go by Uptown now. Willie is my Mississippi childhood family name but Uptown is who I am cause I'm at the center of any city I'm at, ya dig." "Okay," Mario said. "Well, they call me Yo out here cause at dieting I'm a beast, ya dig." Cam finally got a chance to speak. "They call me Cambo cause my momma country as hell." They all laughed as Yo passed the blunt to Uptown. And out here, "address me as kinfolks or fam cause there are a lot of gangs here and some of them use that cuz word. So you don't want to get caught up talking bout shit you don't know. Ya feel me." "Okay, I got you kinfolks," Cambo said. "And oh yeah kinfolks, I got a lot of friends that'll love to meet you. I been telling em about my down south family and they all know how to treat women so get ready to hit the clubs with me." "I got ya kinfolks," Uptown replied. "But first I need to get some rest. That road is a muthafucka on a nigga back." Yo said, "okay kinfolks. I got a big comfortable Cali king size bed. I'ma be at my baby momma house, so you can have my room as long as you like." Uptown said, "that's what's up."

After unpacking, Uptown went to sleep. He slept longer than usual. All night long, he dreamed of a day when he and his loved ones could reunite. He thought about Mona and how he missed her so much, and the thought of having her fly out made him smile in his sleep.

After a good night's sleep, he woke up to the smell of bacon, eggs, and toast. His T-T had made him a good breakfast just like his momma used to make. Even though she had been on the west coast for almost 30 years, she still cooked southern food as if she were still there. They finished eating and decided to smoke a fat junt. Uptown then said, T-T, "This orange juice is good as hell." She said, "yeah nephew, I squeezed it myself. Take a look out back."

Uptown lifted the blinds and saw orange trees, lemon trees, strawberry trees, and a grapevine. California has some of the best soil and sunshine to grow fruit and nuts in the country. Uptown said, "damn T-T, you got a whole supermarket fruit section in yo back yard. That's hard as hell." She replied, "yeah it saves me a lot of money too. Now let's talk about this house situation. You know you can stay here as long as you like. I would love to have you here. You can get a job helping me on the hills here and there." Uptown said, "Thanks T-T, but I'm grown and I need my own spot. But I'ma still help you on bills as long as I'm in this city. If you need anything I got you. In fact, as he reached into his pocket, take this." He gave her a thousand dollars and said, "T-T I'ma hustla and I don't need a job. I'm here to get rich and open up my own business.

I plan to get a big house and to bring some of our family out here to live with us. T-T said, "now that'll be like heaven to me to have all my family come out here to live. That would be a dream come true. Yo momma told me you been hustling since y'all moved to Memphis. I don't knock how you get yours, nephew. I hustle too, a few pills here and there; nothing big but a lil sum - sum to make ends meet, ya hear me. But listen here, nephew, she said. Be careful out here. These muthafuckas out here on that gang banging shit. Don't be in their hoods trying to hustle shit cause they be fucking up newcomers trying to get their sales in their hoods. But Uptown LA is wide open. People from everywhere come here to hustle, but be safe and if there's anything you need to know holla at yo T-T. I got you and love you. Oh yeah, and thanks for the money." "Don't thank me, T-T, I need your help in finding a house. I have another stack for you if you can do that, kinda be my real estate agent." They both laughed as they shared another junt.

After the morning breakfast, Uptown looked out and could see the sun bursting through the clouds. The city was bright and there were so many people. This was much faster than Memphis. Still Uptown was ready to see what LA had to offer. His kinfolk, Yo pulled up and Uptown slumped in the car with him. It was time to get the grand tour. Yo drove through all the neighborhoods, especially the ones you hear about on tv. Then they cruised the beaches of Malibu, Santa Monica, and Venice.

Uptown was so amazed at all the beautiful women out in two-piece swimsuits just lying on the beach. They walked Venice Beach to see all the weird people selling shit and performing for tips. There were lots of vendors selling everything from t-shirts to food and drinks! Everywhere he went, people were hustling. There were even Mexicans standing on the freeway selling oranges.

They decided to stop by a chicken spot called El Polo Loco and grabbed a bite to eat. Uptown asked Yo, "So why aren't you out here hustling fam." Yo said "well kinfolks I used to but now I gots 2 strikes against me and in this state, all it takes is 3 strikes and you're out, just like baseball nigga. But you don't go to the bench you go to the pen for life." "Dam," Uptown said, "that's cold right there." "Yeah it is", Yo replied. "It's a lot of Black and Brown people doing life in prison for lil or nothing shit. So I gave the game up. Now I just hustle cd's, tapes and I rap too. Just enough to get by but at least I'm free, ya feel me." "Dat's what's up kinfolk," Uptown said. "I can respect that." "Plus I got kids so I gotta be out for them. Still I can help you on whatever kinfolks. I know the city and I know who's who; bet that." They finished their conversation and eating and drove over to Yo's baby momma's house on Wilmington in Compton.

Uptown called Cotton to see how he was doing. Cotton picked up the phone as he was cussing and yelling at one of his hoes. He was a muthafucka when it came to pimpin. Uptown said, "slow down low down. It's yo brother nigga." "Oh yeah my bad big bruh, he said. But these hoes trying a pimp's patience. How's Cali big bruh." "It's beautiful," Uptown said. "How you doing in the big D-town." "It's love big bruh. I told you I had a hoe already working down here. Now I gots my hoes on this hot stroll called Harry Hines Blvd. It's plenty of money flowing through this city, big bruh. What's up on the dope game down there," Uptown asked. "Well," Cotton said, "it's way more drugs being sold here than in Memphis. These niggas are well connected. They doing some real drug smuggling in this muthafucka. Also, it's close to Memphis so I'm looking for plugs only, ya dig." "That's what's up," Uptown said. "I'm coming to see you soon seeing that you already got a house and a lil established already in Dallas." "I'm on the way nigga. Can't wait to see ya big bruh," Cotton said.

Hey, get Dee on 3-way. Cotton called and Dee picked up right away. "What's good, bruh," Dee said? "I'm chillin on the westside bruh." Uptown asked, "how's business going in Memphis?" Dee replied, "Everythangs going just like we planned. The work is moving fast and the weed just landed yesterday." "Ok. That's what's up," Uptown said. "How yo pimping ass doing in Dallas, Cotton," Dee asked? "I'm good bruh. My hoes working hard on the Blvd., and I just knocked two Texas hoes, ya dig." "Dig dat," Dee said. "I'll be coming through soon Bruh. I'm on my way to Nashville in a few days. I got some players up there, and then on to the ATL. So, I can get some of them dixie dollars, ya hear me." They all bust out laughing. "That's what's up. The team is in the game as planned. You niggas be safe and stay hard as shit to feed the fam. We got people who need this money and we gotta do what's best for them, ya dig," Uptown said. Dee said, "yeah plus I'm finna have another baby, my nigga. So you know I can't be out here playing no games cause kids can't eat love, ya hear me." "Believe that my nigga," Cotton said. "Congrats tender dick ass nigga," Cotton joked. "And you betta watch yourself in the ATL cause bitches ain't bitches. Check da neck nigga." They all laughed. "Well until we talk again, love ya, my brothers," Uptown said. They all hung up.

Uptown and Yo drove to Watts to see the world-famous Watts Tower. It was smaller in person than in the movies. LA had a lot of famous spots. After all, this was tv land, and 85% of tv was filmed in either LA or New York. As they drove through Watts and South Central, Uptown could easily see that although the big city had a lot of glamor, it still had very poor ghetto's too, just like down south. But the good part was that in LA you could see the rich part of town and it wasn't far away. So, the move up was close and he was ready to move on up like George and Weezie from The Jefferson's. After a quick tour of the hoods of LA, they went back to his T-T house.

She said, "well I found a few spots for you to rent. I talked to my friend. He has a couple of houses and apartments for rent." Uptown said, "well first, I want something not too big maybe a lil two-bedroom apartment in a low-key area. But I need it to be nice, somewhere I can rest but also entertain. And you know you'll be over all the time, T-T. You'll have keys to the spot as well, ya dig." "That's what's up nephew. But I'ma just make sure you is okay at all times. Plus I will come by to cook some good southern soul food for ya sometimes cause out here the food is good but it's fast and quick like the city." "That's cool T-T and whatever you need I gots you too," Uptown said. "Okay, we'll go tomorrow to house hunt and have lunch too." "Okay nephew, it's a date," she said. "And here." She gave him two ounces of some purple strong-smelling weed. She said, "yeah my home girl just came back from Oakland, Cali, with this. It's called granddaddy purp." Uptown said, "thanks T-T, I gotta get up that way some day if they smoking like this". She said, "yeah nephew, the bay area and northern Cali is the mecca of the weed world. It's way better and much cheaper up there than in LA."

Uptown's hustla mentality automatically kicked in. That's another weed plug for him and his team, he thought. He already had his old head in Seattle bringing pounds to

Mississippi. But he understands that the more plugs the more money. It was simple math. "Thanks T-T," Uptown said.

They smoked a couple fat blunts and Uptown got on the phone and called his momma to let her know he made it safely and that he was okay. After that, he called all his brothers and sisters. Family was super important to him and he knew they all missed him as much as he missed them.

After checking on the family, he called Mona. She picked up. "Hey baby, I been waiting on yo call, how's the west coast"? "It's beautiful baby just like you," he said. She said, "you sure know how to talk to a lady and make her feel good." "Yeah, that's my job to make you feel good." Mona said, "thanks bae. So when can I come visit you"? Uptown said, "well, baby soon as I get situated. I gots to get a place to live and that'll be soon cause I'm grown and can't stay with my T-T." "Yeah you better not be staying with yo T-T, Mona said. Cause soon as I come visit, I'm gone be naked all over yo house." They both laughed, and talked for an hour or two, and then said "till we see each other again, love ya" as they hung up.

Uptown missed Mona so much, not cause of the good lovemaking and that was a plus. But because this was his friend and she made him feel like he was a king for real. Still he had to stay focused to ensure that business was first and foremost.

A few days had passed and Uptown got to know the streets and highways of LA a little more. So, he knew where to go and how to get there. He and his T-T picked out a 3 bedroom, 3 bath penthouse off Wilshire Blvd about two blocks from the Uptown area. "See, this is how he got his name. Uptown is the heart and brains of any city. You can get anywhere from there and it's used to seeing out-of- towners, so you won't feel out of place. And people won't be alarmed by newcomers moving into their neighborhood.

It was time to move. Uptown's place was on the 52nd floor. His balcony overlooked the bustling city below where people are moving 24-7. This city was fast and at night it lit up like the stars in the night sky. Yeah he was really excited about his new situation.

After getting his new penthouse fully furnished, he got out and started his plans to hustle. First, he took a fast survey of his surroundings. Close to where he lived, was Skid Row. It was a street close to 4th and Wall Street. There were a lot of homeless people living in tents and cardboard boxes. Most of them come to LA with dreams of making it big in Hollywood or the music industry. In that business, drug use is the #1 reason why people get into situations where they get strung out; all the while lying to their families like they made it. But the truth is that they let the drugs take over and now they too embarrassed to go back to the city or town they come from. So, they stay and deal with their condition the best way they can.

Yet and still, Skid Row got thousands upon thousands of drug users now. Sure they broke, so it's only small packs of them buying, but a lot of small packs makes plenty big stacks. Also the Wilshire area had a lot of tourists pouring into Uptown to go to the fashion district, garment district, and a lot more districts. So it's a lot of shopping and sightseeing. Although most of them wanna watch and have fun, some wanna get high.

Uptown bought a couple pounds of weed and a half brick of coke from his cousin Yo's homeboy. He rocked up half the coke and made powder packs out of the other half. Then he hit the streets with his plan. He dressed like a homeless bum to blend in with the crowd on Skid Row. He got two crackheads to work the block with him, one man from DC named DC and a woman from St. Louis named Pam. They only sold 5-, 10-, and 20-dollar rocks and packs, nothing big, just enough to establish clientele.

He would work the downtown area from 6.00 a.m. till 4 or 5 p.m. Then he would hop the metro train to the beaches like Venice, Santa Monica, and Malibu. Once again, he would dress the part by trading his bum gear for a beach-ready surfer look wearing swim shorts, sandals, shades, and all. He even had a small surfboard he would carry with him. The look was different but the plan was the same; find out-of-towners and sell them drugs. On the beach, weed and powder coke was the thing and he made his packs in 50's and 100's. He would hustle on the beach till sunset then go back to his penthouse, change clothes, and get a lil rest, then hit Hollywood on Sunset Blvd at night working all the clubs and hot spots.

The money started coming in fast and after a few weeks he had established his hustle. His T-T came over one Sunday and he was counting large stacks of cash on the kitchen table. She looked at him and said, "Dam nephew, you must have robbed a bank. How you getting money like this"?? He replied, "I'ma top notch hustla T-T. I know how to take money and make it work for me." She said, "I hear ya nephew, but be careful out here." "I will T-T and oh yeah T-T, I can help you make some extra money too. A lot of customers be asking me bout them pills you be having. Now I don't know the prices so you'll have to let me know what they go for." "I got ya nephew. And oh yeah I wanna make me some of those big stacks you got. I gots tabs, bars, perks, uppers, and downers. Also, I know how to get heroine, meth and Sherm too." "What's Sherm T-T," he asked. "Oh yeah nephew, it's like clear water. People dip their cigarettes and weed in it. Don't smoke with these niggas out here unless you roll it yourself cause that shit ain't no joke." "I got ya T-T.

Thanks for letting me know. Here you go T-T, a lil something for your pockets." He gave her a light thousand dollars. She said, "thank you nephew. I could sure use this, and I'll bring the pills by here tomorrow okay." "Okay T-T," Uptown said. "I'll see ya tomorrow then. Oh yeah, that reminds me, go talk to the realtor and be on the lookout for a big house in the suburbs somewhere. I'm finna have the family come out here to visit us for the holidays. The rent don't matter. I need something big and nice for my momma and family to relax in. I wanna pool in the backyard and plenty palm trees in the hills overlooking the city." "Okay nephew. You trying to do it big." "Yeah T-T, nothing but the best for the fam. That's what I hustle for so they can enjoy life like never before. You know we come from nothing, T-T, and we deserve it." "We sure do Nephew," she said. "Yeah that will make your momma so proud. I'ma get right on top of that for you." "Appreciate that," Uptown said. "We finna win T-T and I promise you we gone make a way cause money is the key to improve our way of living. We from the bottom so it's only up from here." "Okay then, get with ya later." She left with a big smile on her face.

    Uptown finished counting his cash and took a drive to the valley. He loved how the city looked in different areas. While riding thru San Fernando Valley, he stopped by a bar to grab a drink and watch the Lakers-and-Knicks game. While sitting at the bar, this young, beautiful, glistening Hispanic girl sat beside him. She instantly began asking him questions. "What's the score my guy?" He said, "it's 55 to 68, the Lakers lead. She screamed, "yeah go Lakers." Then she said, "are you a Lakers or Knicks fan"? He replied, "nether one I'm a Celtics fan." She then frowned saying, "you must not be from here huh"? Uptown said, "nah baby, I'm from the dirty south." "You okay country boy," she asked. "I love how yall talk." Uptown shot back, "thanks but it's country man not boy, ya dig." "Oh I can see you all man" as she looked him up and down. She said, "do you play ball cause you sure is tall enough." He smirked and said, "I used too but not anymore." "Okay, so what brings you to LA," she asked, flirting. Uptown said, "I came to get famous like everybody else." "So you're an actor too," she said. "Naw I'ma boss. I don't act. I'ma promotor and producer." "Okay in other words, you're an investor of the film industry." He said, "yeah what you said." "Okay I do movies too. My name is Miriam but everybody call me Rosy." "Okay, just like a beautiful flower," he said. "You smell good just like a Rosy." She said, "okay you're a country charmer." Uptown said, "so what movies you played in"? She said, "I did a couple tv shows, a few low budget B-list movies, but now I do adult films." Uptown didn't understand the term adult film so he never questioned it. But in reality, Rosy was a highly paid porn star.

Uptown got straight to business cause he was a hustla first. Fuck friends. It's all about making ends meet, and we know most actors got high and they paid top dollar mainly for privacy. They didn't want to be seen out buying drugs on the streets so they would order their dope.

Uptown said, "so you and your actor friends get high"? Rosy replied, "do we! Actors gotta stay high cause in order to play a role you, you gotta get your high on to stay in character." Uptown said, "cool well I have some of the purest coke in this city. I don't cut it or mix it. It's pure as the snow." Rosy said, "everybody says that. Do you have a sample on you"? Uptown said, "sure but let's go to my car. I'm private bout my dealings and our business ain't for the public, ya dig." Rosy said, I like how you do business; real professional." Uptown said, "that's the only way."

They went to his car and he gave her a gram. She took a blow up the nose and then rubbed some on her teeth. She looked at Uptown and smiled, then said, "yeah this is super good. So do you deliver"? Uptown said, "yeah I do but this city so big and a person gotta be willing to wait cause it's only one of me right now. But I should have a team out here if the demand is there." Rosy said, "you keep good shit like this, the demand will be too much. Me and my friends get high all day every day so I'll be calling you a lot cause I like how you handle your business. I can tell you're a real professional and that will keep customers happy and that we like." Uptown said, "okay bet." They shook hands, exchanged numbers, and parted ways.

Uptown got on the freeway, turning on the 110 freeway then exited on Main Street, and headed for the eastside of South Central. He drove to 88th Street and Avalon on the way to Avalon Gardens housing projects. The gangsters over there knew his Auntie and cousins, so he had a solid ghetto-pass.

Uptown needed to corner to all markets. He sold to tourists, on the beach, Hollywood, and Uptown Wilshire districts. But the real money was crack houses in the hood. So he planned to open up one in every hood and projects in LA, Long Beach, Pasadena, Watts, and Compton. He also wanted a few in Gardena and Altadena. These would be the small stacks being sold, the 5's, 10's, and 20's. The little money added up to big money. Still, he set his sights on the big money markets like Brentwood, Beverly Hills, Malibu, and Baldwin Hills cause he knew big packs make big shacks.

After establishing his markets, just like a good hustla, he went to find new connections. LA was full of em, too, all kinds; Mexicans, Colombians, Peruvians, Dominicans, and even Venezuelans had dope and all of em had neighborhoods in and around LA. The City of Angels is really the city of the plugs you can get and drugs at a discount. So it is and forever will be a hustla's paradise.

First, he went to east LA a.k.a. baby Mexico. They are not too kind to Black hustlas maybe because of the history between Black and Brown gang bangers. But Uptown wasn't from LA so his approach made them feel at ease and comfortable. Like him, they all wanted to make money. It's strictly business and they understood that. Also with Uptown's down south markets, it offered them a more lucrative situation cause most people in LA would rather ship drugs than sell em in the city. That way they are off the radar and make bigger money through distribution price hikes cause the price is always higher than buying in LA and they have means to transport anywhere.

Uptown made a valuable alliance with the Mexicans, Colombians, and Peruvians to ensure he had a lot of options. He made sure the flow never stopped. The key to success is to never run out of product. That's how gas stations get rich. They always have product to sell. Every time a customer pulls up, they can get served. Uptown understood business and he planned on serving the whole country if he could. Ever since he started hustling, he always dreamed big coming from a small town in Mississippi. He never wanted to go small again. He knew selling drugs was wrong and comes with risks, but watching his family struggle and growing up poor made him justify his actions in his mind. Yet and still, he knew deep down his Mu-dear didn't like what he was doing cause although the money helped, she never wanted any harm to come to any of her kids. So, she just prayed for him a lot and asked God to watch over him and judge his young heart and not his greedy ways.

After a few months in LA, everything was going as smooth as a well-oiled machine. His Memphis plug was still giving him work. Whenever they were out, they were buying work from him thru his LA plugs. His weed plug was shipping bigger loads from Seattle, plus Dee had a team in lots of states all through Tennessee, Mississippi, Milwaukee, Atlanta, South-n-North Carolina's, Arkansas, Alabama, St. Louis, Chicago, Detroit, Kentucky, Iowa, and DC.

Cotton was in Texas pimping and hustling in Dallas, Houston, Fort Worth, Austin, San Antonio, Waco and had a plug in El Paso and Laredo. Also he had a crew in New Orleans that was pimping and serving tourists.

The money was pouring in super-fast. Uptown's dreams of being rich was now near reality. He sat in his living room and hand counted 2.6 million dollars in cash. There was so much cash that his fingers turned grey from the ink and his sweaty hands. Half went to the plugs and the rest was his.

Cotton was sitting on a million and a half in Texas and Dee had 8 or 900 thousand in the stash in Memphis. Life was great. They all had plenty money. Their families and crews were all taken care of.

Uptown bought his Mu-dear a big house in Cordova, a suburb outside of Memphis. Cotton bought a big apartment complex in East Memphis, and all his sisters and brothers lived rent free. Dee bought his momma a big house in Atlanta's Buckhead neighborhood and got all his sisters and brothers apartments and cars. They also bought stash houses all over the country so wherever they were, they had homes, apartments, and cars. It was all off the hustle and it made them feel extra good to help their families live a decent life with no money problems. The cash was unlimited. Still a lifestyle like this and with so many people depending on this money, Uptown knew he had to keep it going and get more. Ain't no such thing is enough when you have that many responsibilities. So every day he sat back and thought about ways to make more money. He was a good businessman and knew what he wanted.

He took a trip to the bay-area and drove up the I-5 highway heading north. He enjoyed the ride thru the mountains and Napa Valley. He arrived in Oakland and got a room down by Jack London Square. He had meetings with weed growers in San Francisco, Oakland, and Sacramento. He needed more weed. Weed was selling more than cocaine. Also the weed would allow him to break into the east coast markets like Boston, Philadelphia, New York, Connecticut, and Rhode Island. Weed was the gateway drug that was valuable all over the world and Uptown knew this would be a major boost to his income.

He made agreements in all the bay area cities and secured three good distributors; one in Oakland agreed to trade product for product. They wanted cheap coke for cheap weed. The deal was extra sweet. Now Uptown had high grade weed for a low price coming from 4 major weed cities. That alone made his profits triple.

He liked the bay-area so he bought a penthouse overlooking the San Franciso bay. He could see the Golden Gate Bridge from his living room. He enjoyed the good seafood at Fishermen's Warf, the live shows on Broadway and Market Streets. Plus, he learned about another more profitable drug in Chinatown. They had pure white heroin. It sold for ten times the amount of cocaine, and in Chinatown. They were getting boatloads of the drug. It was a match made in hustlas' heaven. This new product was the key for going from rich to being wealthy. Unlike cocaine and weed, heroin was a body high that customers had to have and they paid top dollar for it. It was the highest costing drug on the market. Turns out, the bay-area was his personal goldmine right by the Golden Gate Bridge.

And the Chinese hustlas were world-connected. They spoke in more than 7 or 8 different languages. They also taught Uptown the importance of opening up legal businesses. They told Uptown that the goal to success is to have plenty legal businesses to hide your illegal businesses. And the Chinese had their hands in everything including restaurants, real estate, clubs, food distributors, car lots, hotels, casino's, warehousing, clothing stores, stores, construction, promotions, computers, entertainment, sports, gambling, insurance companies, you name it. Whatever it was, they more than likely than not were involved in it or got a connection to it. They were the smartest professional hustlas Uptown ever met. So much so, that they even helped him get a fake ID, birth certificate and social security number. They even helped him to get a passport and visa. To top it off, they helped him get A-1 credit with all the good credit card companies. This was all he needed to take his hustle to the biggest level of his career.

He had Dee send him 30 workers from down south and set up trap houses all threw the bay-area. He had spots in Oakland's ghost town, the shady go's, westside to the eastside, in sac-town's, Mack Road, 29th and Garden block and several other major neighborhoods. You name it, he had it.

With good coke from LA, pure heroin from Chinatown and good weed from the bay, his hustle was now international. The earth was his turf and the money was his motivation. Now Uptown started taking flights because his business was too big to be driving everywhere. He had to get to it fast just like how the money was coming in, fast. This was the fast lanes and in the fast lanes, ain't no slowing down. This is how he envisioned the big time would be; big money, big lifestyle and he loved it. The money was coming in so fast he had to pay people to count and store it all.

He had Cotton and Dee send him pictures of themselves and he got both of them ID's made. He overnighted them their ID's and told them it's time to celebrate their success.

His sister had moved to Las Vegas and was getting married to a cool dude from Santa Barbara, cal. named Jim. So Uptown flew in all his family members, Cotton and his family and his hoes too, Dee and his family. A handful of loyal crew members were rewarded with a trip to Sin-City too. Altogether, Uptown paid for 63 flights. He also rented 50 rooms on the top floor of the MGM Grand Hotel-&-Casino overlooking the Vegas strip. His sisters all loved to gamble, so he gave all of them 5 thousand a piece. He spared no expense. He loved his family, so he ordered limo's to take them wherever they wanted to go. But he saved the best for his momma, Mu-dear and his love, Mona. He flew them in in a private jet and met them at the airport with red carpet rolled out. He had roses and a bottle of champagne for Mona. She was so happy, she cried. It was like a dream come true. She missed her man. Uptown had two presidential suites, one for his momma and brothers and one for him and Mona. He rented out the ballroom of the MGM for a dinner party for his sister and her husband-to-be, Jim. He also wanted to show his family and friends that he, Cotton, and Dee had finally made it, and planned on forever being on top, and this was worth celebrating.

    They all sat in the big round shaped tables as Uptown asked Cotton and Dee to stand up as he held his champagne glass to make a toast. "I would like to propose a toast to congratulate my sister and her fiancé. Welcome to the family bruh. Second, I would like to thank everybody who came out. We did this for the family. We love yall. And last and more importantly my brothers, Cotton, and Dee." Uptown got choked up and started to cry. He then held it together and with his head held high said, "y'all the reason for all this. Y'all believed in our dreams. The day I met Cotton, my life changed for the good. You taught me how to go get mine. You made me, Bruh, and I love you for life. Dee, you the most loyal honest nigga I ever met. You showed me how to really survive in the streets. I cannot thank you enough for all the love you showed me and Cotton when we moved up from Mississippi to Memphis. You gave me my name, Uptown Brown, and I became somebody thanks to you. Y'all made my dreams come true and I'll die for both of y'all cause I love yall just that much." They all came together and cried and hugged each other.

"This is a time to let everybody know that with a strong team and love, any dream is possible." Cotton wiped his eyes and said, "we love you too big bruh. We only good as our boss, and you're the boss. I'm the pimp/playa and Dee a true street hustla. We cannot lose our team. We like the Bulls and you're MJ, nigga." They all laughed. Dee said, "now let's eat, drink, and hit the casinos and clubs. We finna party dirty south style in Sin City."

Mu-dear stood up and said, "first let's say grace. Now y'all bow your heads.

> Lord, thank you for this wonderful meal, for the nourishment of our bodies. Thanks for allowing our families to come together in this fabulous city. Yeah, it's Sin City but we God's people no matter where we at. Thanks God for my new son-in-law, Jim. May they stay happy for life. Thanks to my son, Willie, and his friends for all this and all that they do for their families. I know they not getting honest money, Lord, but they hearts are in the right place. Dear Lord, please watch over them and keep them safe and out of harm's way. Father God, you came to save the sinners, Father God and we all was born in sin. So, place your loving arms around every sinner here and protect them. In Jesus' name. Amen.

They all said amen as they enjoyed a meal fit for royalty. They ate, drank, and had a great time together.

Afterwards, they all hit the casinos and went to all of them on the Las Vegas strip from the Flamingo to Ceasar's Palace. They gambled and partied till the sun came up.

The next day, they all drove over to Henrietta's house for a good ole Memphis style barbecue. Uptown was forever trying to find new markets and knew there were plenty in Vegas. So when he got to his sister's house off Nellis and Bonanza, he decided to go right in to see his young nieces, Sheena and Lissy, knowing that they smoked a little weed, and asked them to take him to buy some weed. He also asked them to show him the hood and to give him a tour of those Vegas streets. So, they hopped in the limo and rode the streets. First, they went to the westside, the main Black hood in Vegas, and then went to MLK Street, because of course there was one in every hood in America. Yeah, Dr. King was for the Blacks and that's Black power, ya dig. They rode through all the projects, the PJ's, Gerson Park, Crip City, just to name a few. They then pulled up at a corner store on MLK and Lake Mead called Mario's, a typical hood store where all the hustlas hung out. They copped some weed and bought some good ole fried fish.

Then they rode over to Northtown, a mixed hood with Blacks-n-Latinos. They were getting plenty money on those blocks; a lot of 24-hour bars they would hustle at. Then they drove thru the notorious Donna Street where the crips were, and them niggas were dangerous. They were right behind the Silver Nugget Casino. They had that area on lock.

After riding through Northtown, they drove to the east side and pulled up at the 28th street projects. The Mexicans had that project on lock. They got money but were known for their murders. They continued to drive going east on Bonanza Street and they made a left into some projects called the Big Rogus. That project was Mexican and Black people. It was live. A lot of money came thru there. They also had a smaller section a few blocks over called the Lil Rogues. It was all Black. Then they drove down Boulder Highway where there were a lot of small casino's and weekly hotels, a lot of prostitution and junkies. Uptown thought, yeah this Cotton's type of block. They went through a few hoods close to the strip like Naked City, a project behind the Stratosphere Casino. They hit a couple more known hoods and then returned to Henrietta's house.

As they came in the door, Henrietta said, "dam bruh, where yall been, gambling"? "Naw sis," he said, "me and my two beautiful nieces went to find me sum good to smoke. You know I gotta have my weed." "I know bruh," Henrietta said, "and look at they lil asses high as a kite. Y'all know y'all some Browns smoking wit' cha dam uncle." They all laughed. "Now yall come on get some of this good Memphis style dry ribs. We got everything ready." Earl worked the grill while the women fixed all the good sides like corn on the cob, baked beans, slaw, spaghetti, salads, home fries, baked potatoes, mac and cheese, greens, corn bread, and dinner rolls. It was a true feast.

They all ate, drank, and smoked good till it was time to hit the casino's again. Like I said, ain't no sleeping in Vegas. The show must go on.

After another all-nighter on the strip, Uptown planned a trip just for him and Mona. They started by going to the jewelry store in the Wynn Casino where Uptown bought Mona a 10-karat diamond ring. He said, "when I retire from the streets you gone be my wife. She was so happy. They then had a candle-lit brunch at the Peppermill Grill in front of the river. When they finished eating, they drove up to Hoover Dam and took a helicopter ride overlooking the dam, the Grand Canyon, Mount Charleston, and the world-famous Vegas strip. It was so magical to fly over the city like that. They felt like they were on top of the world.

After a few hours in the air, they landed and headed back to their penthouse at the MGM where Uptown had room service put rose petals and candles all over the room. They made love all night and in the morning. It was the best night of all.

The next day was the big wedding for his sister. Everything was beautiful, his sister most of all. After the wedding, it was time to go and get back to business. Everybody said their goodbyes as they headed to the airport. Cotton flew back to Dallas, Dee back to Atlanta and everybody else back to Memphis.

Uptown rented a car and headed south on the I-15 till he got on the I-10 then to the 110 and then exited off to the Wilshire district to his place. He had enjoyed his time with his family and friends and couldn't wait to buy a big boy house in LA so he could fly everybody out and show them how they do it in the City of Angels.

He got right back to his business calling all his plugs. He had to make up the time spent in Vegas. And like they always say, "what happens in Vegas stays in Vegas, and that includes your money, ya dig. So after leaving a big bankroll in Vegas, he had to double his orders and turn up production to the max. He needed to bounce back. After talking to his Chinese connections about business, he started putting them all in family members' names. Before long, he had a lot of legal businesses; a moving service, a few 18 wheelers, a promotion company mainly cause of the going away party he threw. He and Cotton opened up strip clubs in Dallas and Jackson, miss. He and Dee opened up a clothing store at the Underground Mall in Atlanta, and a barbecue spot in Nashville. He opened up a couple beauty shops and beauty supply stores in Memphis, a limo service in LA and Vegas, a car lot in Milwaukee, and a soul food spot in Little Rock, Ark. Everything was going smooth, but we all know in this game the smooth will turn buff in a New York minute.

CHAPTER 8

THE TOP OF THE MOUNTAIN COMES FAST, BUT THE FALL COMES FASTER!

After a few years on the west coast, Uptown decided to go check on his brother, Cotton, in Texas. He went to LAX and boarded a Southwest airlines flight to Dallas Love Field airport. He arrived in the DFW at 6:00 o'clock p.m. and jumped in a cab headed to the strip club they owned off Harry Hines Blvd. Cotton didn't know he was coming so it was a surprise. Security didn't know who Uptown was so he gave Uptown a hard time.

Uptown said, "look big neck nigga. I'm your boss and by the way you fired." The security guard laughed and said, "this nigga a joke." Uptown said, "get Cotton to the door." He went and got Cotton and told him what Uptown said. Cotton came out cussing saying, "I'm the boss and can't no strange nigga tell you shit." He then sees Uptown's smiling face. He dropped his cigarette and ran to hug his big brother. He was so happy to see Uptown that tears started to run down his face. The big neck nigga was shocked. Cotton turned to him and said, "this my family and he's my boss so if he said you fired, get lost big back bitch"! The security guard said, "dam Cotton it's like that boss"? Cotton said, "nigga you still here." Uptown said "naw naw bruh. He didn't know. He get a pass. I ain't that low down." Cotton said, "okay big bruh," then he said, "you betta thank big bruh for yo job and from now on you call him boss too. In fact, call him big boss and me just boss, you got it big back"? "I got ya boss," he said.

Cotton said, "now big bruh let's go to our office. And, how you gone sneak up on a pimp like that bruh. You know I hate surprises," Cotton said. Uptown said, "I been missing you bruh, plus I needed to take a vacation from the west coast. Ain't shit like being around yo family, ya dig." "I can dig it big bruh," Cotton said. "I been down here in Texas for years and the only people I really know is my hoes and a few of those already broke bad and went back to Memphis and Mississippi. I guess them hoes got homesick, ya dig. Anyhow business is good down here. I gots new hoes, new plugs with plenty thugs selling my drugs ya dig." Uptown laughed and said, "nigga you should've been a rapper all you do is rhyme." Cotton said, "yeah if Pimp and Too Short can do it, so can pimp Cotton. I would've got a grammy for best pimp talk of the year, ya feel me." "Yeah you're a true superstar, bruh."

Uptown said, "So I need the grand tour of the big-D bruh, let's get out and see the city." "Okay let's do it bruh," Cotton said. "Let me get my driver," Cotton said. "Driver so when you get a driver," Uptown asked, "when I started getting real money, big bruh. I'ma v.i.p., a very important pimp ya feel me," Cotton replied.

They went to the parking lot and got into Cotton's 600 Benz with v-12 under the hood. Uptown was impressed. Cotton rolled like the president with a security in the front and back of the Benz. You gotta roll like this in the dirty D. Niggas know I gets money plus I own this strip club and suckas be chick hatin on a playa; mad cause they bitches wanna be my hoes ya dig. Still we some street niggas and we ain't no local brokers. We international playas, hustlas, bosses. They too slow to get at me. I'm cross country, coast to coast like butter and toast, from main to Spain every hustla and hoe know my name, a true legend like dat," he said, as they drove these streets of Dallas smoking fat blunts from the back of the Benz behind tinted windows.

Cotton said, "Look big bruh, Willie's Chicken. You got a chain of chicken spots down here." Uptown said, "let's stop and taste that chicken." Cotton replied, "naw nigga that ain't the best in the city. It's Rudy's chicken that's the best in Dallas. It's in the hood, good bird by Black women and it's where all the locals go." "Okay, Uptown said, cause I'm gone be hungry as fuck after all this smoking." They drove past the Cotton bowl. Cotton said, "Look I got a football stadium named after me down here. This my new home."

They pulled into the hood to famous MLK Street. They knew how to find the hood in any city just look for Dr. King and you'll see his dream. They pulled up to the car wash, all the crackheads ran to the Benz. They all knew Cotton's car cause he always came through and showed love to the junkies and young niggas who were out there washing cars. They jumped out like hood celebs, passing out flyers and 20-dollar bills with the strip club logo on both. He knew how to promote his business and the strip club.

After getting the dust knocked off the Benz, they drove down Malcolm Blvd for a lil bit then got back on the freeway and headed to the notorious Oak Cliff neighborhood then started hitting blocks. Cotton said, "yeah bruh, this the most gangsta hood in the D. These niggas straight killas over here. It's money too but they stay on the news for shootings, robberies, and all types of shit." Uptown said, "yeah, this our type of environment. Reminds you of the LMG in Memphis, one of the most dangerous hoods in America. See street niggas love being in the streets, it's really simple math; wherever it's the poorest part of the city, its gone have the most crimes. Cause poverty breeds more people trying to eat so they do what they have to, to feed they families. That means a lot of drugs being sold, a lot of break ins, a lot of hoes, a lot of robbing, a lot of stealing, a lot of hustling, etc.. When you broke, you ain't got time to be standing around, gotta go get it." Cotton said, "see this area is where half my shack go. These niggas moving that dope big bruh and they know I'ma street nigga just like them. So we have a good business understanding, plus if I have an issue with any nigga anywhere in the city, these Oak Cliff nigga's gone pull up and handle any nigga, ya dig." Uptown said, "I can dig it. Yeah you on point down here bruh." Cotton said, "yeah I learned from the best, you big bruh. They hit a few more blocks, hollered at a few of Cotton's crew, then they headed to big-T's; a hood type swap meet or as they say down south, a flea market.

They hopped out the Benz and walked through Big T's passing out flyers to the strip club. They then left a stack of flyers at a couple booths inside Big-T's. Then Uptown said, "let's go eat I'm starving nigga." Cotton said, "so whatever you wanna eat I gots ya big bruh. What you got a taste for bruh?" Uptown said, "since we down south, I want some downhome good soul food. On the west coast they got good taco's, burgers, and seafood, but the soul food ain't shit like the dirty south." Cotton said, "I know the perfect spot." They drove a few blocks and pulled up to Sweet C Georgia Brown's. Uptown said, "yeah they some Brown's, so I know the food gone be good." Cotton laughed and said, "yeah I come here a lot. They know how to burn in here plus they give you a lot on your plate to make sure you get your money's worth."

They went in and sat down and enjoyed a wonderful southern dinner. Uptown said, "yeah that hit the spot bruh. I haven't tasted soul food like that since I left Memphis." Cotton said, "they ain't got no soul food spots on the west coast"? Uptown replied, "a few. They got Mama's Soul Food in LA, a couple spots in Oakland, but soul food was started in the south so ain't no place better than the original, ya dig."

They drove a little farther and hit a few more hoods. It was starting to get dark outside as night fell. Uptown said, "I gotta shower and get some rest if I'ma hit the club tonight bruh." Cotton said, "bet. We finna swing by the club so we can change into my low-key car and to my castle, ya dig." "I hear ya, King Cotton," Uptown said. They went to the strip club switched from the Benz to a Volvo station wagon. Uptown said, "Dam it's clean but this ain't no pimp's ride. You must've bought this from a trick or White Jim." Cotton said, "In fact, I did. I gotta be low key. I live in Plano, Texas in an almost all White neighborhood. It's a nice big house with a 4-car garage, 5 bedrooms, 6 baths with a pool-jacuzzi in the backyard. Only me and my bottom bitch live there. I got a house in Addison, Texas for my hoes. Don't nobody know bout this house but me, my bottom bitch and now you bruh." They headed north on the tollway north and got on the George Bush turnpike.

They exited off the freeway, hit a couple lights then went into Cotton's gated community. Uptown said, "shit nigga, you living way better than me." Cotton said, "yeah right, all that money you making on the west coast. I bet you got a mansion in Hollywood." "Not yet," Uptown said. "I got a penthouse loft in Uptown's Wilshire district." Cotton said, "yeah that's fly. Uptown is living in Uptown LA. That's boss shit." "Yeah you gotta come visit some time," Uptown said. "Yeah man, my hoes can't wait to hit Hollywood Blvd. You know I got a team of stars so we gone shop when I hit LA." "That's what's up bruh," Uptown said.

They chilled, smoked a few blunts then Uptown took a hot shower, went into the guest bedroom, and fell fast asleep. He was tired from the flight and all the smoking and riding.

After a good refreshing nap, Uptown got up, got dressed and they headed to the strip club. It was 12:40 a.m.

and the line was wrapped around the corner. It was packed. As they entered through the back door, they headed to the office. Cotton had a window that acted as a mirror on the outside so he could see out but you couldn't see in. He and Uptown watched the action and the house lady came in to let him know what was going on, and give him all the dancers stage fee's, the club money and the bar's take. Cotton also had his runners selling powder packs with weed sacks. They only sold 20's 50s, and 100's packs. He had one in the men's bathroom and one in the ladies bathroom. They also sold blunts, loose cigarettes, condoms, lighters, breath mints, female hygiene, perfume, cologne etc.

    On top of that, Cotton had his personal hoes working the v.i.p. rooms, turning tricks and hitting licks. The money was rolling in good. Uptown said, "I see ya bruh, you really doing the damn thing. Yeah big mama would be proud of you bruh." "Thanks," Cotton said, "yeah like you said, gotta get more and more. By the way, I been good on the shipments but it ain't coming fast enough bruh." Uptown said, "yeah I know bruh. Dee said the same thing in Atlanta. I be wanting to move faster but I have to wait on the plugs to do their things. I be thinking of using the Greyhound or the Amtrak trains, cars, trucks etc.. Still it's about location and timing." "I can dig it bruh," Cotton said. "Coming way from the west coast is a lot of miles between us."

    "Yeah speaking of that, what's them plugs you been telling me bout in El Paso," Uptown asked. "Yeah, I been buying there when I get the load bruh," Cotton replied. "So why not up the load," Uptown asked. Cotton shot back saying, "I was waiting to talk to you and Dee first before I commit that much money cause this is about us and not just me." "Well we'll get Dee on the line tomorrow and go over the numbers and make it happen cause I know Texas got them plugs too. It's also on the Mexican border too, just like

Cali. So I know the loads are big. Everything's bigger in Texas, ya dig." "Okay it's a go, but for now let's go and party with the strippers and the crowd. This our club and we the attraction, ya feel me." They moved through the crowd greeting customers, popping bottles, and passing out bottles of Moet to the high rollers-n-big spenders. Cotton was the host with the most and the crowd loved him and his shit talking on the mic. They partied till the sun came up.

Meanwhile in Memphis, a young female walked into the DEA's office with something she said that'll make the officers happy. They said, "now how are you gonna make us happy?" She said, "I know about a drug ring that's operating in almost all the states in this country, but they started right here in South Memphis." A tall red headed detective named O'Kelly said, "Now look young lady, if you're looking for us to drop a charge of yours this better be worth it." "Oh it's worth it and no I do not have a case, I'm doing it cause my cousin is a victim of human trafficking by this group and our family is trying to get her home but all she sees is the money and lifestyle."

"Ok, okay, so who are they," Detective O'Kelly asked? "Their names are Cotton and Uptown," she replied. Det. O'Kelly said, "yeah we've been looking for Cotton's ass for years. So who the fuck is Uptown"? "That's his partner," she said. "Okay, tell me more," he asked? "Well, they are running drugs and a lot of it too. They got 100's of workers and a lot of money". "So where the fuck they at," he asked? "They be everywhere. Cotton lives in Dallas, TX, and Uptown lives in California. I don't know which city; I think LA or Oakland." "So how do you know all this young lady," he asked? "I'm ashamed to say this, but I used to be a working girl for Cotton." "Working girl, you mean you used to be one of his hookers, right"? "Well, yeah I was 19 years old and poor so I made bad choices, don't judge me. But I'm older now and I need to right my wrongs and bring my cousin home to her kids and family: "I'm sorry ma'am. Sit down and let us gather more information."

O'Kelly pulled up the file on Cotton on his computer. "Okay, he is Mr. Ian Jones a.k.a. Cotton, born in Hernando, MS. He moved to Memphis about 10 years ago. He been on the run for a minor drug offense for 4 years. He has 3 brothers and 4 sisters. His mother. passed away 10 yrs. ago, no kids no wife. Sounds like a pimp to me."

"Now first let us contact our DEAs office to see if they've heard of our fugitive, the infamous Cotton. "Where the hell did he get a name like Cotton." "Maybe he's soft on his hoe's like Cotton," one officer poked. "Naw he's a Cotton-picking nigger from Mississippi," Det. O'Kelly said. "Well however we finna pick up this Cotton and make prison uniforms out of his ass." They all laughed.

The young lady didn't laugh at the racially motivated jokes cause although she was mad at Cotton for how he treated her, her cousin still was a Black person and she hated to see how happy White police love to fuck over a Black person. But what was done was done, can't take it back now. The way she looked at it, Cotton used his own rope to hang himself.

Det. O'Kelly called the US Marshall since it was across state lines, the case becomes federal and the feds don't play. They only go after the big dealers. So, now the game takes a turn for the worst unbeknownst to Cotton. He had really pissed off this young girl so bad that she's willing to help send him to prison just to get back at him for sending her back to Memphis. A woman scorned is bad but a hooker's revenge is devastating, even deadly at times. Most pimps who get caught, these hoes is the reason! They teach them to be cutthroat for their asses but like everything else, that has two sides cause when they get mad at their pimps, they'll cut their throats too. It's a dangerous game, but when you're blinded by dollar signs, you don't see the danger till it's too late.

      Meanwhile back in Dallas, Cotton, and Uptown wake up around noon after a wonderful night in the strip club. They got Dee on the phone and was telling him about the El Paso plug. Dee said, "That sounds good and that he met some Cubans from Miami that had cheap numbers, 150". They said "bet, we can use all the plugs to stay well connected so they could keep the power alone, ya dig." "So, what's the plan," Cotton asked? Uptown replied, "let's go meet your plug now. Ain't no sense in waiting. Let's go get it. Gotcha boss." So Cotton got the contact on the phone and they agreed to meet in Houston, TX for a sit down. They packed their bags and headed south on I-45.

Cotton picked Houston cause he had a few hoes working down there and he knew the city a lil bit. So it made him feel more comfortable. He had dealt with the Mexicans before, but only for a couple keys and 30 to 40 pounds of regular weed, nothing big". Now he wanted a real load, some big numbers, big weight, so this had to be done right. Ain't no middleman bs. They wanted to speak to the boss to get an understanding.

They passed the Huntsville prison on the I-45 which was the Pasadena prison that executed more convicts than any other state in the country. Cotton said, "Dam bruh, look at that old ass prison. I'd rather be dead than in prison bruh." Uptown said, "don't say dead bruh. Ain't shit worse than being under the dirt. I rather not do either but I'll choose jail over being dead any day." "We different bruh," Cotton said. "I'ma pimp and ain't no hoes in the can nigga." Uptown said, "it's hoes but them hoes got poles." They both laughed. They passed a huge statue of Sam Houston, the man who the city was named after. They drove a little bit more then got on the I-610 then to the I-10 and exited downtown. They went and checked into the W-hotel. They always got rooms in the downtown area cause that's the heart of every city and that heartbeat is what keeps all cities pumping. They unpacked, got settled in and then arranged to meet the plugs at Al Poppa, an upscale seafood spot.

Cotton had his hoes posted in the back strapped with guns just in case they tried any funny shit. The Mexicans were cool though only two spoke English but they had translators who conducted all the important business. In Mexican tradition, they toasted the deal with a shot of good tequila saying salute as they all tapped glasses and took a stiff shot. They agreed to have a look at the weed in El Paso, Tx. so they'll know when to ship it to Memphis and Atlanta. The weed wasn't cheap indoor type weed. It was some Texas light green brick style weed that only sold for a couple hundred bucks but in the country it sells cause in small towns any weed sells. But for the price they was paying, profits was worth it. The coke was good and cheap, plus they had some cheap black tar heroin too, so the deal was going to open up a lot of doors. Also it's a down south plug so they already had ways to ship the loads to Memphis and Atlanta.

 After the sit down, they headed to the Galleria Mall on Gessner-and-Westheimer St. They did a lil shopping cause they planned on hitting a few clubs that night. Cotton loved high fashion. He wore only the best clothes money could buy and even had his clothes tailored to fit only his style. He had a wardrobe meant for a king. He had all the high-priced labels like Gucci, Fendi, Louis Vuitton, Prada, etc. If it was high, he had it. Also his jewelry was top of the line; Rolex watches, big diamond rings-n-chains, and everything from his hat to his socks had a name brand on it. He had to be the center of attention any and everywhere he went. That's how he attracted so many hoes. He would show them what money looked like and if they wanted the finer things in life, they should get with him cause as he would say everybody loves a winner and he looked like the champ!

Now, Uptown was a more laidback low key all business type of nigga and he dressed the part to a tee. He preferred a polo shirt and jeans, nice loafers, no bling, and nothing flashy. He only dressed up to hit a club and even then it would be a button down, sports coat, nice slacks -n- wing tips or square toes. He dressed like a professional and for the occasion. And since they was going to Club Maxie's, a known hip hop club, Uptown wore his black Chanel frames and a diamond chain.

They went to their rooms, got dressed and ordered a stretch Benz limo. The limo came and picked them up and Cotton ordered the driver to take them to Bissonnette St, so Cotton could pick up 4 hoes who were in Houston working for him. They jumped in the limo and Cotton said, "y'all been down here a week. I know y'all got some money for daddy." They all said we sure do, as they handed over big bank rolls to Cotton as he counted the money. When he got to one hoes' money, he said, "damn bitch, you been out here all this time and this all you got? It's less than half of what these other hoes got. Is you out here on dope or selling top to bottom for 5 dollars; which one is it bitch". She said, "naw daddy the police hot as hell down here and I been on my rag too." Cotton said, "what that mean bitch. That's only one hole. You got two mo holes, now where's my doe hoe." She said, "I'll make it up when we get back to Dallas." Cotton said, "no the fuck you won't bitch" and told the driver to turn around drop this hoe back on the blade and then told her, "don't come back till you get my muthafuckin bread hoe"! She said, "but daddy, I got dressed to party at the club with y'all." Cotton said, "well dance your ass off and get my money and then we can party anywhere you want, but business first bitch. Now get out and go get it." She got out on the street with tears in her eyes. Uptown laughed and said, "now that's pimping 101". Cotton said, "can't let no hoe shortchange me. I work too muthafuckin hard on the Blvd. to starve.

They pulled up at Maxie's. The driver opened the door and they jumped out like super stars on the red carpet.

Uptown gave the door man 100 dollars to skip the line. So they went in v.i.p. and got a table. They ordered 20 bottles of Dom Perion with sparkles. Cotton sent the DJ a 100-dollar bill to let the club know that Memphis' most valuable pimp was in the building. The DJ got on the mic and said, "we got Memphis champs in this bitch tonight. I see you making easy-money, pimping-hoes in style." Then he started playing some 8-ball, followed by some 3-6 mafia. The club was jumping. It was a rap-a-lot event.

Uptown and Cotton's section was the liveliest in the club. They were smoking the best Cali buds and drinking the best champagne. The women were jocking hard. It was recruiting as usual with Cotton. He would let them know off top he was a pimp and a hustla; wasn't no faking. So if she chose, she already knew what it was.

Uptown's only interest was getting money. He would meet a nice-looking woman and let her know, "look I have a wife at home. All I'm looking for is fun tonight, but I don't do hoes. I don't pay for sex. I just have it and I'm gone. If they agree to those terms then she and her friends can roll with him back to his room for more fun, more kush and more drinks. Most of them respected the fact that he kept it 100 so they parted and sucked and fucked him anyways.

After Maxie's closed at 3 a.m., Cotton had two more new hoes bringing his total to 5 hoes. Uptown had two club hoppers who came along for a good time. They headed to a strip club called Harlem Nights. They partied there till the sun came up, went back to the room, kicked it some more, and then went to sleep. They got up around 3 p.m., called the airport and booked the next flights to El Paso. The last flight left at 6:30 p.m. It was only an hour and 15-minute flight. They packed their bags. Cotton had the limo driver drop the hoes back off at their rooms close by the hoe stroll. The two new hoes followed them also. The two fun girls Uptown had took a cab right after the party was over. Both had men at home waiting on their messy asses.

They got on the plane and before long they touched down in El Paso around 7:50 p.m. They got a room at a hotel right next to the University of Texas El Paso. They went to a Walmart close by to buy UTEP gear cause in El Paso, it's 90% Mexicans so Uptown figured it was best to look like students or alumni so they would fit in around town. They bought t-shirts, hats, and backpacks. They arranged to get with the plug the next day. In the meantime, they took a cab to go get some good Mexican food and see the city.

El Paso looks a lot like the west coast with palm trees, hills, and clay style houses. The culture was all Mexican. They had a strip mall they called The Plaza. It was full of outdoor vendors selling everything: clothes, food, toys, shoes etc. Also the border crossing was right there. You could drive or walk across a bridge right into Mexico. The only thing that separated the US from Mexico was a small river called the Rio Grande. Yeah, it had some small fences here and there but you could literally throw a rock into another country with ease. After a little sightseeing, they headed back to the room. Tomorrow was too important to be out lollygagging around.

When they got back to their room, Cotton's cellphone kept blowing up. He said damn, "what this hoe want. Now she know I'm out on business." Cotton answered the phone, "what is it bitch"? His bottom hoe said, "daddy, daddy in a crying voice. They just hit the club, they raided the club." Cotton said, "slow down and calm down. Now repeat that." She said, "baby the feds just hit the strip club and my neighbor said she believes they in our house." Cotton's jaws dropped. "What, what the fuck?!! Where you at baby," he asked? "I'm in North Dallas at a tricks house. Baby I'm scared. What do we do"? Cotton said, "give me a second to gather my thoughts. Ima call you back with instructions then." "Okay" she said. Call me right back okay." "Bet," he said.

    Uptown noticed the look on his face and asked, "What is it bruh, what's wrong." Cotton said, "man bruh, the feds hit the club and I believe they at my house too." Uptown said, "damn bruh, that's fucked up." Cotton said, "So what the fuck I'ma do now." Uptown said, "shit nigga you run, hell, we run cause I know if the feds are on you like that, they gotta know bout me and Dee too. The feds do their homework before they go after a nigga." "Dam bruh, how the fuck did I get on they radar," Cotton asked? "It might be that drug warrant but still that wasn't a lot of dope. That's petty shit." "Naw bruh, somebody snitching," Uptown said. "It's always a rat in every household no matter how clean you keep your house. If there's something to eat in that house, a rat gone find its way in. And we been eating good lately bruh. It was only a matter of time." "Still bruh, we gotta keep on pushing and moving. They gotta catch us. Ain't no giving in. We got the funds to go anywhere on the planet so we gone be good. Let's get this money, stack our bread, and stay on the move cause it's hard to hit a moving target." "Shit you been running over 4 years now, Uptown said, "Now calm down, call yo hoes, and tell em to pack there shit and go to New Orleans. They need to work down there for now. They

can wire you yo cash for a while. You gone lose a few but that's the game. You gotta stay lowkey from now on. No more flashy shit bruh. This shit too serious. No more clubbing and partying. Only taking care of business and dip."
"Bet," Cotton said.

Then he called his bottom bitch and told her to leave everything at the house and go get the money he buried in a ranch outside of Fort Worth and take a Greyhound to Jackson, Mississippi. Then he called his brother, Man-Man and let him know what was going on and to shut down the Jackson, Mississippi strip club for now.

They booked two flights to Jackson, Ms. for the next morning. They met the plug at a house in an El Paso suburb and agreed to the terms of the deal. And as a good faith deal, Uptown gave the plug 150 thousand up front to let them know they meant business. They headed back to the room. Cotton was a nervous wreck. He was cool in Dallas but now he had to uproot and live state to state. No more balling just staying under the radar from now on.

The next morning, they boarded their flight and landed in Jackson, Mississippi. Man-Man had a stash house in Clinton, Mississippi. While there, they had all their family members come visit them to let them know the situation. Mona also came down to visit Uptown. When they got to Jackson, they all had stories to tell about how the feds done hit this house and that house and yeah they knew about Uptown and Dee too.

There was a lot of panicking and uncertain thoughts, a lot of crying too. Their families were so worried-and-stressed cause they didn't want to see them go to prison. Then amongst mess and madness, Uptown stood up and spoke like a born leader. "Look fam, we feel yall pain and concern but please don't stress or worry. We gone be alright we knew the consequences of our actions. We knew one day the pigs would come after us but that's a part of the game. It's the pigs job to catch us and it's our job not to get caught. And so far, we been good at it. Still the feds are better than local pigs but still they pigs and we just gone keep on getting better at not getting caught. In any event that we do get caught, we still gone be family at the end of the day. Still money gotta be made and bills gotta be paid. So ain't no slowing down. We still gone take care of all you." Then Uptown's sister spoke. "It ain't about the money bruh, we just don't wanna see you or Cotton and Dee go to jail." Uptown said, "well, we in it now and we'll deal with that whenever it comes. We got lawyer money put away so we good. Just live and pray for us okay sis." She said, "you're always so calm and cool. Don't shit scare you." Cotton said, "if you scared to live you already dead."

After the speech, everybody relaxed and Uptown told them to keep an eye out and to use prepaid phones and to buy a new one every 30 days. Never pay a bill and never call on a phone that has their real name on it.

    After they kicked it at the stash house with their families, Uptown and Cotton took Man-Man's girl's car and headed east on I-20. They drove for 6 hours into Atlanta. They had a condo in Lithonia, GA, just north of the city. They called Dee and told him to meet them at Varsity Hot Dog right off I-75 not too far from Peach Tree St. Dee lived in Buckhead so he wasn't too far. They both pulled up around the same time. Dee was happy to see his two partners in the grind. Dee pulled up in a blue 4 door Maserati. He jumped out and said, "y'all in a Honda now. I know Uptown ride lowkey but you a pimp Cotton this most definitely ain't yo style.

Cotton said, "I know bruh, "I know. Anyhow look bruh, we gotta talk real business and we down here cause we couldn't do it over the phone." Dee could see the expression on their faces. It wasn't a friendly visit, this was serious. "So lay it on me," Dee said.

Uptown spoke first. "The feds on us bruh and 9 times out of 10 they on you too". Dee paused for a second and then dropped his head. "Now it all makes sense. Both my baby mommas been blowing my phone up so hard that I had to block both of em." Cotton said, "yeah they probably tried to warn you." "Let me call them bitches right quick." Dee called his daughter momma first. She picked up the phone and went off saying "dam bitch ass nigga you blocked me. I could've been dead or your daughter could've been in trouble. You just don't give a fuck with yo weak ass. Anyhow nigga, this ain't bout me nigga this bout you. The fed's been to my muthafuckin house. They looking for yo ass nigga. You need to lay low nigga. As bad as I hate yo black ass, you are a good baby daddy and our baby girl misses you." Dee said, "I'm sorry for blocking you and look from now on get a prepaid phone to contact me. I'm finna go underground for a while drop off the map, but I'll stay in touch and send you some money for my daughter, okay." She said "bet, be safe and stay out the streets."

Then he called his other kids momma and she said the same thing, the feds been through there and they know his full name and that they been all through the LMG looking for him too. After calming her down Dee just sat there stunned saying, "dam bruh, we got to go on the run." Uptown said, "yeah but we got a heads up on em so we just gotta move smooth now, no more flashy balling; only low-key cars, and oh yeah, since we can't be traveling with all this fucking cash, we can buy big diamonds, I'm talking 10 to 20 karats. That way we could have a million or two in our front pockets and they sell everywhere." Cotton said, "dam you smart nigga. You should've went to college." "Yeah maybe," he said. "I would've made a legal million." Dee said, "so we buy the diamonds. How we gone pay the plugs"? Uptown said, "we keep the re-up money in cash and we buy diamonds with our profits." Cotton said, "well let's get to buying ice then."

    Uptown said, "first we gotta find a jeweler who gone take all that ice you got Cotton out of your watches, rings, and chains, sell the gold for more ice. Go and get all your jewelry too, Dee, and we only want Dee diamonds. Then we go get wedding rings with big rocks in them from Lennox Mall and get the diamond out of them too. So let's get to it."

    They first went to a hood jewelry store in the DeKalb Mall and got the ice taken out of Cotton and Dee's jewelry, told them they'll be back with bigger ice and they wanted to get the ice out of those rings too. After that, they went and sat down to eat at Gladys Knight's Chicken and Waffles. It reminded Uptown of Roscoe's in LA.

    After eating, it was time to go break the bad news to Dee's family. He had moved his whole family to Atlanta. His momma lived around the corner from him. And just like Uptown and Cotton's family, they were devastated; they all cried. But Uptown assured them that everything was going to be alright. Still they knew life was going to be different from now on plus they weren't going to see Dee for a while. Things were about to get very serious now. Dee hugged his family goodbye and hopped in the car with Uptown and Cotton. They headed back to Lithonia, GA. Dee smoked a blunt and said, "so what now."

    Uptown said, "We wait here on two plugs, one from LA and our new load from El Paso, pay them, have our Memphis crew on point to catch two more loads then we fly to Milwaukee, WI. We will lay low for a few weeks while the stash gets moved then go to Cali or on the east coast, somewhere big where we can get lost and still get money." "Who in Milwaukee, bruh," Dee asked. Uptown replied, "My uncle and cousins. They some straight up home team from Hernando, Mississippi. People who know how to lay low, it's perfect for now, plus we already got a team up there."

Dee said, "okay bet, but first I gotta go put my Atlanta team on point so that soon as the 3 load get dropped, they can get it cause we ain't got time to be stalling, ya dig". "Bet that," Cotton, "you drive cause I need to smoke." Uptown said, "naw no smoking in the cars from now on. Remember we on the run. Yeah, our license legit but we don't need no slip up's. Besides, this your city Dee; you drive us nigga." "Got ya, boss man," Dee said.

So they rolled through all the hoods in the ATL and then pulled up on Peach Tree St. They stopped at Justin's, a spot owned by Puff Daddy a.k.a. P. Diddy, and got a bite to eat. Then they headed back to the spot in Lithonia.

The next day the plugs dropped the loads off; one on Buford Highway and the other in Marietta, GA. The crews handled the business & Uptown paid the plugs. After the business was taken care of, Uptown booked three flights to Milwaukee for that same day. He didn't want to spend another second down south it was too risky.

They finally boarded the plane heading to Milwaukee. They all tried to stay calm as they landed in Milwaukee at around 8:45 p.m. They hailed a cab and took it to his Uncle's house right off 29th and Clybourne St. This was his Mu-Dear's brother, a down to earth Mississippi/Memphis nigga who been in Milwaukee for almost 50 years. He knew the city very well and was well connected. He had a plush bar in his basement. In Milwaukee, almost all the houses had basements. They sat around and had shots of Remi Martin. He told Cotton he knew his momma Big Momma, and his daddy too. That was a surprise cause even Cotton didn't know his real daddy. He explained to Cotton that his father was the White man who Big Momma bought the house from. He also owned the corner store that Cotton and Uptown used to go to after school. Then it all made sense to Cotton. No wonder Big Momma said, "stay away from that White devil." Also, he would always call me Son. "I thought that was a figure of speech but dam that's deep. Why she never told me? I knew my momma was a hoe turned pimp. I wouldn't have judged her". He said, "It wasn't that she was ashamed, she just didn't want you to look at him as a father cause he paid her to get rid of you.

"You was her last child and she kept you cause she loved you before you was even born. That's what made her stop hoeing, and then she became the best pimp in Mississippi. Dam that's deep ole school. After they all got drunk, Uptown pulled his Uncle to the side and said, "look Unk I gotta be 100 with you. The feds looking for us so I gotta be on some low-key shit while I'm here. We family so I gotta be honest with you bout our situation." Uncle Yale said, "that's cool nephew, besides me and your momma already talked about this before you got here. So I already knew the business. You need to call her because she so worried about you." "I will tomorrow Unk," Uptown said. "Okay, look nephew. I got a spot in Brown Deer. It's a nice house ducked off by itself. The only neighbor is a blind dude about a mile away from the house. Plus it's right off the freeway so you can get in and out the city real quick. I used it to take a few of them young sack chasing chicken heads to when I'm bored. I can dig it Unk. Here's the keys. It has 4 bedrooms. Don't look like much on the outside but it's plushed out on the inside. And oh yeah I got a Lincoln Continental in the garage too. You can drive it too. The tags & insurance all legit. Gotta buy yo own food though. I don't cook there, I just get eat there" and they both laughed. "Yall can crash here for tonight and I'll take y'all to the house in the morning. I gotta go to my stash spot and find the keys.

They slept on the couches in the basement till the sun came up. Uptown could smell good bacon frying in the pan. He could hear feet above his head. Then he walked up the stairs to the kitchen to see his cousins Maylee and Cubby and their kids. They all came to see Uptown. Maylee had made big breakfast for him and his friends. She said, "good morning cuz. I started to wake you but didn't want to wake your friends." He hugged both his cousins and their kids. This was his family that he didn't always get a chance to see cause he was always in the streets when they would come to Memphis. Maylee said, "yeah, I know y'all was gone need something to eat after drinking with Unk all night. He always gone get you drunk cause his bar stay stocked. So, how long you in town for cuz"? Uptown said, "about a month or two." She said, "Cool, I'll get a chance to kick it with you while you're here." Uptown said, "sure will cuz cause I came to see y'all and nobody else." "Okay, now tell yo boys breakfast is done. I gotta go take the kids to school and go to work. You know I own a daycare cuz"? "Oh yeah, that's what's up cuz. Do yo thang? Gotta eat and we Brown gotta get that money, believe that cuz."

Cotton -n-Dee came upstairs to a beautiful breakfast with orange juice and all the trimmings. After they finished eating a comforting meal, they all got in the car with Uncle and headed to the house in Brown Deer. The ride was short so it wasn't long before they were there. They soon realized what things they would need and after getting settled in, went to the local Walmart for food, supplies, hygiene products, prepaid phones and a lot of Packers and Bucks sports gear. They headed into the city around 4 o'clock when Cubby got off work so he could show them around the city.

He took them through all the hoods in Milwaukee. The eastside was where all the Italians stayed, northside where all the Blacks stayed and the westside was a mixture of Blacks and Whites. Milwaukee is best known for its beer, Harley Davidson, Happy Days and a lot of pimping and murders. Yeah, they are off the chain in Milwaukee. Also, there is a lot of gangbanging and drug slanging just like any other major city. You got your good, bad, and ugly sides of the city. But still, Milwaukee was a lively city where a lot of people with roots to the south end up. It's like that in most cities where their Blacks got ties to the south. When we came to this country as slaves, we came to work the cottonfields and they only grew it in the south. So if you are Black, no matter where you at in this country, your family started in the south somewhere. And what most people don't know, your last name is the name of the slave masters who owned your family. Yeah, it was a dirty game, yet we gotta play it till the end my friends.

Now that Uptown knew the city a little bit more, he could sit back, relax and plan and plot on his next move. As they say "make yo next move yo best move cause you slip you could lose," and in this game he was playing he stood to lose his freedom. So he had to make the right moves, ya dig."

Every day that passed, he would think of ways of ducking the feds.

Back in Memphis, Det. O'Kelly called a meeting with the DA, DEA, local and federal police, US Marshalls, bounty hunters, you name it. If they had a badge, they was at this meeting. He was so upset when they didn't catch Cotton or Uptown in Dallas that his blood pressure went up. He thought he had them but he was one step behind. Now he wanted to get the media involved; put them on local and national most wanted tv shows like Crimestoppers, 528-cash, and America's Most Wanted, but in order to do that, he had to convince his bosses that they were national threats.

Det. O'Kelly put up a big Memphis ring screen and turned off the lights, then he said "thanks for coming to this meeting. I'm prepared to show evidence and prove that the focus of my investigations is major drug traffickers and not your everyday on the corner drug dealers. These men are a danger to this community and this country. My colleagues and I are calling them the dirty south cartel, and this is operation dirty south. These are the subjects of focus. The man in charge is Willie Brown, age 30, 6 ft. 5 inches tall, and weighing in at 231-lbs. He was born in Hernando, Mississippi, and goes by the street name, Uptown. He moved to Memphis 11 years ago. He's the brains of the operation, the leader. They all listen to him. His whereabouts are unknown. He keeps a pretty low profile. He has 12 brothers-n-sisters, all of whom still live in the Memphis area, so does his mother and. father.

Next up is his childhood friend, Cotton, who goes by the legal name of Ian Jones. He's 29 years old and was born in Hernando, Mississippi, also. He moved to Memphis about 10 years ago. He has 4 sisters and 3 brothers. Some live in Mississippi, some in Memphis. He's a known pimp with working girls throughout the south. He's the main focus of our investigation. We believe he has a strip club in Dallas, TX. He has ties to the Texas, Mississippi, and Tennessee areas.

Then, there is Dino Smith who goes by the street name, Dee, originally from Memphis born and raised. He has ties to Nashville, Little Rock, and Atlanta. He has one brother and 4 sisters, all in the Atlanta area. His mother's whereabouts are unknown. Father lives in Memphis. Dee is a member of the notorious LMG mafia street gang. He also has ties to the TTO street gang and the 4-V grind hard street gang. These are the leaders of the ring. Under them are lower hustlas and crew members working in a lot of states transporting drugs from Texas and California to almost every state in this country.

They are making a mockery of our great judicial system and thumbing a nose at the law. In other words, they give us a big fuck you finger saying catch us if you can. And trust me, I will and put them away for a very long time. So I'm asking you respectfully, my intelligent colleagues to give me the resources I need to go after these major offenders cause taking them off the streets saves lives. They are dealing death through cocaine, heroin, guns, human trafficking, sex slaves and a lot more. This is the worst crew on our streets and we pledged as officers of the law to keep our streets safe. This meeting is why we come to work to go after the bad guys. O'Kelly cut the lights back on and everyone in the meeting stood up to shake his hand. He had won them over.

The next day Uptown, Cotton and Dee were on America's most wanted and on every most wanted show in the country. They even put them on the FBI's top ten most wanted list. Things got very serious then. And like clockwork, all their plugs changed their numbers on them. They all loved the money that they was getting but all the heat they didn't need. They were too hot to deal with. They went from making millions to not making a dime overnight. These were the dark times!

CHAPTER 9

YOU CAN RUN BUT YOU CAN'T HIDE!

They got all the updates from their families in Memphis. It was time to leave Milwaukee. They couldn't fly cause it was too risky so they went to one of Cotton's cousin's houses in Chicago to buy low key cars. They knew they had to split up in order to move low key. Cotton chose to stay in Chicago; it was the 3rd largest city in the country and easy to stay out of sight. Dee had a female friend in Boston who said he could come lay low there. Uptown had to get back to LA, get his money and then he had a low-key spot in the desert part of Scottsdale, AZ. So Uptown headed west on the I-80 and Dee headed east on the I-80. They both shaved their heads, wore fake mustaches, and put on nerd looking glasses.

Uptown put on a suit with a brim with the bible on the dash. Dee made it to his destination. He called his female friend and got the address to her house. She stayed in a hood called Mattapan, it was all Black. Dee was happy to see that cause all he heard about Boston was that a lot of White Irish people lived there. But a lot of blacks and Latinos live there too. But they live in Mattapan and Roxbury, and a few more spots too. Boston was cold too and Dee wasn't used to all this cold weather; first Milwaukee then Chicago now Beantown. He had to go buy some warm cloths.

They all had about a half million worth of diamonds and a couple hundred thousand in cash and gold each. First thing Dee did was take his girl on a shopping spree then he had a 5-karat put in a ring and a gave it to his new girlfriend. He had to spoil her to make sure she kept her mouth shut. Cotton on the other hand, posted up in Chicago's wild 100's and had his bottom hoe come up and continued to change his hoes over the phone till all of em broke bad cause they kept asking when he coming to New Orleans. He would always lie knowing he couldn't step foot down south plus he knew he couldn't 100% trust them hoes.

Uptown made it to LA after 2 1/2 days on the road. He snuck into his penthouse at 2:30 a.m. got his money out the safe, and then headed to Donna's house on 54th and Avalon. She told him, "nigga be careful. The feds been to her house looking for him." He said, "I know family, I just came to tell you goodbye and give you money." He gave her 35 thousand. She said, "you sure you not gone need all your money." He said, "I got more than enough." She said, "you should go to Mexico." He said, "that's what they expect; everybody go there. I got a plan, kinfolks, I'ma be alright." "Take care yourself," she said. He said, "I will." They hugged then Uptown got on the 110-freeway exit going east on the 1-10. He drove 62 hours through the desert till he reached Phoenix, AZ. It was 9.a.m. He drove through Mesa, Temper, Camelback road, and then to Scottsdale. He had bought a house on the outskirts of town with no neighbors. The house was a western style flat made for the hot desert weather. It was perfect for hiding out; it was miles away from any roads and tucked behind the mountains. You could see someone miles away if they were coming to your house.

Uptown ordered everything that came. He didn't go out for nothing. It was a lowly life but he knew he had to live like this for a while until it cooled off with all the most wanted bs.

After a few months, he got used to being to himself. He learned to like nature and the outdoors. He would go into the desert and enjoy the sights, then he would hike up the mountains to take advantage of the cool air up there. He would talk to Mona and his family a lot, watch a lot of tv shows, and sports. Every now and then he would drive to the Indian casino on the reservation. It was low key and he could get in and out without being noticed. Uptown got used to his way of life and it was how he had to live in order to stay focused.

In Chicago, Cotton was having a kinda difficult time adjusting to this new life on the run lifestyle. All his life he been the center of attention. He was a pimp. He stayed riding around knocking hoes, talking to women, hustling and being a people person, clubbing every night, and feeling the sun come up. He never really slept only took naps; then he was back in the streets. Now he was confined to this house sitting around waiting on other people to do this and that for him. He had money but started to feel like everybody was using him cause they knew he couldn't go out and do things for himself. So, after 3 months of being cooped up in the house, Cotton started going out to clubs. He liked this club called The Click and another one called the 50 Yard Line. His bottom hoe started living in North Chicago. They wasn't hunting for no money, but she got boxed in hustling chicks, because this was all she knew.

One day Cotton was driving late at night coming from a club, he had offered to take a young lady home who stayed off 57th and Justine Street, a known drug and gang area. Before they made it to her house, the Chicago PD hit the lights and pulled him over. The car was legit, but Cotton had been drinking, smoking and you could clearly smell it. On top of that, the young lady had a small bag of weed and a pocketknife on her. As soon as they got Cotton out of the car to pat him down, she slid the weed and knife under his seat. They put Cotton in the back seat of the patrol car then searched the car. They found the knife and the weed and then made the young lady walk home. They took Cotton to the Cook County Jail on 24th and California Street. They booked him on driving under the influence and misdemeanor possession of weed and a deadly weapon.

His bond was one thousand dollars. He called his bottom hoe and she rushed to the jail to pay the cash bond. Cotton had a fake ID so he was super nervous. They put him in a tank with nothing but gang bangers. There were Latin kings, Micky Cobras, Black P. Stones, 4 Corner hustlas, Black Souls and Simon City Royals. Cotton was in the tank for 10 minutes when this big stocky dude asked him, "what you is, people or folks?". Cotton knew what that meant. He shot back, "neither one. I'm from Mississippi. I'ma pimp not a playa or Mack, just straight pimping. I run with a gang of hoes, my nigga." The dude said, "dig dat. I respect that." After that, the whole tank knew Cotton was a cool cat from down south, and he didn't have any issues with nobody. He was a born people person.

After 36 hours, they called his name. He had made bond. He left out the tank headed to the release area of the Sap. Cook County Jail was big so it took time doing everything, even getting out mainly. There were thousands of people coming in and out of this huge jail. When he got to the desk to sign his bond, he had to take another fingerprint before they released him. This one was a national check for warrants called the National Criminal Search Computer. it takes a few hours, so you go into a holding cell until you are cleared. Then and only then could you get your clothes and leave. The wait was nerve-wracking for Cotton. Cotton was sweating bullets and after 4 1/2 long hours, the CO called his name. Cotton tried to play it cool as he walked up. The CO said, "You have a warrant under the name Ian Jones." Cotton's heart dropped. He said there's been a mistake. I'm Peter Coleman from Los Angeles, Cali. I'm here visiting my sick aunt. The CO said, "Well you have a warrant out of Memphis, Tenn, and you will remain here till we contact Memphis and let them know about your arrest. Then you have the right to fight extradition. But for now, you'll return to the tank and wait for Memphis authorities to come pick you up so you can go there and answer to the warrants they have on you."

Cotton just sat back and was shocked. He returned back to the tank. He got in his bunk, put the blanket over his head and cried like a baby. He knew he had fucked up and there was no getting out of it.

Meanwhile in Memphis, Det. O'Kelly's phone rang. It was a detective from Chicago. He said, "Mr. O'Kelly, we have your fugitive, Ian Jones here in the Cook County Jail." "That sounds great," he said. "He goes by the name Cotton and he's a major drug smuggler here in Memphis," O'Kelly said. "We've been looking for him for over 5 years now. Thanks, I'll be on a flight to get him in the morning." "Okay, the Chicago detective, said. I'll have him ready for you."

O'Kelly called his bosses yelling, "he fucked up, he fucked up. He got arrested in Chi-town. I'm going to pick his ass up in the morning. One down and two more to go."

The next day, O'Kelly left Memphis International Airport at 7:15 a.m. and landed at Chicago's O'Hare Airport at 9:05 a.m. He and two federal agents contacted Chicago's federal field office to assist them in the transportation of one of America's most wanted and the FBI's top ten most wanted.

That morning, Cotton's face was on every news station in the country. The niggas in the tank were like "dam country-P. You a celebrity. You a real live kingpin, a true drug lord and you don't even act like it. Dam, you sure fooled us. We thinking you a southern Don Juan but in reality you more

[176]

like Freeway Rick Ross. That's hard my nigga." Cotton said, "Yeah, I hustle dope, hoes, whatever it takes to get the cake, ya dig." The cops interrupted and called him by his street name, "Hey Cotton, Memphis here to get you." He dapped all the niggas in the tank and headed down to the detective's office where Det. O'Kelly was waiting on him with a big smile on his face. He said, "so, Mr. Cotton or Ian whichever you like, it's an honor to finally meet you, Sir. It's been a long time since you've been to Memphis huh"? Cotton just looked at him stone-faced. He knew not to talk to the police without a lawyer. O'Kelly just kept on talking trying his best to get Cotton to say something, but he just kept his mouth closed leaning back in his chair. After about 30 minutes or so, Det O'Kelly said "well you ain't got to talk. There are a lot of people talking for you." They got in an unmarked car and headed to the airport.

All Cotton could do was think about what a fool he was for going out that night. Now three days later, his whole world had ended. He already had instructed his bottom bitch to go get his money and diamonds if he ever got caught. Plus she was the only person he could truly trust in Chicago. After landing in Memphis, they got on I-55 and took the Sam Cooper Highway heading to the federal holding facility in Mason, Tennessee.

Uptown got the word that Cotton had gotten caught. He packed what he could and called Dee. He told him to get rid of his phone and to leave Boston right away. Uptown knew he could trust Cotton but he didn't know if they had his phone or not and if they did, they would know he was talking to Uptown and Dee. So, he couldn't take any chances. So he packed what he could and drove to Albuquerque, New Mexico. He drove around the Black community and saw a young mother at the bus stop. It was so hot outside that he pulled over and offered her a ride. She said, "look I don't ride with strangers, plus I got my kids with me." He said, "that's why I asked. It's hot out here and I didn't want y'all to be in this heat waiting on no bus." She said, "appreciate you sir but I taught my kids never to speak to strangers so that means I gotta follow my own advice if I want them to listen to me." Uptown said, "I respect that lil momma. You're a good mother."

    He pulled off. He got a block down the street then busted a U-turn and headed back to the bus stop. He got out the car then sat at the bus stop with the young lady and her kids. She said, "I know you trying to flirt and I'm not interested." He said, "you too young for me, I'm here to do God's work, my good deed for the day." He handed her an envelope with 5 thousand dollars in it. She said, "wow, thanks sir." He said, "Now I want you to get in that car. It has good A.C. blowing. The title is in the glove department. Write up a bill a of sale and then take it to the DMV. Get it in your name and get you some insurance." He gave her a slightly used Mazda.

    Uptown was smart. He knew he couldn't drive far on the run; it was too risky. So, he gave the young lady his car and walked to the Greyhound Bus Station. He walked 4 blocks in the hot sun till he made it to the bus station. He didn't know where he was going. He just looked at the schedule and bought a ticket to the next bus leaving out to a major city. The neon sign said bus leaving to Miami in 15 min. So, he got his ticket and waited in line to board the bus. He got a seat in the back where he could stretch his long legs. Then he got his pillow and blanket and went fast asleep.

    In Boston, Dee was driving by the ocean when he got the call and immediately he threw his phone in the water and bought another prepaid one. He drove around for an hour wondering how he was going to tell his girl he had to leave. He knew he couldn't take her with him, so he decided it was best that he just left. He got back to the house. She was still at work. So he packed a bag and took a cab to the Greyhound in a suburb outside the city. He got a ticket to New York City. He left her a letter on her refrigerator saying "look baby, I'm sorry to have to tell you this but I have to leave. It's not about you or us, it's my situation. I loved the brief time we shared together but I'm wanted by the feds, and I don't want to bring no harm to you or your family. So I have to go. Don't ever fall in love with a man in these mean streets cause he gone leave either by going to prison or getting killed. You're too sweet of a woman for that. Please find you a working man who stays out of trouble and loves you for you. I know it's hard to say goodbye but someday you'll thank me. Take care and thanks for all the good times we shared." He waited till he settled in New York to call her from a blocked number. He left her the car and 20 thousand dollars with the letter.

  She picked up the phone and could not believe it. "Why you leave me, she asked"? "Baby go read the letter on the refrigerator and you'll understand," Dee said. Then he hung up the phone.

  Dee arrived in New York and decided to get a place in Harlem. It wasn't long before he found a small apartment. He liked the neighborhood. It had all kinds of people in it, and in New York you don't need a car cause the subways take you everywhere. So he never had to worry about getting pulled over in a traffic stop, it was public transportation from then on.

  Dee got a lil studio apartment off 108th and Lennox Avenue. It was in the center of everything including the world-famous Appollo Theater which was a few corners away. All the Black businesses were close by. The subway to Manhattan was one block away. People were coming and going 24/7. This was perfect for a person on the run, plenty of tourists, and millions of out-of-towners. The city that never sleeps is most definitely a city you could get lost in. He went out and bought plenty of Yankees, Knicks, and Giants gear.

Uptown had taught him in order to blend in and go unnoticed, you gotta look and dress like a local. Dee learned from the last situation in Boston to always get his own place. He also learned to never get too attached to no female while on the run cause at any minute, you might have to drop everything and leave. So from now on it was just fun and one-night stands for him. He bought a wedding band so if a woman saw it she knew off the top that this wasn't going to be a long-term relationship. Dee lived like that in Atlanta. While there, he would only date club hoppers cause after having two crazy baby mommas in Memphis, he was living his best single life there.

He would hit all the liveliest clubs in the area like the Compound, Magic City, and Jazzie T's. Dee missed that but New York had a lot of good night life to offer and he planned on checking out a few.

Uptown arrived in Miami days later. It took 51 hours to get there. The bus stopped at several different cities from Dallas to Alabama to Florida. On every stop there would be a guy out selling drugs right in front of the Greyhound building as if he worked for the company. Shit was crazy. Uptown would buy a blunt, walk over to a fast-food spot like McDonald's or Burger Kings and grab a bite to eat. Then he would smoke and hop back on the bus. It wasn't as bad as he thought it would be. He bought a D.V.D./c.d. player with some headphones and watched movies and listened to music.

Uptown grew up listening to the Blues and ole school soul music in Memphis. They called that form of music pimping music with artists like Willie Hutch, Bobby Womack, Al Green, The O'Jays, the Isley Brothers, and Aretha Franklin. Still, the Mississippi in him loved the Blues. He was a Delta boy at heart, the birthplace of the Blues. See, Mississippi knew the true history of the Blues that started from old Negro hymns that the slaves used to sing while working the cotton fields in the south. This is something they brought with them from Africa. They just changed the words to English cause they weren't allowed to speak African. Before Negro hymns, all these people knew was English European music like Mozart and other opera sounding bullshit. The Blues started all music like R&B, rock and Roll, jazz, pop, disco, rap, and country. In fact, country ain't nothing but the White man's blues.

Uptown loved what he saw in Miami. It's a beautiful city with sunshine, colorful houses-n-buildings, nice palm trees. They weren't as tall as the ones in LA, but they seemed cleaner with white sandy beaches. It reminded him a lot like southern California only it was flat land and no hill-and mountains. Also, it was humid, that hot sticky sweaty heat. In LA, it was sunny and dry with a cool ocean breeze at night. Yeah, Cali had the best weather, but Miami had the best look and best-looking women too. If a woman ain't a dime or close nine, she better find another city to go to cause Miami is the land of the supermodel, bad bitches only, ya dig. Uptown didn't want to stay in South Beach because there were too many police who patrol that area. So, he got a small one-bedroom apartment across the bridge in North Miami. He went and bought all plush furniture, cause although the outside of his spots looked bad considering the area, it was the inside that always looked like a home in Beverly Hills. They were lined with leather sofas, marble tables, granite kitchen counters, California king sized beds, flat screens in every room, China plates, and Italian rugs.

It may have looked like a dump at the front door but once you came inside, you felt like you were in a baby mansion. He loved to decorate; something he learned from his sisters and momma. Just because you live in the hood, does not mean you cannot classy up the place.

Uptown went to the beauty supply store and bought a dreadlock wig. He had to change his appearance. There were a lot of Jamaicans, Haitians and Bahamians that lived in Florida, and most all of them wore dreadlocks. So, it was the perfect way to move through the city looking like a regular nappy dread basta. Then he went to the Bal Harbour Mall to cop him some Dolphins, Heat and Hurricanes aka da gear, sticking to the strip to look just like a local. With it being so sunny, he also bought a lot of sunglasses, also good for staying lowkey. He didn't wear any high-priced clothes because he couldn't be dressing like he had money living in North Miami. That's the quickest way to get yo ass robbed. Uptown's a certified street nigga, so he knew how to move. It's all about staying off the radar; only if Cotton had stuck with the plan.

Speaking of Cotton, he was in the fed joint in Mason for a week when his Jewish high-priced lawyer came to visit him. Cotton said, "look man. You been paid. What took you so long to come visit me"? Looking at Cotton with round rim glasses hanging from his big ass Jewish nose, he said, "Mr. Jones, I'm a very busy man. I have clients who are in trials and others out of state but trust me, your wait will be worth it." Cotton said, "what the fuck that mean"? He said, "Mr. Jones, you're a high-profile case. You are one of the FBI's most wanted, you and your crew. This is not about winning but about not getting a life sentence cause you're charged with human trafficking, drug trafficking, conspiracy, money laundering, kidnapping, and promoting prostitution across several state lines. This is serious, Mr. Jones. Also, many of your crew members are already here and a lot of them are cooperating with the feds. In street lingo, "they snitching to save their own asses. I as your counsel strongly advise you not to talk over these recorded phones about your case and never ever, I mean never ever talk to nobody in here about your case. These dudes in here will switch on their momma to get out."

Cotton said, "I noticed that in here. My brother told me the feds act like the state pen. In state prison, you can get your ass killed for snitching, but in here they get rewarded with a get out of jail card when they tell. Not me though. I'm not cut like these soft ass niggas, plus I love my family. I can't have nobody wanting to hurt my family cause I told on them. Nah, I was raised by my Big Momma and Big Momma didn't have no rats in our home. She was too clean for that bullshit. I'ma stand firm. I did the crime, now I gotta do the time. It is what it is."

"I'm glad you feel like that way. That makes my job a lot easier," the lawyer said. "Now you don't have a long criminal record, so your points shouldn't be that high." Cotton was confused. "What points," he asked. "Well, in federal court, it's your criminal history. Each felony has a certain amount of points and those points determine how much time you'll be facing." "Something like your priors in the state system," Cotton asked? "Yeah sort of like that," his lawyer replied and "how do you know so much about how the state system works? Did you ever go to state prison cause if so I need to know." "Naw," Cotton said, "my brother stayed in and out of prison when I was growing up, so he put me up on how things work in case I ever went to prison. Still never thought I'd be in this fucked up position."

"Well," his lawyer said, "you could've and would've made a very successful businessman cause you made a lot of money with what you do. But unfortunately for you, selling drugs and women are both illegal. I know you did it to take care of your family but with a mind and talk like yours, you would've made it no matter what career you chose. Now let me go try to work out a deal so you don't go to prison for life. Until then, don't stress. Sit back, do your time, and don't let the time do you."

Cotton headed out of the meeting with his lawyer. He knew he was going to prison but for how long? All he could do was wait and wonder. He would spend days just daydreaming about all the fun he had, all the money he made, all the cars he used to buy, all the bitches he used to fuck. Speaking of bitches, it's been almost 2 months and he hadn't heard shit from his bottom bitch. She had over a 100 thousand dollars' worth of diamonds and 42 thousand in cash that belonged to him. Now he can't find her. First he was worried fearing she got robbed in Chicago. But then his sister came to visit him telling him she went over her momma's house in North Memphis and her momma said she came by and gave her some money for the kids and said she's moving to St. Louis. Cotton couldn't believe she broke bad with all his money and diamonds like that. He thought he could trust her. She had shown him that no matter how much a person say they love you, you get in a jam and their actions will speak louder than their words. He reached out to his brother, Man-Man, to go find her tramp ass.

After about a month and a half, he located her working at a strip club in East St. Louis called the Pink Slip. He asked for a lap dance and told her he's new in town and he and his homeboys got a room at the Doubletree Hotel across the bridge, and if she wanted to make more money, to come through for a private party. She came through around

3:00 a.m. When she entered the room, she went to the bathroom to get dressed. When she came out, she asked "how am I supposed to dance. Ain't no music"? Man-Man and two of his goons just stood there with stone faces. Then the big nigga grabbed her and put his hand around her mouth. The other nigga started to duct tape her feet and hands. Then he put a sock in her mouth and taped her shit shut. Man-Man pulled out a big 40 Glock and pointed it to her head and said, "look bitch this a message from Cotton. Where's his diamonds and money? And before you start screaming, just know we know where your momma and kids at in North Memphis. How you think we found your dumb ass. You gone cross a nigga who was good to yo stupid ass. He know where all yo family live. You a dumb hoe.
Now scream for the police if you want. I'll go to jail but trust me, your family gone pay. So I advise you to tell us what we want and give us all the money and diamonds you have left and everything will be alright." Then he ordered the big nigga to remove the tape off her mouth so she could speak. In a whining crying voice, she said "I'm so sorry. Tell Cotton I do love him with all my heart and that I wasn't trying to cross him in anyway. I was just scared. I didn't know what to do. I didn't know who to trust. I didn't know if the feds was looking for me, I just didn't know. So I left Chicago and came to St. Louis. I was too afraid to go to Memphis."

Man-Man said, "ok, okay you was scared. What about the ice and bread, bitch. That's why we here. He gots lawyers and family who needs that money, and if you love him like you say you do, you know his sister and you know where they stay. You could've pulled up on them. They hate yo ass now but still you knew he was in jail and would need that money for bail even though he can't have a bond, but he need lawyer fair for sure. Now enough of this small talk. Where's that money at." She said, "I have an apartment here on the southside. It's under the carpet under the wood panel at the foot end of the bed. But I have a dude who lives with me and he the DJ at the Pink Slip. I know he should be heading home soon, so you gotta get in and out fast." Man-Man said, "naw bitch, you gone call him and tell him that you'll be working this private party for a few more hours and that you need him to wait on you so you'll feel safe leaving with all this money on you." She got on the phone and told the DJ to wait on her at another hotel near the Doubletree.

The two goons got the address and keys and went to the apartment. They returned in 30 minutes. Man-Man counted the cash first. It was only 6 thousand dollars. He said, "dam bitch. Where's the rest of the money." She just held her head down. Then he looked at the diamonds, it was about 15 or 20 thousand dollars' worth left.

Man-Man choked the Glock and said, "bitch I should kill your low-down ass. That man trusted you with his life and this is how you repay him. You ain't worth a killing. You had a boss and you so dumb and disloyal you don't know how to keep it 100. You're a zero bitch and give me that jewelry around your neck. Matter of fact, give me them rings, dat watch, those earrings and all the money you made tonight, which was about 14 hundred. And remember, if you go to the police, we know where your entire family live. You might not give a fuck bout Cotton, but I hope yo heartless ass care bout your kids, momma, and family."

They cut the duct tape and took her to her car and told her to call her boyfriend. She said, "what if he asks about the money, my jewelry and the stash of cash and diamonds at the house." Man-Man said, "tell that trick you got robbed. Tell em that you not from St. Louis so them niggas was targeting him. Blame him for it and make him feel guilty. he'll try to pay you so yo slow ass will be okay. And remember, you ain't seen or heard shit you got it bitch"! She shook her head and drove off.

They jumped into their car and headed south on 1-55 till they reached Memphis about 3 1/2 hours later. Coming across that M bridge always made them feel safe. He stopped by Waffle House for some breakfast and then gave the goons 15 hundred a piece. He then went over his sister's house in Walker Homes to wait on Cotton's call. They only talked in codes cause all phones are recorded. Man-Man taught Cotton this as a young kid when he was doing time in Parchman Prison in Mississippi.

Cotton called about 6 p.m. Talking in code, he asked, "Did you go to the concert in St. Louis?" He said, "yeah but it wasn't that packed only 6 thousand people showed up". Cotton said, "Okay, okay what bout the after party"? "Oh it was one. Had to leave cause too many niggas, ya dig." Then Cotton asked, "so how many bitches numbers yall get"? Man-Man said, "shit, bout 15 or 20 in all". Cotton dropped the phone, then said, "yeah that promotor ain't bout shit." Man-Man said, "shit bruh I know that's right, but I'll find other entertaining events to go to. How you holding up in there, bruh"? Cotton said, "I'm good bruh, just waiting to get my day in court so I can see how long these crackers trying to throw me away for". Man-Man said, "bruh, you gone be alright. The family gone always be here for you just like you was there for us." Cotton said, I already know that big bruh. Look, call the rest of the fam and let em know I need some lawyer fair. Let em know the situation. They said their goodbyes as the time ran out on the collect call.

Man-Man knew when he said the other fam that he had to call Uptown and Dee to get some more money for the lawyer after that no-good hoe fucked off all his

[187]

bread. So he contacted Uptown's sister, Verdean a.k.a. Zolly, and she gave him a number so he could get at him.

Uptown didn't notice the number so he didn't pick up till Man-Man texted him. He answered the phone saying, "what do OG." Man-Man said, "shit bruh good to hear your voice my nigga." Uptown said, "you talked to Cotton, how's he holding up"? He said, "he good. Lil bruh a Souljah. He know he gotta do some time and he taking it one day at a time. That's why I'm calling. He need you and Dee to send him some lawyer fair. The bitch, the one he called his bottom bitch, that hoe ran off to St. Louis with some trick ass DJ nigga and blew almost every dime and every diamond. But you know I pulled up on that hoe and took what she had left, which was 6 thousand, and 15 to 20 thousand worth of diamonds. Bottom bitch my ass, I should've put that bitch in the bottom of the Mississippi river"! Uptown said, "wow that hoe ain't shit, and come to find out it's a hoe that started all this federal investigation shit. That's why I don't trust hookers. They only around to be sluts and tell on a nigga when they get mad. Anyhow, look bruh, call my sister, Gladys. I'll have her give you 30 thousand and I'ma tell Dee to get another 20. That should take care of the lawyer. You, go sell that ice and give yo sisters a lil sum-sum and keep the rest.

Man-Man said, "bet bruh man. Thanks for everything." Uptown said, "Bruh we family. We gone take care our own." Man-Man said, "bruh, be careful cause Cotton said there's a lot of workers and crew members in there with him that's already cooperating. So stay moving and stay safe, Bruh." Uptown said, "I got you OG. You stay safe too, and you gotta stay free to take care lil bruh cause you know how it goes. He need you more than ever and tell em I love `em". They said their goodbyes. Uptown hung up and crushed the phone under his feet.

He always bought new phones just in case. He knew he could trust Man-Man but he just didn't trust cell phones.

    He called Dee and told him the business with Cotton, and Dee told 'em where Man-Man could pick up the cash for the lawyer. Dee said, "dam bruh. I hate that bruh got caught up like that. This shit so dam crazy bruh. We was just on top of the world 6 months ago, now we on the run living day to day. Life's a bitch." "Tell me bout it," Uptown said. "You know that low down dirty bottom bitch of Cotton ran off and spent almost all his cash and diamonds"! Dee said, "for real, that nigga had bout a half a mill worth of ice. That hoe should've got shot for dat shit." Uptown said, "yeah Man-Man said he should've dropped that bottom bitch at the bottom of the Mississippi river"! They both laughed. Dee said, "yeah, Man-Man don't play." Still, listen big bruh? It's been a minute since I seen you, maybe when this shit die down a lil bit you could come visit me in New York. I'm super low key up here bruh. Plus, this city so big and crowded that you meet new people almost every day that's not from here. It's like everybody in the world trying to get here. You can hide right out in the open and no one will ever notice. People here ain't like in the south, mid-west, or west coast. Nobody walks up and say how you doing, cause they don't care. All they care bout is getting through the crowd. It's a lot to see here, and oh yeah I got a plug buying good name brand clothes in bulk, straight from the manufacture overseas for the super low. Then I ship it to Memphis and Atlanta for my people to sell at a discount. I triple my money and my people make good money too. It's like this: I buy a hundred pair of jeans at 10 dollars a pair. I charge my people 30 dollars a pair. They sell them for 50 dollars a pair. The price tag has 80 dollars on it so the customer thinks he or she getting a great deal so everybody involved is happy. That equals to easy money, and I just started but it's something to do, you know hustling just in my blood bruh. Gotta keep it coming, get more and more like you taught me bruh. So if you want in, I could send you a couple cases of all new fly gear to sell down there in Miami, you know. New York is the fashion capital of this country. They get all the latest gear first and they get it cheaper too."

"I'm cool right now", Uptown said, "if I need ya I'ma hit you up on that but I haven't been here long enough to be out hustlin clothes. Plus I ain't got nobody in Memphis I could trust to sell them for me. So until then, I'll be alright, but thanks bruh." Still, Uptown knew his Bruh Dee like a book. He knew the only reason that he's selling clothes is that his money is getting low. He knew that Dee had two habits that'll run through a bankroll and that's gambling and hoes. Dee not a trick that buys pussy from hookers off the street but he'll meet a bitch and all the partying is on him; weed, shopping, eating, dating. You know, shit niggas do to get the pussy. So if you doing this every other day for months it'll take a toll on a bankroll, especially when you no longer making that big money.

Uptown's only habit was weed. He'll show a woman a nice time but he wasn't a trick. While on the run, he's been telling women he's broke living off a disability check and that if they was going to kick it then they riding in her car and that some dates she gone have to pay. See, unlike Dee, he didn't use his money to get women cause he was blessed to be tall, dark, and handsome. He knew his worth and Cotton taught him to play and not get played, ya dig.

Still freakness was not his weakness. He only focused on staying lowkey and staying free. He had Mona sneak up once a month when he wanted some real female companionship, but when she wasn't there, he only went out with two other women: one from Liberty City. She was a newly divorced woman who only wanted to be dicked down with no strings attached. The other one was from Hialeah, an ex-model. She was a beautiful dark-skinned Cuban that was married to an ex-NBA player but he lived in LA with his new Boo. They had 3 kids together. Both women knew what it was and there were no feelings involved. They just hung out, had fun, and returned to their day-to-day lives.

    See, Uptown only dealt with women on his terms and women respected him for his honesty. The only lie he told them was his name and where he was from. If a woman started asking too many questions, he quickly cut them off. His personal business was never a topic. He knew how to converse. He had the gift of gab, also something he learned from Cotton. Also, women loved that Uptown knew how to treat a woman. When women went out with him, he made them feel important. He would listen to them, console them, and he would make them smile and laugh. They had fun when they were with him. He didn't really do clubs but would go out and dance with them from time to time. He would take them to concerts, comedy shows, plays, and sporting events.

    Also, he was a smooth romantic nigga; candlelight dinners, beach picnics, champagne in front of a fireplace, walks in the park. Plus, he knew how to cook 5-star meals, breakfast in bed, but also loved to go out to eat and try new foods. In Miami, there's a lot of different cultures. He loved the Jamaican jerk chicken, the Haitian curry lamb stew, the Bahamian ox tails. Miami is the Latino capital of America. There are more Spanish speaking people in Miami than any other spot in this country. That made Uptown want to learn how to speak it, so he could understand his surroundings more. He liked Miami, but he missed LA and his heart was in Memphis. In Miami, he had to keep a super low profile but in LA he wasn't on the run and he enjoyed his lifestyle. In Miami, he had money but didn't want to bring any unwanted attention to himself. So playing broke was kinda weird, but fun at times cause he grew up broke so it wasn't nothing new to him. He always went to the ghetto in every city he visited. In Miami, he would go to Overtown, Little Haiti, the infamous Pork and Beans projects, Carol City, everywhere the poor Black and Brown people were at. Uptown felt at home here. These were his type of people, people born in the struggle just like him. He could relate to those who understood life was hard and you gotta have a strong will to survive and thrive when you are raised in the hood with no money. That's what makes people grind harder cause they were born hungry and starving, everybody in life trying their best to eat.

    Things were going well. He had been in Miami for almost a year. He knew the city well and he wasn't on nobody's radar. Then he got some bad news that shook his heart. Dee had gotten arrested in New York. His sister talked to Dee's mother and she told her what happened. Dee sent some counterfeit clothes to Atlanta to this nigga, and the nigga got caught selling the shit without a license. So instead of taking his charge, he snitched on Dee and they caught Dee at the FedEx shipping another package to Memphis. They took him to the fed joint in New York and then sent him to Atlanta then on to Memphis. He's now in Mason, Tennessee with Cotton. Shit was bad now. Uptown had to up and move again, same situation.

    Meanwhile in Memphis, Det. O'Kelly couldn't wait to interrogate Dee. He had him in a small room slightly darkened with drinks and cigarettes. He said, "so Mr. Dee, you a hard man to catch up with. You know why I'm here and you know what I want to hear." Dee said, "look I don't know shit, but I'm Black, in jail and I want some weed. Anything else, I don't know." Det. O'Kelly's face turned red as he got highly upset that Dee was talking shit. He said, "cut the bullshit. Where the fuck is Uptown? You tell me where he at and I can make sure you don't get a lot of time." Dee said, "look you Irish red headed pig. I ain't no snitch, so fuck you"! Det O'Kelly slammed his fist on the table and yelled out, "go ahead be hard, I'ma make sure you don't see the light of day till you old and gray." Dee said, "look I'm done talking. Talk to my lawyer and let me go back to my cell. I think they bringing chow and you ain't talking bout shit." Det. O'Kelly told the CO to get this muthafucka out of his face. The CO grabbed Dee by the arm and rushed him back to his pod.

    He got back to the pod and told the rock man to send Cotton a kite. He wrote telling him to meet him at the gym after chow. He had been in Mason for a week and a half and hadn't seen Cotton. So later that day after chow, Dee walked in the gym and saw Cotton over in the corner talking to some niggas. Dee snuck up behind him and hugged him. Cotton turned around and smiled and said, "what's up bad"? Dee's smile instantly turned to a frown as he noticed Cotton had a black eye with black and blue bruises on his face. He said, "bruh what the fucks up. Who did this to you"? Cotton said, "Bruh don't sweat it. I had got into it with this nigga. The nigga tried to bully a pimp, so we got em up. The nigga pulled a pimp's hair like a bitch but we squashed it. He know I ain't no hoe ass nigga though." Dee said, "Where the nigga at now." Cotton said, "the big, tall nigga that's on the basketball court right there." Dee said, "oh yeah that big ass nigga jumped you." Cotton said, "yeah but I held my own, ask any nigga."

    All Dee could see was Cotton's fucked up face. He knew Cotton was a mixed breed pretty boy but wasn't a fighter nor was he a violent person. He was a lover not a fighter. Dee said, "look Bruh, we in prison. You can't let no nigga make your face look like that and his face ain't shit wrong with it. You gotta take your respect in blood in prison, fuck the trouble. Our respect is everything in here." Cotton said, "So what you wanna do." Dee said, "wait right here." He walked over to Big Chuncey a.k.a Ced, Greg's big brother. He's the other leader of the LMG mafia gang. Dee walked up and gave Big Chuncey a handshake. He said, "what's up, home team you good"? Dee said, "hell naw big homie. This big ass nigga jumped on my bruh, my charge partner, my nigga." Big Chuncey said, "I knew I seen that high yellow nigga in the hood before, but he said he ain't affiliated." Dee said, "he not really. He from Mississippi. He close family with Uptown. He our family, ride or die with me." Big Chuncey said, "well if you and Uptown rockin with em then he the L and don't nobody put they hands on the family; its murda. You know how we rock." Big Chuncey called over 4 or 5 souljahs and told one of em to give Dee and Cotton two big shanks.

He said, "tell Cotton to come here." Cotton pulled up. Big Chuncey said, "look my nigga. I didn't know you was part of the family. You fucks with my homie Dee, so from now on you LMG and we got yo back on whatever and who ever. Now look, this gone put us in the hole but it's gotta be done to make an example that don't nobody fuck with us and when they do, it's blood on the floor. This how this finna go down. Me and two of my hittas gone take off on the nigga, we gone get him to the ground then you and Dee gone cut his face up. Make sure you cut him deep, give him some scars he'll have to look at for life. Every time he look in the mirror, he gone regret that he ever put his hands on you. We gone do it in front of this whole gym. Every nigga, every gang and every CO will know the LMG don't play." Cotton said, "bet." Dee said, "you know I'm ready big homie, let's go"!

Big Chuncey and 5 of his souljahs walked onto the court and one of the souljahs grabbed the ball. The nigga said what's up Big C; we in the middle of a game Bruh. The nigga knew Big Chuncey and he knew how dangerous Big Chuncey was. Big Chuncey said nigga, "look here, game over nigga. it's yo day to get put on the bench. Then a souljah swung hitting the big nigga in the back of the head. The nigga tried to fight back yelling "what I do to y'all"? Big Chuncey drew back and landed a punch right on the nigga jaw sending him to the ground. Big Chuncey stomped him in the face knocking out his front teeth. Then Cotton and Dee ran over and started to cut and stab the nigga in his face and head. Blood was everywhere.

    The cops ran up and pepper sprayed the crowd. After backup got to the scene, they handcuffed Cotton, Dee, Big Chuncey and 3 souljahs. Two of them got away. They sent them straight to the hole for 23-hour lock down; 1 hour for rec and shower. When they got to the hole, the Captain said, "y'all nearly killed that man. I'm charging all yall asses with assault." Big Chuncey just laughed. He knew the ropes. Dee wasn't shaken either cause he knew it was just a write up.

    Cotton was unsure, this was his first time in jail. Big Chuncey waited till the captain left and then he yelled out, "now that's how you handle business. When we get out the hole they gone know y'all some real hittas and you won't have no more issues with no nigga, if so, it's on again. We don't fear no nigga. If we gotta smash and crash, so be it, that's how this shit go." Cotton could tell by the sound in Big Chuncey's voice that he loved hurting people. He was a dangerous gangster that didn't mind seeing people bleed. He was a stone cold killa, a man who you didn't cross. Still, Cotton was happy he had made his respect in jail. Prison is a place where either you are a predator or prey; a real-life jungle where even a lion would get got. You gotta use your mind and muscle to survive in a dog-eat-dog world like prison.

After it turned dark, Big Chuncey said "hey y'all I got some fye kush, send y'all lines." Cotton knew how to fish from 201, the county jail. They smoked and got high all night. That really relaxed Cotton as he talked shit and went to sleep.

In Miami, Uptown was in a confused state. Where would he go next; he couldn't go back to California and couldn't go to Texas. He thought about Detroit. He had a lot of people he knew up there, niggas from west side, eastside, and a few bitches on Joy Road. He thought Detroit because if he got up there he could get into Canada, but that border crossing ain't kind to Black people. Then he thought about Mexico cause he had learned enough Spanish in Miami to actually live there, but Mexico is too dangerous, niggas get kidnapped and killed down there all the time.

He thought about New Orleans cause he visited there plenty times and would easily fit in in all of the cities, but New Orleans is super-hot with niggas killing for nothing. That brings a lot of police around when your city is known for having one of the highest murder rates. So he chose to take a speed boat to Cuba. It was right off the coast of Miami. He liked the food plus he met a few people while in Miami that's back in Cuba cause they got deported. That was perfect.

He paid a Cuban speed boat owner to take him there the same day. The ride was fun. It was like a scene straight out of Miami Vice, this was a nice boat. Uptown had his shades on and the water was splashing on all sides. The speed boat was cutting through the water going 180 miles an hour. He could feel the wind smashing against his skin. This was a big step, going into a whole new country. Still it was exciting cause he had heard so many good things about Cuba, the cigars, the colorful homes, the beautiful old school cars, the white sandy beaches, the food and of course the beautiful

Brown and Black women. They approached the island. It was almost nighttime.

    The city of Havana was lit with plenty lights like Las Vegas and just like las Vegas or Atlantic city, plenty of casinos too. As the boat docked, the owner told him about a good low-key bed and breakfast spot on the outskirts of the city. It was about an hour taxi ride, but it was worth it for a good private night's sleep. That's just what Uptown needed to relax his nerves. He reached the bed and breakfast, which was really somebody's home they built in the back of their house. It had nice little rooms with a bath with a shower; real lowkey with a yard in the back. Uptown unpacked his bags and laid down. It had been a long day. He had to uproot right then and there. He gave all his things to his neighbors. They were surprised by all the nice things Uptown had in his apartment. Uptown didn't care about all that material bullshit. All he cared about was staying free.

    He was so sad to hear that Dee had gotten caught. Now his two closest friends were locked up, shit his brothers were in jail. This was so messed up. He was super depressed and stressed out. Still he knew that now the main focus of the feds was going to be on him. So, now he had to be extra careful. He still had plenty of diamonds and a lot of cash, yet he still had to play like he was super broke to keep the takers away from his stash.

    Uptown awoke to the sun shining through the windows. He could smell the good breakfast being cooked. He got up and looked out the window to see a beautiful banana tree right by his window. He reached out and picked him one. It was warm cause it stayed hot all year round in Cuba but it was so fresh. He peeled the banana. It tasted so good.

He took a quick shower, got dressed then headed downstairs to get his free breakfast. They had Cuban dishes like eggs and shrimp, banana pancakes with pork and rice, black beans with chopped beef and American waffles-and-bacon. The food was amazing. Uptown knew how to talk in Spanish, so he told the nice lady that he loved her cooking and would like to pay for his room for two weeks up front. He then gave her a 100-dollar tip in American money that was a lot. Still he knew he had to get his American cash switched over to Cuban cash, so he got into a taxi and headed to the casino in Havana. He played a little craps and blackjack but in all honesty, was trying to get his money with Cubans on the bills, that way he won't look like a tourist.

After a day at the casino, he walked the beach buying gear to fit in. Baseball and soccer were the sports teams they supported. So, he got what the locals were wearing. After getting his clothes and hats, he went and bought 5 prepaid phones with plenty phone cards. He just had to check on Dee and Cotton. He knew Dee got caught and like Cotton, probably needed help with lawyer fair.

He only trusted his sisters to handle important business like dealing with money and lawyers. They were always on point with taking cake of whatever situation it was. They were his lifelines. He called his sister, Lyne a.k.a. Pauline and told her to get at Dee's momma to see if he needed anything. She said, "I gots you Bruh, love ya."

Then he called Mona. She was so happy to hear from him. Every time he changed his number, she would think the worst until he called and she could hear his voice. She said, "Hey baby I miss you, plus I got some good news. He said, "What's the good news." She said, "Baby I'm pregnant." Uptown's heart dropped. He was happy but he was on the run, so it was bittersweet. She said, "so when can I come and have fun in the sun with my baby daddy." He said, "baby I'm not in Miami anymore. Dee got caught in New York so I went ghost. Mona was sorry to hear that. "So, when can I come where you at," she asked. He replied, "Soon as I figure some shit out. Just be patient and know I'll always have a way for us to get together but where I am now you can't take a bus ride." She said, "ok, Daddy, I'll wait on you; you're worth it."

They talked for about 2 hours. Mona was so happy, and Uptown loved the fact that he was going to be a father. But he knew one day he'd be in prison and that alone had him sad knowing that he wouldn't get a chance to see his first child grow up.

After dwelling on it for a while, he needed to clear his mind. He hadn't smoked any weed since he'd been in Cuba, so he walked the beach trying to find some. He noticed some young cats chillin smoking what smelled like some good kush. He pulled up and asked, "mane tell me y'all got some of that fire for sale." One of the niggas said, "Depends on if you police or not." Uptown said, "I'm no pig, let me hit the blunt and that'll show you I ain't the law." The other nigga said, "Look chico, in Cuba the cops smoke weed, do coke, and shoot dope, you gotta be from America. Uptown said, "Yeah I am." the young niggas said, "What part you from"? Uptown replied, "LA." They both yelled, "shit you from Cali, you Mr. Hollywood huh? So what brings you to our island, Cuba ain't near bout as glamorous as LA."

Uptown was quick on his response said, "my baby momma from Cuba and she's pregnant so I came with her so I could be with my family. She got deported. So here we are now. Do I have to tell you more and can I please buy a 20 bag of that weed". They said, "I guess you cool," and sold him a fat bag of that sticky icky, no stems, no seeds.

Uptown matched a blunt and got their numbers. He wanted to buy a nice amount but didn't trust them enough yet. The weed made him more relaxed. He walked the beach some more and saw a help-wanted sign on this big fishing boat. He didn't really need the money, it was more about networking. Meeting new people always opened up more opportunities. And when you are in a new place, you need to get with people who know the place. The boat was called El Cinco cause it had 5 big storages on it. They mainly fished for shrimp and oysters, but they sold and caught all types of seafood. The owner was this fat guy named Pablo. He ran his boat with his two sons, Manny and Tonyo. They had about 4 other workers but needed more cause the fishing business is big in Cuba. The port was filled with boats of all sizes.

Uptown introduced himself and said he didn't know much about fishing but he's strong and willing to learn. Pablo said, "The pay ain't good but you'll eat good and you'll get paid on time. Uptown said, "As long as I can pay my bills I'm good. Then Pablo said, "So when can you start?" Uptown said, "Today if that's possible. "No chico, tomorrow you can start." Uptown noticed everywhere he goes everybody used the term chico. He figured it was kinda like when Mexicans say migo. So he knew it was a word he had to develop on his own. Communication is all about fitting in, and after being on the run for so long, he started to get good at blending into new environments.

He went back to his bed and breakfast before it got too late. Uptown didn't do the late-night shit. The only time he would go out late was to a club and it always was with a woman. Being in Memphis, he learned that if you're a man out pass 10 o'clock you better be on a date with a woman or you gone get harassed by the police. And that's true all over the world especially when you're a Black man. He settled in for the night, smoked good, got a good night's rest, and got up early the next morning. He ate a good breakfast and headed to the port for his first day of work on the fishing boat. Right off the top, the smell of all the fish turned his stomach. Pablo gave him some nose plugs and said "you never get used to the smell of fish, but here is your wetsuit and rubber boots. Keep em on as long as you're on this boat. And when we get back, we have a shower on the lower deck of the boat."

    Uptown liked that cause he couldn't imagine getting into a taxi smelling like fish. They set sail at 7 a.m. The seagulls were out everywhere. They went far out till you couldn't even see Cuba no more. They had these huge nets and cages that they threw into the water. The waves were stronger in the middle of the ocean than they were on the beach. Uptown was taller than all the other workers, so he was in charge of all the jobs that the shorter workers couldn't reach. Every time the nets and cages were lifted out of the water, there were thousands of shrimp, oysters, and fish.

    Uptown's a businessman and a hustla at heart. He saw all that seafood and thought about nothing but dollar signs. All this free money in the ocean. Dam only if he could've gone legit before he got on the feds' radar. The shit he now knows. The work was hard but it was fun too cause they would be smoking weed and drinking.

    Pablo loved his cigars. Cuba was known for having the best cigars in the world. They were super expensive in the US, some going for as high as a couple hundred a piece.

    Uptown had gotten used to work on the fishing boat. After a couple weeks, he left the bed and breakfast and moved into a small bungalow not too far from where his job's boat was docked. He would get extra food and feel his refrigerator up and sell the extra's to the street vendors. He was getting used to being in Cuba, plus Cuba didn't have an extradition treaty with the US. So, even if they knew where he was, they weren't going to come get him and Cuba wasn't going to detain him. So, he felt he had it made; so he thought.

Meanwhile back in Memphis Det O'Kelly was focused on getting Downton in a cell. After months and months of pressuring the feds to up the reward money, they finally made it 50 thousand dollars. Three weeks later, they got a call from a guy in Miami only known as Hector. Hector said, "the money was cool but what he really needed was a green card." He said, "get him the green card and he'll get him his man." Det. O'Kelly said, "give him a few days to get in touch with immigration and he'll have that card for him."

A few days later, he got the green light and it was a go. Det. O'Kelly and five of his officers met up with three federal agents and they flew to Miami. They were met at the airport by Miami police, federal, state and ICE officers. They set up headquarters in an office building off Collins Avenue. They had a meeting to discuss the operation and Det. O'Donell handed all the lawmen in the room a picture of Uptown. He told them that Uptown is a major drug dealer whose been on the run for years.

He said, "look this man is smart. He knows how to stay out of sight. We got intel that he's somewhere in the Miami area and if they don't act fast he could be gone in a New York minute." Det. O'Kelly said, "we have a confidential informant on the way here with his whereabouts." They talked some more and went over plans on how to take him down without shots being fired. Then Hector showed up. He said, "before I say anything, I want to see my green card and get it in writing so I can show my lawyer. Det. O'Kelly handed him the green card and all the paperwork. Then Hector began to tell them what they been waiting to hear. He said, "Uptown is in Cuba going by an alias. He works on a fishing boat called the El Cinco. It goes out Wednesday through Sunday. He's off work Monday and

Tuesday and usually he only walks the beach. He never goes out at night. One of the federal agents asked him how he knew so much bout Uptown. Hector said he used to work with him on the boat before coming to Miami. He said that he didn't want to go back to Cuba. The work is hard and the pay is pennies. He can work a fishing boat over here and make 10 times the money he made in Cuba. He said, "I really didn't want to snitch on Uptown but I didn't want to go back to Cuba either." So he made the choice to get a green card so he could work and send money home to his poor family.

Det. O'Kelly said, "look Hector. I don't give a fuck why you did it. This information better be correct cause if it ain't you gone get yo ass deported. And if you come back, you gone be put in prison. You got that migo." Hector said, "I got ya chico. He'll be on that boat I bet my life on it." Det. O'Kelly said, "yo life in this country is on it."

The federal agent said, "we gotta alert the US Coast Guards cause we don't have an extradition agreement with Cuba. So we gotta wait till the fishing boat is in open waters before we can make an arrest."

They set it up for the next day. They sent out lowkey boats to scope out the fishing boat first. The next day they made the boat ride to open waters close by Cuba. They had undercover fishing boats all around the island. They didn't know where Uptown's boat would be working that day, so they waited till the boat was out of Cuba's jurisdiction.

That day was beautiful. Uptown had got to work early, so he was in a good mood. He had just bought some good kush from his young chicos and ate some good Cuban food. He and Manny were high cracking jokes. Pablo was smoking a fat cigar and talking shit as he normally does. The sun was shining and fish were biting. Everything was lovely.

Uptown texted his family and told them he loved and missed them. He then texted Mona and told her the same thing. Then out of the blue, the US Coast Guard speed boats came rushing from all sides. They yelled on the loud-speaker, "you're in international waters, stop this boat now." With guns aimed at the boat, Pablo rushed to the deck to address the coast guard. Pablo said, "we out here fishing. Our business is legit. Fuck them pootos" as they boarded the boat.

Uptown was hoping that they was there for illegal fishing areas. But after they all had everybody on deck, another speed boat pulled up, and Det O'Kelly, two US Marshalls, and 3 federal agents got on the boat. Det. O'Kelly walked right up to Uptown and said, "hey there Mr. Uptown Willie Brown. I have been waiting to meet you for years." Uptown's heart dropped to his draws. He couldn't believe it. After years and years of being careful, he was finally caught. He had had nightmares about this very day and what it would be like. Now he knows and it was as painful as the dream.

His boss, Pablo came running up saying "yall got the wrong man. He from Havana, he's my primo, my La Familia. Det. O'Kelly said, "he's from Mississippi and wanted in Memphis, Tennessee." They all looked at Uptown and said "chico, is it true"? He said, "yeah, Pablo it's true but thanks for all y'all did for me." He then asked, "can I hug my boss before y'all handcuff me." Det O'Kelly said, "go ahead, we in the middle of the freaking ocean. We not worried about you going nowhere."

Uptown hugged Pablo and whispered in his ear saying that he had diamonds and cash in his bungalow. He said, "buy you a new boat. It's a gift and remember to always put family first." Pablo cried as he hugged Uptown. He had grown to love him like a son, now he was going to be gone.

Pablo promised he would stay in touch for life. Det. O'Kelly then said, "enough with all that lovie dovie stuff. Cuff his ass and let's get off this stinky ass fish boat." They got Uptown onto the Coast Guard's boat where they had a mini holding cell for prisoners. It's like a jail on water.

As the Coast Guard sped back to Miami, Det. O'Kelly called the feds to set up a flight for as soon as they made landfall. He didn't want to waste a second. He was ready to talk to Memphis news to show them he had caught one of Memphis' most wanted. He already had the US attorney set up a press conference and all the local and federal officers would be there.

It was time for Det. O'Donell to go on live tv. As soon as they landed at the port of Miami, five cars picked them up and drove them to a private jet that was waiting at a clear port. Uptown looked out the window of the jet and said, "dam they spending good money to get me in a cell." Det O'Kelly said, "we sure are, you're not your everyday catch, you're a big fish. Imagine that; a kingpin working on a fishing boat in Cuba. I can't make this shit up." Uptown said, "well you got me, but I'm not guilty. I'm not a kingpin, I'm not even a drug dealer. I work for a living." Det. O'Kelly said, "yeah you sale plenty work for a living. But save all that I didn't do bullshit. I finally got all y'all asses in a cell, and you can tell all that shit to a judge. I'll see yo Black ass in court in a year or two."

The flight landed at a clear port outside of Tunica, Mississippi. As they made the ride straight to the federal building in Memphis across the street from 201 Poplar, the press conference was already set up. They put Uptown in a holding cell as Det. O'Kelly took the podium. All the news stations were there. Detective O'Kelly let the captain speak first, and then he took center stage. He began speaking with confidence, "today the Memphis PD along with federal agents from Tennessee and Miami along with US Marshalls and ICE captured Memphis's most wanted drug trafficker. Mr. Willie Uptown Brown was caught in open waters off the coast of Cuba where he had been hiding for years. He was working on a fishing vessel and was taken into custody without incident. Court records will show that Mr. Brown and his organization brought cocaine, marijuana and heroin to Tennessee, Mississippi, and about 35 other states. These men are dealing drugs that cause most of the violence you see in our communities. It is our responsibility to keep the streets safe, and with this arrest, we're doing just that."

"Now that Mr. Brown is off the streets, that mean less drugs will be on the streets. I would like to thank all agencies involved in this operation. It was a collective effort of good law enforcement not just here in Memphis, but in Miami and other states. Also thanks to the community for their help in bringing these dangerous criminals to justice. We truly believe we can cut crime down in our city but we got to work together to rid our streets of these drug dealers who are preying on the weak drug users. With that being said, thanks for your time, and we will continue to enforce the laws of the land and protect the city from traffickers who are looking to make a fast buck while the city suffers. Not on our watch, not now, not ever. Thanks and have a blessed and safe day."

As Det. O'Kelly left the podium, the lights and cameras turned off. He turned to his partner and asked, "how did I do"? He said, "like a Hollywood star. You should get an Oscar." He just smiled. He knew the city would be watching. It was his moment. He gloated for a while and then headed to the holding cell where Uptown was being held.

Uptown was sleeping. He kicked the door and said, "Hey Mr. Brown, we both famous now." Uptown said, "naw you might be but not me. I'm just a country boy who caught a case." Det O'Kelly said, "naw, you're the biggest criminal I ever caught, and thanks, you might have just helped me get a raise." Uptown said "who me, if I had my way you'd be a security guard at the mall." Det. O'Kelly said, "yeah I bet I would in your dreams, but get your shit talking ass up. Time to go be with yo homies in Mason, Tn."

So, he handcuffed Uptown and threw the flap in the door. They took a van straight to Mason. When the barbed wire fence closed behind him, Uptown felt his freedom leave his body. It was official. He was in prison. Det. O'Kelly handed him to the CO's and said, "I'll see you in court Mr. Uptown." Uptown said, "fuck you, you red-headed Irish bitch!

After getting dressed out, they took Uptown to his pod. He walked in and looked around. Niggas were staring trying to size him up and figure him out. He walked to the cell assigned to him. A fat light light-skinned Muslim dude came in the cell and said, "Hi my brother. My name is Abbas. What's yours"? Uptown said, "They call me Uptown." Abbas said, "I'm yo cell mate. I'ma get out your way, and let you get yourself together but if you need anything I'll be in the day room." Uptown said, "bet that." He got unpacked and then headed to the day room to take a view of his new surroundings. He was from the streets so he knew plenty niggas who had been to jail and prison. He knew niggas was in gangs, niggas was clicked up, niggas was in all types of fucking shit. One of the niggas who was at the card table walked up to him and said, "What's good hombre, where you from." Uptown said, "I'm from the LMG." The nigga said, "ok; a lot of yo homies just crashed out, they in the hole now."

Uptown said, "Do you know they names"? The nigga said, "It was big Chuncey and bout 4 or 5 of his homies. They butchered a nigga in the gym a few months ago. They still talking bout that shit. Yeah y'all LMG niggas some real live gangstas.

Uptown felt good to hear that, but he didn't want any negative attention, although he did like the fact that he already had respect just cause he was affiliated with the L. He knew Cotton and Dee were there but didn't know what pod they were in. He asked a few niggas but everybody kept acting like they didn't know them. Then one day at chow an LMG nigga named Jimny Duke came and sat by him. He said, "you Dee's charge partner right"? He said, "yeah that's my brother. Where he at"?

He said, "oh yeah, they shipped him and big Chuncey to FCI Memphis out there by the penal farm for sticking on this nigga in the gym." Uptown said, "okay I heard bout that, all yeah. Do you know Cotton"? Jimny Duke said, "yeah he still in the hole. I heard he got bout 3 or 4 more months before they let him back on the compound". Uptown said, "look homie get word to him and let em know I'm down here". He said, "shit nigga, he probably already know. News travel fast in jail, plus yo Black ass been all over the news and newspapers." Uptown just shook his head like dam no wonder niggas just be looking at him. They all know his situation but fuck it, he here now and gotta stand firm.

He finally broke down and called his Mu-dear. He dreaded this day, this call. He never meant to hurt her, but once she picked up the phone, and he heard his momma scream, he broke down in tears. He couldn't hold it no more, all the emotions just flowed out of him. She said, "Son I love you no matter what them news people say. They don't know you. You my child, and I'll always be here for you." Uptown said, "Momma I'm so sorry bout all the pain I put you through. You tried to warn me but I let the money control me. Now I gotta pay for my crimes, but please forgive me, momma. I just tried to provide a better life for our family." She said, "I understand son, I truly do. But you always gone have my love and support right or wrong. Now you gotta ask God to forgive you. Get you a bible and pray, talk to God. He will listen. They can have your body but in Jesus, your spirit can be free. Now bow your head and let's pray." She prayed for her son as they both said amen. Then the phone said you have one minute remaining. He said, "I love you Mu-dear." She said, "Love you too son, take care and I'll be there to see you soon as the visitation form get approved.

Uptown hung up the phone, went to his cell and got in his bunk. He pulled the sheet over his head as he cried in silence. His cell mate saw the expressions on his face, so he left the cell to let him get it all out of his system. Abbas had been in prison for 17 years so he saw how newcomers get when they realize it's all over. Uptown knew his life as he knew it was over. This wasn't a lil bullshit charge, he was facing life in prison, and in the feds life means life; ain't no parole. You die in prison.

After he let all his emotions out, he just tried to get in jail mode. So, he went to the law library to learn about his case. He had his sisters to contact a good lawyer to represent him. He went to the gym to work out and play basketball. He got word from Cotton who told him Big Chuncey and Dee got maxed out cause they kept catching write ups in the hole and that he'll be out the hole in a few months. He also said to stay away from haters cause in the feds there are a lot of rats running around on the compound. Uptown sent him a kite back. He was happy to hear from his brother, but still reality set in. Dam, they were in a fucked-up position. But like Abbas told him, at least they still alive. So Uptown was happy to wake up every day. One day Uptown was in the cell just talking shit with Abbas. He said, "so celly, the whole Mason knows what I'm in here for, but I don't know what you in here for." Abbas said, "well normally brothers don't share what their charges are mainly cause dudes be snitching, but I can feel you're no rat so I can tell you."

"I was a lowkey dude living in Covington, Tennessee. I had a wife and kids, life was good. Then this dude broke into my house and stole all my kids' gifts for Christmas. I was young and dumb seeking revenge. I called myself gone go set his house on fire. Well the fire department came to put out the fire and a firefighter fell through the roof and died. So they charged me with arson and murder. They gave me life plus 120 years. I been locked up for 17 yrs. I lost my wife, my kids, my family, my freedom, and my life. If it wasn't for Allah and Islam, I don't know what I would be doing right now."

Uptown said, "Damn my nigga, my bad my brother that's deep. I know you've seen it all in here." He said, "yeah I'm just back here on my appeal, I'm at a fed joint in Washington state. Whenever they hear my case, I'll be getting shipped back." "Oh," Uptown said, "so what the fed joint in other states like"? He said, "well different states have different politics. Usually, you stick with dudes from your state. It's called a car and I'm in the Tennessee car. I ride with them if it's state against state but I'm also a Muslim so I roll with the Islam community too. They got camps, U.S.P.'s and maximums depending on your time and history, which will tell where you go. Camps are laid back but U.S.P.'s are dangerous brothers. Fighting and killing each other, the max is 23 and 1 lock down. Don't nobody want to go to max. They lock you down like a zoo. Brothers lose they minds on max. So if I was you, I would just stay away from gangs, never gamble, and never do drugs. Those are the main reasons brothers be fighting and killing."

Uptown said, "Thanks for the knowledge Abbas," and he said, "No problem I had to learn too. But you know Allah can open his arms up for you too brother," Abbas said. Uptown said, "thanks I respect your religion but I was raised Christian by my Mu-Dear, so I'ma honor her and stick with my faith." Abbas said, "I feel ya brother."

They became real cool. They knew how to respect each other's space. Abbas taught Uptown a lot about how to do time and not complain, but to just live life.

After two months, they finally approved all Uptown's visitors. His Mu-dear and Mona came together. Mona was starting to show her pregnant belly. She saw Uptown coming through the door in the visitation room, and just broke down crying. She was both happy and sad. She hated to see him in a prison uniform. She ran and hugged him so tightly that she didn't want to let go.

After a long embrace, he hugged and kissed his Mu-Dear and his Mona and they sat and talked for a while. Then his Mu-Dear said, "I got some bad news son." Uptown said, "What bad news." She said, "your daddy Ike-Lee is on life support and his family is going to pull the plug tomorrow. I'm sorry son." He started to cry but had to stay strong. He had heard Ike-Lee was sick but didn't know it had come to this. He gathered himself, he couldn't be crying and whining in the visitation room area with all these hard legs. His Mu-Dear said, "he'll be in a better place and no more suffering. He's old and his kids love him. He had a blessed life." Uptown said, "yes ma'am. Ima be strong." They enjoyed their visit but the hardest part was when it was over and you know you can't go with your loved ones. No matter how long a person be locked up, he never gets used to that.

    A few months passed and all his sisters and brothers would come to visit him. He and his siblings were really close, so the visits would be so emotional. His sisters would cry every visit. This was their brother who had taken care of them. He was their hero but now he was in a position to where they don't know if they'll ever see him as a free man again. It was extra painful for them. He just would always tell them no bars or fences gone stop the love they have for each other. He always knew how to uplift their spirits, still nothing could fill that void they had in their hearts. Prison affects more than just the person who's locked up.

    After a few months, Cotton got out the hole. Uptown was happy to see his brother from another mother. He convinced the CO's to move Cotton into the pod with him. He told them he was going to keep him out of trouble. Cotton told him about the sticking situation. He said, "man it had to be done. Dude was asking for it." Uptown said, "look bruh, we facing life and can't be in here going to court from the hole; it only makes you look bad." Cotton respected that and chilled out as they worked on their case.

    After getting the evidence they learned that the heat started from an angry ex-hooker of Cotton's who was mad about getting sent back to Memphis. That started a domino effect. Workers, crew members and even a few plugs who were drivers got caught and started to snitch. It was a no-win situation.

    After talking to their lawyers, they decided it was in their best interest to just plead guilty and try to get a deal. Still the feds ain't like the state, they don't have a set time. The judge can agree or not agree to a plea and give you what he or she wants. So after a year and a half of going to court, it was finally sentencing day.

> Uptown, Cotton and Dee's' entire families were in the courtroom. Also the U.S. attorney, the Prosecutor and Det. O'Kelly were there. The US Prosecutor laid out the case by stating these three men were more than your average drug dealers. They held from Mississippi and Memphis, but they had drugs running all over this country spreading death and destruction. They were trafficking major amounts of drugs through buses, trains, ships, planes, and cars. Also they trafficked women for sexual sales. They destroyed countless lives with their criminal careers. We as a society have to send a strong message that if you choose to deal in drugs, violence, and mayhem, you will be punished to the fullest extent of the law.

Then, the defending attorney began to speak.

> These lawyers as a collective stood up and spoke about how bad and evil these young black men were. But look around this courtroom, they have a lot of family and friends to support them. They are not killers. They grew up in poverty; two from Mississippi and one from South Memphis. These are some of the poorest communities in this country. All they ever wanted was to live better not just for them but for their families too. We judge them yet we don't give them proper education or affordable housing to choose a better way out. But now you want to throw away three lives for what; making some money when in this country a White man can embezzle billions and he only gets 5 or 10 years. Where is the justice in that? We the counsel respectfully ask that you consider there unfortunate upbringings and that this is really their first serious offence.

Then the judge said, "Can the defendants please rise." Uptown, Cotton and Dee all stood up. They all were super nervous. This was the moment they all had nightmares about. How would the judge see them as poor men looking for a way out or a menace to society who only dealt drugs to do dirt. Then the old gray-headed, White, red-faced judge spoke, "I understand that you young men grew up poor but usually poor people grow up hard workers. They don't choose a life of drugs and human trafficking to support a lifestyle that only adds to the destruction of our youth. So this court doesn't believe you didn't have a choice, you always have a choice. And you young men just happened to make the wrong one."

So, with that, he sentenced Dee to 550 months, Cotton to 820 months, and Uptown to 636 months in prison. Cotton got the most cause he had pimping charges added on. The whole courtroom broke out into screams, yelling, and crying. A few family members added up the months and passed out.

Cotton began to curse out the Prosecutor and judge. Det O'Kelly was smiling with a devilish grin on his face. The lawyers just shook their heads. This was a true railroading of some young black men but sadly it's standard in courtrooms around the country.

Dee got shipped to Pollock in Louisiana. Cotton got shipped to Beaumont, TX a.k.a. the bloody Beaumont. Uptown got shipped to Atlanta U.S.P. They all were in the south for now but when the feds are involved, you move around a lot. And, with how much time each of them had, they knew that at any point they could be shipped to the other side of the country. Their lives were over. They'll be old and gray if they make it out of prison.

So in other words, the game for them was officially over. All they would do is rot in prison and think about how they fucked their lives up. They made plenty of money going state to state cross country hustling, but in the end, they realized that in this country ain't no way to break the law and think the system won't make you pay for it.

SO, THE MORAL OF THIS STORY IS:

No matter how high you rise in the dope game, you always will fall no matter who you are. The game ain't a winners' game, it's a lose lose situation. But sadly there are millions of men and women in this country who are willing to risk freedom and safety for that almighty dollar, and it's been like that since the beginning of time. The love of money is the root of all evil and as long as there are greedy people in this world, the prisons and jails will stay full of lost souls chasing that pot of gold. Yeah, they went cross country hustling but like that old saying "all money ain't good money" and it's sad that sometimes good people learn the hard way!

The End

Northmemphispublishinghouse@gmail.com

www.northmemphispublishinghouse.com

Made in the USA
Columbia, SC
14 November 2023